"What the hell do you mean breaking into my house...

"putting wiretaps on my phones, setting up surveillance equipment? Are you completely insane? I ought to call the police right now and turn you in—you could lose your license for this! I can't believe the arrogance—"

Ky smiled. "Getting over your crush on me, are you?"

It was such a ridiculous thing to say; his smile was so unexpected and sexy and charming. For a moment Amy could do nothing but gape at him. Once she recovered, she answered, "By the minute."

"That's good," he said, "because from now on neither one of us is going to have much time for flirting. Now, what I need from you is—"

"All right, that's it." Amy flung up both hands in a gesture of defiance and spun on her heels toward the door. "I don't need this. Get out. You're fired!"

Dear Reader,

Sometimes good things are over too soon, and that's how you'll feel about Rebecca Flanders' terrific trilogy, Heart of the Wolf. But first you get to read the irresistible last volume, *Shadow of the Wolf*. This is a book that will have you on the edge of your seat as Amy Fortenoy and Ky Londen fight for their lives— and their love.

Next month welcome a bright new talent to the Shadows pantheon. Kimberly Raye will be making her first appearance with *'Til We Meet Again*. Luckily for readers everywhere, her second book will follow in just a few months. And in two months look for reader favorite Carla Cassidy's newest Shadows novel, *Mystery Child*. I think you'll love it.

As always, I hope you'll enjoy your journey to the dark side of love—courtesy of Silhouette Shadows.

Yours,

Leslie Wainger
Senior Editor and Editorial Coordinator

Please address questions and book requests to:
Silhouette Reader Service
U.S.: 3010 Walden Ave., P.O. Box 1325, Buffalo, NY 14269
Canadian: P.O. Box 609, Fort Erie, Ont. L2A 5X3

REBECCA FLANDERS

SHADOW OF THE WOLF

Published by Silhouette Books
America's Publisher of Contemporary Romance

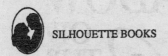

SILHOUETTE BOOKS

ISBN 0-373-27059-3

SHADOW OF THE WOLF

This edition published by arrangement with Harlequin Books S.A.

® and TM are trademarks of Harlequin Books S.A., used under license.
Trademarks indicated with ® are registered in the United States Patent
and Trademark Office, the Canadian Trade Marks Office and in other
countries.

Printed in U.S.A.

REBECCA FLANDERS

has written over seventy books under a variety of pseudonyms. She lives in the mountains of north Georgia with a collie, a golden retriever and three cats. In her spare time she enjoys painting, hiking, dog training and catching up on the latest bestsellers. She is currently working on her next book and always enjoys hearing from readers.

PROLOGUE

New Orleans, Louisiana
July

"This is Amy Fortenoy, reporting live from the scene of what appears to be another bizarre murder, similar to the ones that took place last month. The victim, identified only as a white female between the ages of twenty-five and thirty, was found near the French Market about six o'clock this morning. Her throat, like those of the two previous victims, had been cut with a jagged-edge instrument. Though the body was found partially clothed, police say there is no evidence of sexual assault...."

August

"Another body has been discovered tonight with its throat cut, a young man this time. This is the second victim this month of the so-called Werewolf Killer, known as such because of his propensity for attacking only during the full moon, and because of the brutal nature of the crimes. But Channel Six Action News has learned exclusively tonight of a particularly bizarre piece of forensic evidence that has been a part of each of these murder scenes. Black animal hair—yes, animal hair, like that of a dog—has been found on each body...."

                         *   *   *

September

"The grim total of the werewolf killings rose to six this
morning with the discovery of a body in Jackson Square.
The victim is thought to be a homeless man of about forty
years old and, like the others, died of wounds to the
throat. Last night's rains will no doubt make the collection of forensic evidence very difficult, but police have
confirmed the similarities between this death and previous victims'—the brutality of the attack, the nature of the
murder weapon, which is still being described only as a
'jagged instrument,' and yes, the presence of black animal hair on the body. While the pathologist admits that
the animal hair taken from the scene has been classified
as belonging to the canine family, he is adamant in denying the possibility that it could belong to a wolf. Meanwhile, ASPCA officials report a dramatic increase in the
number of black dogs being turned in to shelters and
caution against a general panic over the possible link between these killings and black dogs. This is Amy Fortenoy for Channel Six Action News."

October

"This beautiful harvest moon behind me is an eerie
backdrop to the scene of yet another violent slaying by the
man we've come to know as the Werewolf Killer. With
Halloween only a few days away, it seems inevitable that
the death toll will begin to rise even higher."

November

"This is Amy Fortenoy live from the banks of the Mis-
sissippi River, where the discovery of the partially sub-

merged body of a middle-aged woman brings the total death count to twelve for the Werewolf Killer. Detectives and forensic specialists have been here for hours, securing the scene and collecting evidence, but this time it seems the killer has left them more to go on than on previous occasions. The crime-scene investigators have spent a great deal of time photographing and taking plaster casts of the footprints that were left on the riverbank, and this is what we want to show you. Can you get that close-up, Paul? As you can see, many of the tracks—there's no other words for them—are clear enough to be read even by an amateur like me. The clear imprint of a rubber-soled shoe—can you see that?—apparently belongs to the victim. This one near it may belong to the attacker—a large print, apparently a bare foot. But these others—these are what are fascinating—appear to have been made by a very large animal. A dog... or a wolf. Is this someone's idea of a sick joke, or has the Werewolf Killer begun to take his nickname seriously?"

December

"In New Orleans, Louisiana, a serial killer holds the city under siege. During the past six months, attacking only under the full moon, a man the media has dubbed the Werewolf Killer has claimed a total of thirteen victims. Amy Fortenoy with our affiliate in New Orleans has that story."

January

"This is Amy Fortenoy, live outside the mayor's office, where, at a press conference this afternoon, Deputy Police Chief Devereaux denied the accusation that the police department has failed to give its full attention to the werewolf killings because the victims so far have been

homeless street people. With the discovery of the fifteenth victim yesterday, the public outcry has become
understandably intense. The police department insists that
it is doing everything in its power to bring the killer to
justice, while continuing to caution the media against ex-
ploiting the so-called 'sensationalistic' elements of this
case. Meanwhile, the death toll continues to rise. Back to
you at the station . . .''

CHAPTER ONE

Mardi Gras
March

Amy Fortenoy manipulated the controls of the tape editor until the smooth, too-handsome-to-be-true features of Deputy Police Chief Marshall Devereaux came into center frame. She muttered, freezing the tape, "There you are, you smug, self-righteous son of a—"

"Oh, real helpful, Fortenoy." Her producer, Janice Waters, paused to look over her shoulder. "Let's start a war with the police department. Guaranteed to get you lots of publicity. Of course, you won't be getting any interviews..."

"Watch this." Amy let the tape play through.

"Before we go any further," the deputy chief said with hands upraised in the manner of a born politician, "I'd first like to express my sincere disappointment with certain members of the media who, although repeatedly cautioned to use discretion regarding certain sensitive aspects of this case, have nonetheless chosen to turn this series of tragic and senseless killings into a virtual circus—"

"Me!" exclaimed Amy indignantly. "He's talking about *me!*"

"Who else?" said Paul Shelton, her cameraman. "You're the one, after all, who made the Werewolf Killer what he is today. With a little help from your friends, of course," he added smugly and perched on the edge of the desk to admire the results of his work as it flickered across the screen.

Amy frowned. She didn't like the way that sounded, any more than she had liked it when Marshall Devereaux had said virtually the same thing earlier that day. Of course, from Devereaux she had cause to take offense, while with Paul...well, he was one of her own. He knew, as well as she did, that it was all part of the business.

"To remind you, once again," Devereaux was saying on tape, "that disturbed individuals such as this very often thrive on the publicity engendered by their crimes."

And that was where Amy came in. She leaned forward to mark the tape. "Excuse me, Deputy Devereaux," she called out clearly from the back of the room. "Surely you don't mean to suggest that we should cease our coverage of the activities of this 'disturbed individual,' as you call him?"

Paul swung the camera to Devereaux. She marked a cut. Close-up on Devereaux's angry face. "What I mean to suggest, young lady—"

"Young lady!" Her voice was practically a squeal. "He called me *young lady!*"

Paul grinned. Janice frowned. The tape rolled on.

"—is that without the insistence of certain members of the press upon turning an otherwise unremarkable series of killings..."

Chaos erupted from the pressroom, but it was, once again, Amy's voice that rose above the fray. It was sweet and polite, laced with Southern sugar—a tone those who knew her well did their best to avoid. "Could you describe to us, sir, what you would consider a *remarkable* series of killings?"

Janice exclaimed in amazement, "What an absolute jerk!"

Paul's grin broadened as he watched the action unfold on the screen. "Nail him, babe!"

"Now, this is a perfect example of how my words are twisted every time I come before you people," returned Devereaux angrily.

"You people!" Janice was practically chortling with delight. "That man is going to hang himself by his own—"

Amy held up a hand for attention as Devereaux went on, "What we have is a sick, deranged individual preying on the weak and helpless among us, who, for some reason that's totally inexplicable to me, has been glorified by the media into what very nearly approximates a cult hero."

"Well, I resent that," muttered Paul.

"Cut it," Janice told Amy, but Amy had already marked it for editing.

"The press has all but convinced the public there is a *real* werewolf out there, a man who changes into a beast during the full moon and tears people's throats out. But worse, there is a strong possibility you've actually convinced the *killer* of it, as well. And that's all we need, isn't it? A deranged killer who's convinced of his own invincibility?"

"Well, I never," murmured Paul, feigning insult.

Amy ignored him.

Devereaux continued, "You might recall that it wasn't until the media started bandying about the term *werewolf killer* that this maniac actually began leaving evidence suggestive of a wolf at the scene—"

"Now that's a downright lie!" exclaimed Janice indignantly. "There was animal hair on the first body!"

Amy simply frowned at the screen.

"Those ridiculous paw prints, which our forensics people had no difficulty dismissing as a hoax, the widely publicized claw and teeth marks..."

"*We* didn't widely publicize them," complained Paul, disgruntled.

"Not to mention the fact that the number of killings has actually increased with each successive cycle, as though the killer is becoming emboldened by his own success. I attribute this directly to what I can only call the media's exploitation of a tragic situation. Let me be clear on one thing, people—I will not have panic in the streets."

"Might not the quickest way to avoid that," Amy spoke up on tape again, "be to make an arrest in the case?"

Devereaux's contempt for her, and the press, in general, was clear through the tape. "That, of course, is at the top of our list of things to do."

"Oh, great," groaned Janice. "The man is dog food."

Someone else called out, "Do you have an update on the progress in the case?"

But Amy overrode him. "Is it true the FBI has been called in?"

Devereaux glared at her. "It is customary for the FBI to take on a consulting role in all cases of this sort. We're working closely with federal investigators and expect a break in the case very soon."

Amy had the last word. "Hopefully, before the next full moon."

Devereaux looked at her long and hard, and then turned his gaze to the assemblage in general. "Are there other questions?"

Amy turned down the volume.

Janice gave a rueful shake of her head. "I assume he didn't have anything else important to say?"

"You heard the best parts."

"The man is such a jerk, it's almost no fun to torment him. Okay, put the best parts together with a nice little narrative, and we'll run it at six and eleven. What else have you got?"

"At the moment, nothing. But I'm going to try to get a quote from the mayor tonight. If I can snag it in time for the eleven o'clock show, I'll let you know."

Janice lifted an eyebrow. "The mayor, huh? How do you plan to arrange that?"

"Simple. He's going to the Governor's Ball tonight. So am I."

Janice gave her a grinning thumbs-up and left the editing room.

Paul said, rising, "Governor's Ball, huh? Boy, I wish my folks had money."

"Money," replied Amy, running the tape backward, "is nothing. Connections, on the other hand, are everything."

"So, is your dad going to be there or what?"

Amy did not look up. "No."

Amy's father, Byron Fortenoy, the internationally renowned cardiac surgeon and researcher, inventor of the synthetic reflux valve that had saved countless thousands of lives, rarely found time in his busy schedule to visit among mere mortals anymore. His name, however, still carried more than enough influence among the New Orleans elite to guarantee his daughter anything from a bank loan to Saints tickets merely for the asking. Sometimes, such notoriety was a pain. More often than not, however, it was incredibly convenient.

Amy said absently, studying the frames as they moved through the editor, "Anyway, I'm only going for the quote. You know how I hate these Mardi Gras balls. And it's not like there won't be a half-dozen other reporters there.''

"Yeah, but none of them who are on first-name basis with the mayor. And none of them," Paul added pointedly as he turned for the door, "who have the Werewolf Killer in their pockets."

Amy shuddered. "Did anybody ever tell you you have a creepy way of putting things?"

He shrugged. "Hey, in this business, if you don't learn to laugh, you spend your life crying."

"Boy, that's the truth," Amy murmured, focusing on the tape.

Amy had been a crime reporter for WLAK's Channel Six Action News for the past four of her twenty-nine years. In that time, she had covered gang slayings, child murders and child murderers, rapes, molestations, abuse, home invasions, drive-by shootings, arson, bombings. Whatever twisted evil lurked in the hearts of men and whatever violent or obscene way they chose to express it, Amy had seen it all. She had quickly learned that to allow herself to become emotionally affected by the stories she covered was a short road to self-destruction, and she was careful to maintain a professional detachment in every situation.

Until now.

"Paul?" She glanced up as he opened the door, trying to keep her voice casual. "You don't think...I mean, Devereaux couldn't be right, could he? About us—about *me*—encouraging this guy?"

Paul scowled sharply in a mixture of annoyance and amusement. "Come on, babe, you know he's just trying to torment you. If you ask me, he's just jealous."

Amy tried to relax. "Of my good looks, no doubt."

"You better believe it. Hey, if I weren't married..."

"In your dreams, sweet thing." Grinning, Amy turned back to the editor. But her amusement faded as she watched the frames scroll by and she said again, "Hey, Paul."

He looked back. "I'm on my dinner break," he reminded her impatiently.

Amy said thoughtfully, "What *was* all that garbage about the forensic evidence, anyway? I never heard anyone declare those paw prints a hoax before. And he out-and-out lied about animal hair on the bodies. Until today, no one said anything about teeth and claw marks on the bodies. It was as though he was trying so hard to tell a lie, he tripped all over the truth."

"And this is unusual? Devereaux wouldn't know the truth if it jumped up and bit him on the ankle."

"But would we?" she wondered, only half to herself.

"Huh?"

"Did you ever hear the phrase, 'Methinks he doth protest too much'?"

"Come on, Amy, I'm going into serious sugar deficit here."

"It's just that...maybe I've been going about this whole thing the wrong way. Maybe the truth has been staring us in the face the whole time."

"What? That the killer really is a werewolf?"

Amy didn't smile. "That the police really don't know *what* he is."

Paul looked confused.

"Think about it, Paul." Amy's expression was serious. "A serial killer in one of the most populous cities in the country evades detection for ten months. Fifteen people dead, and not a single witness. The FBI, local police, all the crime detection capabilities of the modern age are involved, and there's still not so much as a computer sketch or a psychological profile of this guy. Devereaux aside, you don't really believe for one minute the police are *that* incompetent, do you?''

Paul frowned. ''So what are you saying? That they're covering up something? Hardly a new theory, Ace.''

''Exactly.'' Amy chewed a thumbnail thoughtfully. ''Police and corruption. We've all been pursuing that angle. It's politically motivated because all the victims are homeless and the police are heartless. The evidence is being tainted because the police are careless. Competition between law enforcement agencies is hampering the investigation. But, Paul—'' she lifted eyes to him that were dark with worry ''—what if the simple truth is that the police are doing their best, and they still can't find him?''

Paul regarded her gravely. ''Now, *that,*'' he told her, ''is damn scary.''

''Yeah.'' She released a breath. ''No kidding.''

They looked at each other for another long moment. Finally, Paul said, ''I, uh, wouldn't mention this theory of yours to anybody just yet.''

''Right.''

He turned toward the door again, then looked back. ''I'd rather it be a real werewolf,'' he said.

Amy smiled, though the expression was faint and empty of humor. ''Yeah. I know what you mean.''

''On the other hand, it's not as though something like this has never happened before.''

Amy, who had started to turn back to the editor, glanced at him in confusion. ''What?''

''That a serial killer eludes detection for months on end in one of the most populated cities in the country,'' he explained. ''No witnesses, no clean suspects, nothing.''

Amy was interested. ''Oh, yeah? When was this?''

"London, 1888," he told her. "They called him Jack the Ripper."

"Great," she muttered, pushing back her smooth blond hair with her hand. "I think I'll put that in my story tonight. Citizens of New Orleans, there's hope—London survived Jack the Ripper, we can survive the Werewolf Killer."

He shrugged. "As long as we aren't prostitutes or street people, that is. Say, do you have a date for that wingding tonight?"

"Don't need one. This is business, not pleasure."

"My tennis partner is getting a divorce, you know, and I'll bet he's available on short notice."

Amy should have seen that one coming. Paul was always trying to fix her up, and his wife was no better. What was it about happily married people that made them incapable of letting their friends be happily single?

She said, "When he actually gets a divorce, let me know. Meanwhile, the party's black-tie."

"Oh."

Paul sounded disappointed, and Amy guessed his friend did not have his own tux.

Then he cheered. "Anyway, Cindy says for you to come to dinner next week."

"Is the tennis partner going to be there?"

"I guess not, if you're going to take that attitude."

"I'll call Cindy."

Still Paul hesitated. "You don't, uh, need a camera for that interview tonight, do you?"

Amy looked up at him and grinned. "You big baby. No. I'm not going to drag you across town to the Governor's Ball and no, I'm not going to make you put on a tux. Go home to your wife. You're off duty."

Paul returned her grin and kissed his fingers to her. "You're a prince, Fortenoy, an absolute prince. I'll name an offspring for you."

"You'd better go before someone sees you hanging around and puts your name on the assignment board."

"I'm out of here. And be careful crossing Canal tonight—you'll be hitting the worst of the parade traffic."

Amy waved him away, smiling, but she was deeply immersed in the editor now and did not look up.

Amy Fortenoy had spent her life laboring under two handicaps: her looks and her family name. Amy was blond, petite and cute in a business that valued tall, svelte and striking. Her shoulder-length hair was the sun-drenched color of a three-year-old's and the texture of satin, her nose a perfect button, her face round and ingenuous. Her eyes were large and fringed with thick dark lashes, and the only thing that kept them from being breathtaking was the fact that they were more hazel than green. She had flawless Fortenoy porcelain skin, and a perfect size-six figure, which was due as much to her own efforts and the demands of the camera as it was to the Fortenoy genes.

In a business that values physical attractiveness at least as much as it did ability, if not more—there were, after all, very few ugly news anchors—being a cute blonde might not be considered a disadvantage. But *cute* was the operative word, and Amy was a reporter. She was tough, ambitious, alert and perceptive. All she wanted was a chance to prove what she could do, yet she had spent her career fending off advances, fighting the stereotype and being offered jobs as the weather girl by station directors who took one look at her and wondered if she could read...or if it mattered.

But the prejudices she fought in the work force were nothing to the disapproval—indeed, the disappointment—with which she had to contend in her own family. The Fortenoys were a grand old Southern family who bred tradition, snobbery and intellectuals. Amy had two brothers and three sisters, all of whom had earned at least one Ph.D. in suitably exalted subjects like philosophy or mathematics. Two were university professors, one was a doctor like their father, one was a museum curator, one was the director of a major European symphony orchestra. Among her cousins, aunts and uncles were bank presidents, Supreme Court justices, research scientists and poet laureates. Not one of them worked in television. Most of them, in fact, did not even own television sets, and those who did, only brought them out on the occasion of a presidential election or a particularly compelling PBS special.

Amy's Grandmama Fortenoy still lived in one of those wonderful old antebellum houses on St. Charles Avenue, shaded by creeping ivy and oaks dripping with Spanish moss. On Sunday afternoons she served tea from bone china that had been in the family for three hundred years, and friends and relatives and the social elite would gather in her high-ceilinged parlor with its small brocaded chairs, and speak, in their soft sugared accents, of things lofty and genteel and utterly civilized. The Werewolf Killer would never be among their topics of conversation. And if, by chance, some well-meaning soul asked about "poor little Amy," throats would be cleared, eyes would be averted and the subject delicately changed.

Amy was a source of bafflement and embarrassment to her family, but no more so than they were to her. Sometimes she felt like a changeling, and she could no more understand how that most carefully regulated Fortenoy family tree had come to produce her than they could.

Amy had wasted far too much time and energy early in her career fighting the tide of other people's prejudices against her, but when she had finally realized she could do nothing about either her looks or her family, the solution to her difficulties was clear: She simply started using both to her advantage, instead of allowing them to work against her. No one expected a petite, blond, wide-eyed young woman with a sparkling smile and bubbly personality to be a crime reporter. And nobody expected her to be any good at it. Thus she was not only allowed into places a more experienced-looking reporter could never go, she actually, more often than not, had the door held for her as she went in. No one expected Byron Fortenoy's daughter—Joseph Fortenoy's granddaughter—to sully her hands with anything as distasteful as the news. She was therefore privy to certain information relevant to scandal, corruption and white-collar crime that would be guarded furiously from an "outsider."

People expected Amy to be dumb, so she played dumb. They expected her to be helpless, so she acted helpless. They wanted her to be a socialite, a dilettante, a hothouse flower, and she was more than happy to play the part—when it suited her purpose. Only one thing mattered to Amy Fortenoy: success. And she knew that with the werewolf killings, she was as close to that elusive goal as she had ever been, maybe as close as she would ever get.

So, if she was a little obsessed with the case, there was more than one reason. If, like Devereaux had suggested, she had been a little overzealous in reporting the story, she had good cause. After all, the story of a lifetime only came along once, and this was hers.

* * *

Amy was on the air at six, giving her report and showing the tape. There was, of course, nothing new at all to report—the full moon was still almost two weeks away—but it was important to keep the story in the public eye. To her credit, she did not make Devereaux look like too much of a jackass on the final edit, and she left in the part about the sick, deranged individual being glorified by the media. She was trained to be fair, after all.

She left the studio at six forty-five, which left just under an hour to get across town, put on her party dress and get back downtown in time to get a quote from the mayor for the eleven o'clock news. She would also love to get a reaction to Devereaux's remarks this afternoon from the chief coroner, and it was possible she would be able to catch him at home if she didn't spend too much time at the party. He had been ducking her calls all day.

During Mardi Gras, Amy gave up trying to drive to work. It was impossible to keep up with which streets would be closed for what parade or for how long. It was easier and faster to simply take public transportation. She took the St. Charles trolley as far as Jackson Square and then had to walk a block and a half to catch the streetcar to Midcity. Ordinarily, this was no problem; the streets were well traveled and well lighted, and Amy enjoyed the brief walk. It gave her the chance to unwind from a busy day or, as tonight, to organize an even busier evening. But for some reason, she had forgotten about the parade.

Mardi Gras in New Orleans. Music, laughter, crowds and lights, extravagant costumes, gala parades. To the several hundred thousand visitors who packed the city streets every year, Mardi Gras was magic, pure and simple. To New Orleans residents like Amy, however, Mardi Gras was traffic jams, missed appointments and dancing

in the streets until 4:00 a.m. when she had to get up at six.
To her, there was nothing romantic about the shoulder-to-
shoulder bodies that screeched and waved and cheered
and blocked the sidewalk as she tried to elbow her way
past, nothing thrilling about the towering floats and har-
lequins on stilts and fire-eating jugglers that inched down
the street, blocking off both foot and vehicular traffic for
six blocks in each direction.

The noise was deafening. A Dixieland band blared its
trumpets in her ears as it passed less than five feet in front
of her; the stereo speakers on a float a dozen yards behind roared out a marching tune. Grinning masks bobbed
and leered, street lamps glinted eerily off of glass eyes.
The air was alive with writhing strips of pink and purple
confetti, dragons and mermaids danced in the street. Behind her, the door to a pub opened and a new mass of
screeching, jostling, beer-cup-waving bodies spilled out.
Amy felt as though she had stumbled into a madman's
nightmare and she thought, *I don't need this!*

Gauging a break in the procession between a float fea-
turing a giant Poseidon and a gaggle of acrobats in silver
suits, Amy prepared to dash across the street. Her foot
had barely left the curb when something grabbed her hard
from behind.

"Hey!" she cried. Amy tried to spin around, but
someone held her firm. She tried to jerk away, but an iron
arm clamped around her ribs, dragging her back and
jerking her off her feet.

She cried out, struggling. No one in the jostling, excited crowd seemed to notice. She wrenched around,
flinging out a hand to strike, but stopped, gasping and
disoriented, as she found herself staring into the grinning
face of a wolf.

He might have blamed it on the reaction of Voodoo, the
half mutt, half black Lab at his side, but it was more than

CHAPTER TWO

Ky Londen knew something was wrong when he was
halfway up the stairs. He might have blamed it on the reaction of Voodoo, the half mutt, half black Lab at his
side, but it was more than that. The minute they reached
the landing and the door to Ky's apartment came into
view, man and dog froze in place. The dog dropped into
a half crouch, pressing himself against Ky's knee, his
hackles rising. Though there was absolutely no visible
reason for it, Ky felt his hackles rise, too.

Ky's apartment was on the second floor of what once
had been a fruit market on the corner of Rampart and
Canal streets. The first floor was home to nothing but rats
now, completely boarded up and always locked. The entire building might have been condemned long ago had
not the Historical Preservation Society taken a particular, and in Ky's opinion, inexplicable, interest in the place.
Ky had stayed because the rent was cheap and because the
historical society could occasionally be persuaded to foot
the bill for improvements that kept the building, for the
most part, on the right side of health-code standards. Security doors did not, unfortunately, fall into that cate-
gory and on more than one occasion Ky himself, having
forgotten his key, had opened the door with a well-placed
shove of his shoulder.

The apartment was reached via an ironwork staircase
that might once have been used as a fire escape. The

scarred wooden door that faced the alley was closed, just as he had left it. There was no sign of forcible entry. Nonetheless, someone was indisputably inside. Voodoo knew it, and so did Ky.

He had never worried about intruders before. He didn't have anything anyone would want to steal, and personal safety was the least of his concerns. But this was different. Now he was worried.

He reached down and placed a restraining hand on Voodoo's neck, signaling the dog to stay put as he moved forward carefully. The big black dog looked fierce, but he was no hero, and was more likely to melt into a puddle of admiration at the intruder's feet than launch an attack. Some people kept dogs for protection; Ky spent far more time protecting the dog than the other way around.

He took the remaining steps silently, and the closer he got to the door the harder his heart beat, the drier his throat grew. He paused once to glance back at the dog, but he needn't have worried. Whatever was waiting for him behind that door had terrified the poor animal into paralysis. It was a state with which Ky could sympathize.

With every instinct in his body, Ky knew that what he was about to encounter was unlike anything he had ever dealt with before. Not a burglar, not an escaped convict he had once put away, not a homicidal ex-client. This was...different.

Ky was licensed to carry a handgun. He worked some of the roughest streets in the city, and the people he encountered were not always feeling friendly toward him. However, since leaving the New Orleans police department three years ago, he had not carried a gun. Until now, he had never felt the need for one.

Although he didn't really believe that a gun would have protected him from what was inside his apartment, he would have felt better having one in his hand.

He did not waste time looking around for something that could be used as a weapon. There was no point in plotting a strategy. Ky had lived a rough life in an unfriendly world and had survived for almost forty years on his wits, his instincts and his lightning-fast reflexes. Even if he had wanted to, there was no time to change his *modus operandi* now.

He gripped the handle of the door and turned it slowly. It was unlocked. He flung open the door and flattened himself quickly against the wall, making as small a target of his body as possible.

"I assure you, I am unarmed," a male voice said from inside the room. "Like you, I have no need for crude mechanical weapons."

The voice was deep and powerful, now faintly amused or perhaps bored. The accent was cultured and precise but otherwise indefinable. And something about that voice—or perhaps it was the man himself, still unknown to Ky—was compelling. Perfectly aware that his life might be the price he paid for curiosity, Ky stepped cautiously across the threshold of his own apartment.

It was full dark outside, and no lamps were on inside. The only illumination came from the streetlights and car headlights below the windows that faced the street. Nonetheless, Ky's night vision was excellent. He had no difficulty at all making out the figure who stood before the uncurtained window.

Fight-or-flight adrenaline rushed through Ky's veins. His heart pounded in his throat, his breath was quick and strong. Every sense was more acute than it had ever been.

He recognized the man immediately for what he was. And he had never seen him before in his life.

He was a big man, powerfully built, with a thick mane of silver hair that fell below his shoulders. He wore a patchwork fur vest, which was distinctly out of place for New Orleans, and carried an elaborately carved wooden walking stick. His face was stern and imperious, his eyes crystal blue.

Ky knew he was in the presence of greatness. His knees were abruptly rubbery and he wanted to sit down, but he dared not show any weakness. He thought, *This can't be.*

And yet it was.

He squared his shoulders, closing his fists. He demanded, "How did you get in here?"

The other man smiled, and gestured toward the door. "Locks pose no problem for us, do they?"

Ky's heartbeat jumped again. It was hard to swallow. "Who are you? What do you want?"

The intruder moved away from the window a few paces closer to Ky. Ky stood his ground, but all the man did was lift a medium-size canvas satchel from the coffee table. The satchel was not Ky's, so he presumed the man had brought it with him.

"My name," he said, "is Sebastian St. Clare, and I have a business proposition for you."

Ky said nothing.

"You don't have a business address," St. Clare went on. "I presume I was right in coming here."

Ky said, "How did you find me?" His voice was a little hoarse. He tried to swallow.

"You are a private investigator, are you not?" inquired St. Clare mildly. "How do clients usually find you?"

That was not what Ky had meant and the other man knew it. The rules had been established, and they were simple: St. Clare would ask the questions.

The door behind him was still open. Ky considered turning and leaving. He wondered how far he would get.

Instead, he crossed the room to the kitchen area, opened the refrigerator and took out a beer. He turned, twisting off the cap. "I do divorce cases, insurance fraud and process serving. Which are you?"

"Homicide," Sebastian St. Clare replied.

A fraction of a second's pause in the movement of his hand, but no more. Ky lifted the bottle to his lips and drank. He did not take his eyes off the other man.

"I think we should talk."

"Yes, I think so, too," Ky replied.

"But first..." St. Clare's eyes moved past Ky, toward the open door. "Will you allow that pathetic creature to come inside? Please assure him that I won't bite." He said it with a perfectly straight face.

Voodoo poked his head around the corner of the door frame, ears flat, eyes wary. When Ky snapped his fingers, the dog crept inside, his tail low and his manner anxious, and went quickly to Ky's side. He, too, never took his eyes off the stranger, and he made a wide circle around the carpet upon which St. Clare had trod.

"Might we sit down?"

Ky nodded. St. Clare took the lumpy plaid sofa, and Ky, with Voodoo clinging like a shadow to his side, sat cautiously in the reading chair across the room. Every sense, tangible and innate, was working overtime, assessing and observing, accumulating information and processing impressions, trying to make sense of what could not possibly be sitting on his sofa, lifting the satchel to his knee, opening it, showing the contents to Ky.

The satchel was filled with money. The cash was neatly stacked and wrapped with teller's bands: tens, twenties and fifties. Ky's eyes scanned the bundles quickly as he tried to keep his expression neutral. There must have been over...

"Fifty thousand dollars," St. Clare said. "It represents half the amount we are willing to pay for your services. This is yours now, the remainder due when your assignment is completed."

Ky took another sip of his beer. The dryness in his throat was only partially relieved. "And who was it," he inquired carefully, "that you wanted me to kill?"

St. Clare closed the satchel and placed it on the table. He said, "You are aware of the man they call the Werewolf Killer."

It was not a question, so Ky offered no reply. His thoughts were spinning, and there was no way he could predict what the old man was going to say next. None. How could he defend himself if he didn't know the battlefield... or even if this *was* a battle?

"I represent a consortium that would like to see this reign of terror brought to an end," St. Clare stated simply. "You have been chosen for the task."

Ky could not quite prevent a lift of his eyebrow. "I'm flattered. But we have a very fine police department that specializes in this kind of thing. Maybe you should give them a call."

"Yes," murmured St. Clare, holding Ky in that steady blue gaze. "Your police department. The world has seen how effective they have been in dealing with this menace. Not that they are to be held at fault. They are incapable of stopping this killer, we both know that."

I don't know anything! Ky wanted to shout at him. This whole thing was insane. None of it could be happening, it all had to be some kind of colossal joke, none of it made *sense*.

He didn't say any of that, of course. He didn't raise his voice or tighten in muscles or even breathe hard; he did not in any way betray his agitation, but he wasn't fooling himself, either—St. Clare knew what he was feeling. The old man could smell it.

Ky asked the only remaining relevant question. "Why me?"

St. Clare smiled. "Who else," he demanded simply, "is there?"

"You," returned Ky sharply. "If you want this killer brought to justice and you insist upon taking the law in your own hands, you go after him. Don't come to me with your bag of money and expect me to risk my life for people I don't even know."

"But isn't that what you did every day when you were a police officer? And for far less money than this." He nodded toward the satchel.

Ky brought the bottle to his lips again. "Yeah, well, I'm not in that line of work any longer."

"A story in itself, I'm sure," replied St. Clare politely. "And to answer your question...I'm an old man, as you can see. I would be foolish to take on such a dangerous task at my age."

Ky restrained a snort of disbelief. He suspected the old man could have taken on a dozen men half his age without even becoming winded.

"As for the others," St. Clare went on, "I could send a squad of trained specialists down here, I suppose, but I'd rather not attract the attention, or to be frank, risk losing any of my top men. None of them know the city like you do, its people, its legal customs, its resources. None of them has as great a chance of going undetected by the killer as you do. Besides—" he glanced toward the window "—there is a great deal of water surrounding this city, which often makes it hard for us to track a moving target. I assume, to function as well as you have here, it doesn't bother you?"

With Sebastian St. Clare's first statement, Ky's throat had seized. His breath stilled, his muscles froze and he didn't hear anything after the word *others*. *Others*.

When his breath returned, it hurt his lungs. His voice, when he spoke, was hoarse. "Do you mean...there are more? Others like—"

"Us?" St. Clare inclined a regal nod. "Of course."

It was one of those moments, and there are only one or two at best, where an entire life changes. Whatever happened from now on, Ky would be able to look back and effortlessly determine when everything crossed over, the point at which the life he once had lived became the life he could never go back to, and it was at that moment when Sebastian St. Clare looked at him with clear unsurprised eyes and said, "Of course."

Ky's heart raced. His thoughts scattered in a dozen different directions at once. Part of him wanted to shout "Liar!" and seize the man by the throat and shake the truth from him. Yet another part echoed quite calmly the truth he had always known. *Of course.*

St. Clare too easily read the struggle in Ky's eyes and his expression grew sharp with interest. "So," he murmured, "you didn't know. I had wondered."

"How many?" Ky asked, his voice oddly flat.

"Enough."

Something inside Ky snapped. He flung the beer bottle against the wall. It exploded like a bomb, spewing suds and glass across the room. The dog ran to a corner and began to bark hysterically. Ky was out of his chair shout-

ing, "Answer me, you son of a bitch! Tell me the truth or
I'll take you out, I swear I will! Answer me!"

Sebastian St. Clare was utterly unmoved. Like a pa-
tient father enduring the temper tantrum of a deprived
child, he waited until Ky's diatribe had worn itself out.
Even Voodoo's barking became less certain, slowed and
finally ceased of its own accord.

Ky stood across from him, his fists bunched, his
breathing hard, perspiration beading on his forehead. St.
Clare's calm silence should have infuriated him, and it
did; it also made him feel foolish.

Finally, Sebastian St. Clare said gently, "All in good
time, my boy. All in good time."

Ky glared at him, muscles knotted and breath tight, for
another moment. Then he swung away, feeling impotent
and furious.

"I understand this must come as a shock to you," St.
Clare said. "I confess, it did to me, too, but I've had more
time to adjust than you have. There are still a great many
questions to be answered on both our parts, I think."

Ky turned back to him slowly, his eyes narrowed. "How
long have you known about me?"

"I had heard rumors, but until today I wasn't sure of
any of them. To be frank, it had occurred to me that you
might actually be the renegade killer we're trying to dis-
pose of. The moment I entered your domicile, however, I
knew that couldn't be the case."

Ky frowned sharply. "How?" he demanded. "How did
you know?"

"Dog hair," replied St. Clare simply. "It's everywhere. Our killer would not live with a dog."

Ky stared at him, letting the words roll around in his
head. Then he said slowly, "So you're telling me that this
Werewolf Killer is—"

"Appropriately named," replied St. Clare.

Ky refused to be surprised by anything further he heard. He would not be shocked, dismayed, disappointed or hopeful. Most of all, he would not let anything the man said from now on cause him to lose his temper.

"What makes you think I can do what the best law enforcement officials in this state—hell, in the nation—haven't been able to do for the past ten months? And if I could, why wouldn't I have done it by now?"

"You didn't know what he was," replied St. Clare simply, "until now."

Ky turned away again, pushing a hand through his straight black hair, calming himself. For a time, neither of them spoke.

Then Ky looked back at the satchel on the table. He said, "It's not enough."

"What?"

"Your price. It's not enough."

Abruptly, St. Clare burst into laughter. It was a full, rich laugh, and the genuineness of it caught Ky off guard.

"So," said St. Clare, "you are more like us than I suspected."

He looked Ky over thoughtfully. "You'll take the money," he said, not so much offering an opinion as stating a fact. "But you're right, I have something you want even more."

Ky didn't answer. He dared not.

"Your mother died in your twenty-first year," St. Clare went on. "She must have told you about your father, otherwise you wouldn't have been able to survive this long. But she never told you who he was, and you have spent your entire adult life trying to find out. Looking for him."

Sebastian St. Clare's eyes were steady on his, as cold as the center of the earth, as hot as blue fire. "I have the answers you seek, Ky Londen," he said. "And I may be the only person in the world who does."

Once again, everything inside him grew still. Ky looked very carefully at the man who sat on his sofa. He said, with the same care, "You know who my father is?"

"At present," said St. Clare, "I have my suspicions. They will take time to confirm. And no," he added, reading Ky's mind, "it is not me."

Ky was silent, this time for much longer. When he spoke at last, his tone was utterly expressionless. "So. This is blackmail."

"Not at all." St. Clare seemed genuinely surprised, perhaps even offended, by Ky's choice of words. "I've made you a proposition. You are free to accept or reject it."

"And if I reject it?"

"Then," said Sebastian St. Clare, getting to his feet, "you will no longer be any concern of mine. You seem to have lived a full and busy life before I came into it, no doubt you will continue to do so after I depart."

He picked up his walking stick and moved toward the door. For the first time, Ky was able to see the carvings that decorated the stick. The gleaming mahogany was inscribed on every surface with elaborate renderings of the heads of wolves. Of course.

Sebastian St. Clare walked toward the door, obviously expecting Ky to stop him.

Ky said, "You forgot your money."

St. Clare looked back at him. "No," he said. "I didn't." He opened the door and was gone.

When he was alone, Ky had to grip the back of a chair to remain upright. Voodoo came over to him, pressing against his knee, and whined anxiously. Ky dropped his hand to the dog's head, taking two slow deep breaths, one after another. He pushed aside the thoughts that kept trying to explode inside his head, breaking his concentration, and he forced himself to listen, to breathe, to focus.

After a moment, he turned toward the door, lifting a staying hand to Voodoo, who looked at him alertly. "Sorry, old bud," he told the dog quietly, "this one's too dangerous for you. Hell, it's probably too dangerous for *me*."

Sebastian St. Clare had been right about one thing. Ky Londen might be the only person in New Orleans who could find the Werewolf Killer. But with those same skills, he could just as easily track St. Clare.

He left the apartment, locking the door behind him only because Voodoo was there alone. He went swiftly and silently down the stairs and into the street below, close on the trail of the werewolf.

CHAPTER THREE

At first, Amy thought it was a joke. What else could she think? A man in a wolf costume—*wolf*, for heaven's sake—grabbing her on the street and affecting a kidnapping in the middle of a Mardi Gras parade. It had to be one of her colleagues with a warped sense of humor. That was why, after the initial shock, she didn't struggle as much as she should have or make enough of a fuss to attract the attention of anyone in the rollicking parade crowd.

"All right, very funny," she said, and, with a little more alarm. "Hey! Do you have to be so rough? Who are you, anyway?"

His stride grew so forceful that she trembled. He jerked her up sharply. When he picked her up bodily and began to force his way through the crowd, Amy started to grow frightened. "Put me down!" she demanded and kicked out wildly. The arm that had been around her shoulders moved up to encircle her neck, instead, cutting off her breath, and a cruel, black-gloved hand pressed over her mouth. He was so strong that even with these maneuvers he did not lessen the grip that kept her crushed against his chest. If anything, his hold grew even stronger.

Amy knew then it was no joke.

She couldn't breathe. Those leather-encased iron fingers dug into her face, leaving bruise marks on either side of her mouth. His arm was heavy across her throat,

twisting her head back at a painful angle, crushing her
windpipe. She fought back panic, then tried not to waste
her energy and her precious breath with futile struggles.
He was killing her. Black spots danced in front of her eyes
and the sound of traffic and Mardi Gras music grew
fainter, gradually replaced by a high, thin whining in her
ears.

She had spent enough hours in police stations and
courtrooms to know the most important thing she could
do right now was try to stay alert, to identify her assailant if she could, to pay attention to where he was taking
her, to diligently remain aware of any opportunity for escape, no matter how small, that might present itself. But
all of what she'd known and should have done fled her
head. All she could think of was breathing, of how desperately she needed air, of how terrified she was that she
would never be able to draw a deep breath again and of
what a horrible, slow way this would be to die.

She must have blacked out for a moment or two because the next thing she knew, they were no longer in the
street. She was aware of the creak of door hinges and going into a dank, musty-smelling room and abruptly she
could breathe again; he released her and she tumbled, or
was tossed, onto a torn, soiled mattress in a corner of the
room.

For a moment, she huddled there, gagging and coughing as she struggled for breath and fought back the star-
bursts of dark and light that exploded before her eyes.
When she finally was able to drag a few deep breaths into
her aching lungs, her vision began to clear. She was aware
of a small, brick-lined room furnished with wooden crates
and crumpled newspaper and illuminated with candles, a
dozen or more of them supported in bottles and on bits of
broken saucers. The place had the feel, and smell, of a

cave, but she suspected it was part of one of the old warehouses that were scattered here and there throughout the Vieux Carre. She tried to remember which way they had turned, how many turns they had taken, making an effort to visualize where he might have taken her, but she couldn't concentrate. She was trembling, and she couldn't stop coughing.

"Well now."

His shadow fell over her, causing Amy to gasp and choke on her own breath. She pressed a hand against her throat, trying to ease the ache that turned to fire every time she coughed.

He said, "A rather poor beginning to what I had hoped would be a long and satisfying relationship for both of us, I'm afraid. I apologize."

His voice, so smooth and articulate, startled her. She had expected the coarse, angry roar of an uneducated street thug, not the cultured accents of a gentleman. The monstrous costume in which he was dressed only made the discrepancy more bizarre.

The mask was one of those latex affairs that was far too realistic; covered with gray and black hair, the eyes were glittering yellow, the snout drawn back in a snarl to reveal sharp, discolored teeth. Below the mask, he wore black—black turtleneck, black tights, black gloves and boots, even a black cape. For a moment, while her eyes adjusted to the flickering candlelight, it almost looked as though the wolf head were floating above her in midair, and had she had the breath she would have screamed.

"Here. Drink this."

She noticed that he held a water glass half-full of some clear liquid. She merely stared at it.

"It's quite safe, I assure you," he said. "I wouldn't drink the water here, but I chose the wine myself. And the glass is clean."

Hesitantly, still gasping and choking back coughs, she took the glass from him. She had to hold it in both hands to keep from spilling it. She brought it to her face, just close enough to smell the contents, but she didn't drink. He told the truth: it was wine, at least partially. She did not want to take a chance on what else might be in the glass.

"Oh, for God's sake," he said impatiently. "It's not poisoned. I never poison my victims. It spoils the taste of their flesh."

Amy didn't move, or breathe or even think. She huddled like a rabbit trapped in the glare of headlights, clutching the glass and staring at him, and she knew the purest terror she had ever known in her life.

And then he laughed. "What a foolish little human you are, after all!" he exclaimed. "I had hoped for more courage from you... or perhaps simply more intelligence." He shrugged elaborately and turned away. "Drink or don't, whatever suits you. I was merely trying to be hospitable."

Amy's fingers tightened on the glass. "Who—who are you?" Her voice was hoarse and breathless, barely above a whisper. It hurt to make even that effort.

"You know the answer to that, *chérie*," he replied gently. Was there a hint of a smile in his voice? "You gave me my name, after all."

Amy wanted very badly to drink from the glass. She managed to hold it steady against her chest, no drops sloshing out. "Me?" she whispered. Firmly, determinedly, she put more effort into her voice, making it audible. "What are you talking about? I don't know you."

"Ah, but you do, *chérie*. You've followed my career from the beginning." He seemed amused as he added, "Well, almost from the beginning, anyway. And you were the first—I'm quite certain because I made a note of it—to call me by my rightful appellation. The Werewolf Killer. How did you know, I wonder? Will you tell?"

Amy thought, *No. A nightmare*. And then she thought, *A joke*. A very bad practical joke that had gotten out of hand. Or a deranged fan, would-be copycat who let himself get carried away by the Mardi Gras spirit... Yes, that had to be it. Because otherwise, she was being held captive by a man who had already killed fifteen people, and no one knew where she was. A man who stalked and slashed, who tore out the throats of his victims and left them like so much discarded rubbish by the side of the road... a madman who had held the city under a spell of terror for ten months, just as he now held her.

She looked around the dismal, dank-smelling little room. What were those stains on the floor? And the spatters on the wall, were they simply a trick of candlelight? Was this where he brought his victims, then, before he killed them? And she didn't really have to try very hard, did she, to smell the terror in this room like a lingering miasma, to hear the pleas for mercy that lingered in the ether like ghosts...

Sternly, she stopped herself. She was talking herself into hysteria.

She looked at the glass in her hand. She looked at the wolf-thing standing over her, arms crossed, grotesque head slightly tilted as though in speculation or amusement. She thought, *Better to die of poison*... She took a sip of the wine.

"Well now," he said with obvious approval. "I'm glad you've decided to be civil."

"It's very good," she said. *Keep him talking,* she thought. *Keep your wits about you and keep him talking and you have a chance—small, but a chance—to get out of this alive.*

"A simple Pinot," he replied. "Unpretentious but amusing, don't you think?"

"I don't know much about wine."

"Oh, that can't be true, *chérie.* A woman of your background and education? Don't be modest. In fact, I chose the wine because I knew you would appreciate it. Subtle but elegant. Understated but genuine. Like you."

Amy thought, *Oh, God.* She said, "I appreciate your thoughtfulness."

He seemed pleased. "My pleasure."

She searched, in the flickering candlelight, for the door. There was only one, and he stood between it and her.

"Is this your place? Do you live here?" she asked.

Again he laughed. The sound, though muffled by the mask, was not particularly sinister. It was the laugh of a child—or a madman.

"Hardly," he said. "No one could live in a place like this, not even those poor miserable creatures I send to their eternal rest. How could you think that?"

It was becoming easier to swallow. She took another sip of wine. "Why did you bring me here?"

"To talk. I've wanted to meet you for some time now, and after tonight's newscast, it seemed . . . appropriate."

"You—watch my broadcast?"

"But of course. Doesn't everyone? And why should it surprise you to learn that I, your protégé, in a manner of speaking, am one of your biggest fans?"

Amy felt ill, a cold heavy dread weighing down her stomach, filling up her throat. She said, "Why do you say that? You're not my protégé, I told you, I don't even know you."

"Alas, I am wounded."

With a sudden swooping motion, he bent down and took her chin in his fingers, grasping hard. Amy shrank back, too frightened to even cry out. Wine sloshed on her blouse.

"You know me, *chérie*," he said quietly. His breath was hot on her cheek, and oddly pleasant-smelling. Like fresh grass. His eyes, yellow glass eyes in a hairy-covered mask, were dead and glittering, horrifying. How did he see behind those eyes?

"You were the first to know me," he said, still soft, still low. His fingers were like talons, gripping her chin, bruising the bone. "That's why I have chosen you."

"Chosen me," she whispered, and she had never before imagined she possessed the courage it took to look into those flat yellow eyes and not shrink away. "For what?"

The seconds ticked off before his reply. Life or death, torture or pleasure; she imagined him weighing the options.

And then he said, "Well now, that remains to be seen, doesn't it?"

Abruptly, he released her and moved away. She felt the throbbing imprint of his fingers on either side of her chin and she thought irreverently that she would have to wear extra makeup for the show tomorrow to hide the marks. Then she wanted to laugh. Tomorrow, makeup, the show... she, whose chances of surviving the hour were growing increasingly slim, obviously had much bigger worries.

And with nothing to lose, she lifted her chin, tilting her head back a little to look him in the eye, and said, "You expect me to believe you are the so-called Werewolf Killer?''

"Since that is who I am, yes. I should say so. You have an opinion to the contrary?''

Amy glanced around, not too obviously, she hoped, for something she could use as a weapon. There was nothing. If she broke the glass in her hand, he would be on her before she could get to her feet and would probably use the broken glass to cut her throat. In other circumstances, she might throw the wine in his face and try to dash for the door while he was blinded, but the mask would protect his eyes. The room was small and empty and left her with few options.

She said, "You could be anyone behind that mask.''

"Ah, but couldn't we all?''

He seemed to be enjoying himself. And why shouldn't he? He held all the power.

Amy struggled to keep her gaze steady, not to show her fear. She said, "You might at least let me see your face.''

He chuckled. "I think not. Having done that, I would have to kill you, and I'm sure you don't want that.''

Her heart caught a little on hope. "Isn't that what you plan to do, anyway? Kill me?''

Again the head tilted to the side, assuming a posture of thoughtfulness. "Why, no, actually. I hadn't planned to kill you, not right away, anyway. I have plans for you first.''

He came to her and dropped to one knee beside her on the mattress. The yellow eyes glittered in the candlelight, the bared teeth menaced. But none of that was as terrifying as his posture, so close to her: intimate, powerful, in control.

Amy stiffened and choked down a scream as he lifted his gloved hand to her face, and stroked it tenderly.

* * *

Ky knew that St. Clare was probably aware he was being followed. He was a powerful werewolf with resources at his command Ky could not even begin to guess. At the very least, he might be leading Ky on a wild-goose chase; more likely, into a trap. But not for one moment did Ky consider abandoning pursuit.

A powerful werewolf. The words echoed in his head with a measure of disbelief. In fact, when Ky looked back over the events of the past half hour, he was almost inclined to believe he had imagined all of it. And yet, hadn't he always known this day would come? Hadn't he spent his life waiting for it?

Still, in his wildest reckonings, he had not pictured anything like this.

He wasn't exactly sure what he intended to accomplish by following St. Clare. He might spot his car, get a license-plate number, find out what hotel he was staying at or what flight he was taking home...find out where home was for him and who lived there with him and for how long and how many of them there were and who they were and how they lived and a thousand, thousand other things...

He knew of course that little, if any of this, was a possibility. He would find out only what St. Clare allowed him to find out. But how could he not try?

The old man walked for half a block, then got into a car with a driver. Ky had not anticipated this, which only went to show how rattled he was by events in general; even his normal investigative instincts had deserted him. He had assumed that, since there was no car waiting outside the building, St. Clare had come on foot, but of course a person who was planning on breaking and entering would hardly park his car in plain sight.

Ky hesitated, then decided it would be more efficient to follow for a while on foot while the trail was still fresh, then go back for his car when he had a better idea in which direction St. Clare was headed. He did not, after all, seek another confrontation with St. Clare tonight, so time was not a consideration. He simply wanted to know where the old man was going.

There were a thousand, a hundred thousand sensory clues crowding up the well-worn streets of this ancient city, yet the scent of the werewolf was unmistakable, and Ky followed it effortlessly. Even encased as he was in two tons of metal and disguised by exhaust fumes and fresh rain puddles and the succulent outpourings of open-air restaurants as the car made its way in an unhurried fashion through the Vieux Carre, Sebastian St. Clare left a signature upon the night that was as easy to read as a map.

And then it wasn't.

Ky followed the trail the car left for three blocks—long enough to realize he was being led in a circle, or a square, actually, that would take him right back to Rampart Street. At first he was irritated, and mildly disappointed because he had expected something more inventive from St. Clare. But then he understood.

St. Clare's driver had taken the circuitous route not necessarily to confuse Ky but to avoid crossing Canal Street, which was closed for a parade. The parade, now fully in progress and blocking out both visual and aural clues with its color and raucousness for a good quarter mile in either direction, had swallowed up the last scent of the werewolf.

His quarry was gone.

Amy said steadily, "What, exactly, are your plans for me?"

She should have been terrified. She was, in fact, on some visceral level almost too intense to be recognized, frightened out of her wits. And yet she could deal with it, she could sit here on the soiled mattress and gaze into that nightmarish monster face and let him fondle her, without breaking into hysterical, mindless screams, because of him. Because there was something about him—his touch, his voice, his manner—that didn't seem monstrous at all.

He said, drawing a gloved index finger down her cheek from the edge of her eye to the curve of her jaw, "Perhaps I shall just keep you as a pet."

"That might be difficult. I'll be missed. And, as you might know, I have a few influential friends."

He chuckled softly. "Ah, yes. Your friends. Perhaps then, I should think of some other, more amusing, use for you."

The threat was implicit, the meaning unmistakable. Had Amy been able to see his face, there was no doubt in her mind that he would have been undressing her with his eyes.

She said, "Is that intended to frighten me?"

"Does it?"

"No."

"I'm not certain whether I'm insulted or flattered."

"The Werewolf Killer never sexually assaults his victims," Amy said. "If you were to rape me, you'd only prove to me that you're not who you claim to be."

He laughed. "A rather twisted piece of logic, but oddly compelling. And you're right. I haven't the least interest in 'assaulting' you, as you put it."

"What are you going to do with me?"

He sat back, regarding her with an attitude of what Amy could only imagine to be amused speculation.

Then he said, "I am going to use you, my dear, to bring my story to the world."

Amy lifted the wine glass and took another sip. The wine, the conversation, the urbane manners of the gentleman sitting across from her...it could have been lunch at Arnaud's, cocktails poolside, a casual interview in the lounge of the Ritz Carlton. She concentrated on forgetting that she was not in any of those places.

She said, "I thought that was what I was doing."

"Indeed." He inclined his head. "And you're doing a superlative job. But you only know half the truth. I would like you to know all about me."

Because the reporter in her wouldn't die, Amy said, "I'd like that, too."

He was silent for a time. Amy could feel his eyes on her, the eyes behind the yellow eyes and she wished desperately to see his face...not just for identification purposes, but to *see* his face, to know the man behind the mask.

"Yes," he murmured after a time, as though having reached a conclusion in thought, "I think you may be ready to know the truth. Not the whole world, perhaps, but you...yes. And I would like it if at least one person knew."

Amy said, softly, so as not to break the spell of gentle sadness that seemed to have come over him, "Knew what? What is the truth?"

He looked at her, and though of course she could not see through the mask, she imagined that he smiled. "The truth," he replied, "is that I am a werewolf."

Ky stood on the corner, impatiently trying to see over the heads and around the shoulders of jostling parade watchers, reflexively falling back on the ordinary human senses of sight and sound when his extraordinary ones failed him. There was, of course, no sign of the werewolf, nor of the car in which he had been driven away. There were twelve-foot-high floats and belly dancers and acrobats in the street, there were children riding shoulders and men lifting beer mugs on the sidewalk; it was enough to confuse anyone.

The car had obviously passed this way before the parade reached the corner, but in which direction it had gone was anyone's guess. Whatever residual trace of the werewolf scent that remained was masked completely by the chaos that surrounded him now.

"Damn!" Ky said, and turned to push his way back through the crowd. To be this close, the chance of a lifetime, and to lose him in a Mardi Gras parade...

But St. Clare wasn't entirely lost. Ky had his money, which meant St. Clare would be in touch. No one just walked off and left fifty thousand dollars without following up on the contract. And he had a name, which he had absolutely no reason to believe was a false one. No, St. Clare was too arrogant, too sublimely confident in his own invincibility, to try something as banal as concealing his identity from a private investigator. Finding St. Clare again would not be the problem. Getting to him would.

"Damn," Ky muttered again, and broke through the crowd, turning the corner that led to his apartment.

That was when he caught the scent.

"I see," Amy said.

Her tone wasn't convincing, even to herself, and she wasn't surprised that he was angered by it.

"Don't humor me!" he snapped and got to his feet. "You forget your place, human! I have the power, do you understand that? I am in charge here, and I will not be patronized!''

His fury, though not entirely unexpected, was nonetheless terrifying, like a quick harsh storm that broke tree limbs and blew shingles off roofs and then, as abruptly as it began it was over. The roar of his voice actually hurt her ears and she even imagined—surely she imagined—a gust of wind created by the force of his rage. He seemed to grow larger, more menacing, and when he loomed over her in that horrible mask, she could believe he was anything....

"Is this how you use your power then?" she cried. "Frightening helpless women? Kidnapping them and holding them captive and then terrifying them with threats? Does that make you feel strong? Does that make you feel like a *man?*"

She couldn't believe the words were coming out of her mouth. The minute they were spoken, she wanted to drag them back in. She was antagonizing a madman, taunting a killer who was already enraged. She expected him to strike her, to pull his gun or his knife and finish doing what he had obviously brought her here for. She prepared herself for the worst.

And then he said, quite matter-of-factly, "Now you do insult me. I should kill you for that, but I won't. As I said, I have other plans for you. And..." Again he cocked his head at her, and she imagined a smile. "I admire your pluck. Not that I will put up with a great deal of it, but I did choose you for your spirit, among other things. I can hardly blame you for being true to your nature...any more than your kind can blame me for being true to mine."

Amy felt like a condemned felon upon receiving that phone call from the governor; like that rabbit trapped in the glare of headlights when the car suddenly swerved to miss it. She had been given a reprieve when she had had no reason to expect one and every muscle in her body went weak with relief.

"Your nature?" she managed to say. Her throat felt gummy. She wanted another sip of wine but didn't trust her hands to hold the glass steady if she tried. "And what would that be?"

There was pity and impatience in his tone. "You haven't heard a word I've said. I had forgotten how slow even the brightest human can be. I do the planet a favor by thinning your herd."

He sat beside her again, and she held herself very still, refusing to tremble. He moved closer.

"I am," he said, "a werewolf. My nature is to hunt, to kill, to run with the night and to follow the moon. You think you're very clever for discerning a connection between me and a dozen or so dead vagrants, and I suppose you are, by human standards. But listen to me, *chérie*. You've only found what I wanted you to find. You only know what I wanted you to know. There have been hundreds, do you understand that? *Hundreds*."

Amy felt ill. She liked to think she had been born with reporter's instincts, an innate sense of who was telling the truth and who was lying, when she was being given a genuine lead and when she was being led down the garden path. Those instincts were telling her now that she was looking into the masked face of a madman and a killer, and that every word he spoke was the truth as he knew it. Hundreds. He had killed *hundreds*.

She said, "Why are you telling me this?"

And he replied, "I already answered that. I like your style. I saw you on the news this evening with that piece of horse fodder Devereaux—something will have to be done about him, I'm afraid—and I saw how you stood up for me with such calm nobility of character and it was then it occurred to me—you are a woman of deep convictions and genuine involvement. You, and only you, can be trusted to bring my story to the world."

Still she kept her voice calm, her gaze steady. She thought she was beginning to understand him. That did not make her less afraid of him, but she thought she knew enough to deal with him, or at least to prolong her life until she could think of something to do, some way to escape or to convince him to let her go.

"That presupposes, of course, that I believe your story. That you are who—and what—" she added to pacify him, "you say you are."

He bent a gaze upon her that was long and filled with silent menace. "You try my patience," he said at last.

He got slowly to his feet. "Very well, *chérie.*" His voice was soft, calculating, and even more frightening than a shout. "I shall give you what you want. I'll show you proof. And you may yet be sorry you asked."

His lifted his hand to the mask.

Ky's heart was thundering in his chest and a fine sweat appeared on his upper lip, and he couldn't explain why. He stood still, focusing his senses, but he couldn't make his heart stop pounding. The scent. Strong now, on a southerly breeze, now fainter on still air. The same, only...not. St. Clare...and not.

For the first time in his life, Ky knew what it was to doubt his own senses, to know confusion instead of clarity, to be at the same disadvantage as any one else who walked the street. He had never found a scent he didn't know before. He had never encountered a sensory clue he couldn't visualize. And yet this . . . It left him baffled and unsure.

He had never smelled a werewolf before today, and yet he had known the scent immediately for what it was. This, it was the same, it was like St. Clare, only it was . . . diseased, yes, or in trouble or . . .

No, he couldn't define it, and a sharp pain pierced his head with the effort. It was distinct yet muted, familiar yet—wrong. Frightening.

And even though all his instincts shrieked a warning, even though he knew it was the stupidest thing he had ever done in his life, Ky turned down the empty alley, crossed a narrow street and moved into the darkness, following the scent.

Amy held her breath, watching as his hand moved beneath the neck of the hideous wolf head. She thought he was going to take off the mask. Dread and anticipation warred inside her for what she might see.

But he didn't remove the mask. With a quick snap of his wrist, he jerked a thin gold chain free from his neck and tossed it to her. Instinctively, Amy lifted her hand to catch it.

"Ask the police whether anything was missing from the body of the August victim. Sherry Wilson. Yes, you see, I remember their names, when you are good enough to identify them for me."

The jewelry was warm in Amy's hand, and it made her feel strange to hold it knowing that only seconds ago it had been against his skin. Suspended from the chain was a small heart-shaped locket. On a compulsion she immediately regretted, Amy pushed the catch with her thumbnail and the locket opened. Inside was the blurry picture of a blond-haired little girl of about three. Amy felt ill.

"There might even be traces of blood left yet," he commented matter-of-factly, "that they can identify as hers. Of course, they might also pick up traces of my DNA, which should prove to be very interesting when they try to analyze it."

Amy dragged her eyes away from the locket and upward to him. She was quite sure he was smiling behind the mask.

"Why won't you let me see your face?" she demanded hoarsely. "What's really behind that mask?"

"Perhaps simply another mask." And then suddenly he stiffened. His casual, controlled manner was gone and in its place the alert defensive posture of a startled animal. He spun toward the narrow door, and then back to her. "What have you done?" he shouted at her. "Who have you brought here?"

He threw back his head suddenly, almost as though sniffing the air, and turned again, sharply, toward the door. "How can this be?"

Amy didn't hesitate another minute. The moment he looked away from her, she threw the glass of wine against the opposite wall. When he whirled toward the sound, she plunged past him toward the door. She didn't weigh her chances; she didn't consider her options; she didn't think about it even once. She simply ran, and the unexpectedness of her action, combined with his distraction, gave her the advantage she needed to get almost to the door before he caught her.

She screamed as his hand snatched her hair with such force that her head snapped back. He flung her back with such strength that her feet actually left the ground. She screamed again as she bounced against the mattress. But he was no longer interested in her. He spun back toward the door even as it burst open and then the oddest thing happened.

It was dark outside, and the candlelight in the room provided only the dimmest illumination so Amy could see little of her rescuer's face, only a figure, tall and lithe and crouched in the attack/defense position. He wore jeans and a T-shirt. His straight black hair swept over his collar; his face was in shadows. Amy's captor was directly in front of him, less than three feet; Amy expected him to lunge for the door, to attack the man or to push past him and disappear into the night. But he did not move.

It lasted ten seconds, perhaps a little more, and it seemed like centuries. Amy counted every exploding beat of her heart, every half-choked, stammering breath. She wanted to scream; she wanted to run. But the strange paralysis that had afflicted the two men had her in its spell, as well. They stood there, staring at each other, poised on the brink of conflict or the edge of murder, yet startled, studying each other with a kind of mutual horror.

Later she would decide that was exactly what it was. Mutual horror.

And that was when Amy was witness to something she could not explain and would never forget. There was a sound, a low rumbling sound that seemed to come from the throat of one of the men. A growl, only louder and more fierce than a growl, deadlier and more controlled. And with the growl, something began to happen, and afterward Amy would never be able to describe it with words or even recreate it in her mind; it was more of an experience than an observation.

The man in the werewolf mask seemed to change somehow; she could see little in the dim light and with his body disguised as it was by the long cloak and the mask, but it was as though he were shrinking into himself and at the same time expanding, growing larger and more menacing. The air around him seemed charged and actually appeared to quiver, and there was a hot, electric smell like static electricity filling the room. It prickled on her skin and caught in her chest and filled her with a visceral terror... and wonder.

And suddenly everything exploded. The man in the werewolf mask gave a great roar and leapt into the air, flying—yes, *flying*—toward the man in the doorway with an acrobatic strength that was supernatural. The roar echoed in Amy's ears, hurting them. She screamed and covered her ears, pressing herself back against the wall as the werewolf monster struck out at the man in the doorway. The man went down and Amy screamed again, propelling herself off the mattress and toward the door.

When she got there, her rescuer lay crumpled against the doorframe, his throat covered with blood. The werewolf was gone.

CHAPTER FOUR

The memory of those next few moments was confused by shock, jumbled together, irrational and unclear. Amy remembered screaming into the night, "Help us! Someone, please! Oh, God, help us! I think he's dead!"

She dropped to her knees beside her rescuer and he was not dead; when she touched his shoulder, he pushed against her and groaned, trying to get to his feet. There were running footsteps in the distance, but she could not tell if they were coming toward her or moving away; if they belonged to the killer or to someone answering her call for help.

She whispered, "Lie still, lie still, you're hurt..."

And he mumbled, "Let me go, he's getting away..."

He put his hand to his bleeding neck. Amy saw that his throat was not cut, as she had imagined in that first horrified moment, but marked by three parallel slashes, as though raked by some kind of sharp instrument... or claws. She stared at the injury in shock and fascination before she came to her senses and began to search for something to stanch the flow of blood.

"Thank God you found me. If you hadn't come, I don't know what would have happened. He was crazy..." She was babbling breathlessly, trying to keep him still, searching her pockets and the small wallet-purse that she wore on a long strap across her body for a handkerchief or a tissue or even a scrap of paper with which she could clean his wound. She was aware she was bordering on hysteria, but she was entitled.

He tried to push her away, turning his head impatiently when she tried to dab at his cuts with the scrap of a fabric softener sheet she had found in her skirt pocket. "Lady, leave me alone, get out of my way. Don't you see he's getting away? Let me go!"

He had been stunned by the blow, but now his senses were returning. He jerked away from her clumsy ministrations and, bracing himself against the doorframe, pushed to his feet. By now, a small crowd had begun to gather in the alley, and Amy cried, "Please, someone call the police—and an ambulance! This man is hurt! Someone, please do something!"

"He's gone," said the man, and he slumped back against the wall, dark eyes haunted with defeat. "I let him get away."

Amy looked at him intently. His eyes were deep, deep violet, filled now with a pain that was more than physical, his face sharp-featured and defined by a dark beard-shadow, his coal black hair swept back from a high forehead in a way that made him look both bleak and romantic. There was such a grimness in those eyes, such a determined set to his mouth, that she almost expected an answer to her question as she whispered, "Who was he?"

But he merely returned to her a look that was strained and frustrated and still edged with residual shock, and he said simply, "You know who it was."

Amy opened her closed fist, and looked down at the locket she still clutched there. "Yes," she whispered shakily, "I think I do."

Abruptly, the events of the past hour swept over her in a single, gripping wave. She clapped her hand to her mouth but was able to stumble only a few feet away before the nausea overcame her and she sank to her knees, retching.

People were watching, but she didn't care. He was kneeling over her, sweeping back her hair with one hand, touching her shoulder, and she *did* care about that. She was humiliated, miserable and still very frightened. She was Amy Fortenoy, star investigative reporter of Channel Six Action News, and she was throwing up in the street like a common drunk while everyone watched... while he watched, the Dark Knight who had saved her life.

She was supposed to be intrepid, in control, unflappable. She had always pictured herself in that way; she had convinced other people she was that way; she had always believed it of herself. But she had never been through anything like what she had just experienced. She had never *seen* anything like what she had just seen.

The foundation of her world had been knocked out from under her feet and she wasn't brave at all. She was weak and terrified and she would never feel in control again.

When at last the spasm had passed, her rescuer helped her to her feet, and turned her back toward the building, shielding her with his body from the curious onlookers. She cast him a grateful look.

"Are you okay?" he inquired quietly.

She started to nod, then replied more honestly. "No." Her voice was still unsteady, and she blotted her damp face with the back of her hand. "But I think I will be."

Understanding was in his silence. Then he said, "Did he hurt you?"

Amy shook her head, trying to repress a shudder. "No, I—he only threatened. I was just frightened." She looked up at him, trying to regain her composure with one unsteady indrawn breath. "I'm sorry, I don't know your name. I'm Amy Fortenoy."

He said with a faint smile, "I know who you are."

Even the shadow of a smile transformed his face, making Amy realize that he was a handsome man—more than handsome, striking-looking, memorable—making her wish to see more of it, more of his face, more of his smile. She was actually so taken by his face, by those deep indigo purple eyes, that she forgot what she was going to say for a moment. Then they heard the fast-approaching sound of a siren and they both turned toward it.

Chaos overtook them shortly after that, and by the time Amy realized that she still didn't know her hero's name, he was gone.

"You really ought to have stitches," the paramedic told him as he placed the last strip of adhesive tape across the bandage on Ky's neck. "Why don't you come in with us and let the ER check you out?"

Ky shook his head, wincing a little at the pull of the tape. "I'm fine. They'll just give me a tetanus shot and tell me to see my doctor in the morning. Had one last month and I will, first thing. Okay?"

The young EMT looked unhappy. "I'll have to put you down as 'refused treatment.'"

"You do that."

Ky touched the bandage gingerly as he stepped down out of the ambulance. His shirt was still damp with blood and his fingers came away sticky. He felt a little sick as he thought, *He knows the smell of my blood now . . .*

"Is this character giving you trouble, buddy? Don't take any of his lip, he's known for it."

Ky turned to meet Detective John Handley Sentime the Third, known to friends and family simply as Trey. Ky and Trey had been partners for the last three of his ten years on the police force.

"So they're sending you down to the slums now. Who's wife did you get caught with?" Ky said.

"Yeah, very funny, Londen. Your sense of humor was always the thing I loved best about you. You okay?" He gestured to the bandage.

"Just a scratch. I've gotten worse in barroom brawls."

"What'd he get you with? A switchblade?"

"Could have been," Ky replied evasively as they walked away from the ambulance. He didn't like to lie to a colleague, and he would never have done anything to hinder a police investigation . . . not if he had thought the police had any chance at all of catching his assailant.

He knew there was no switchblade. The only weapons the man who had attacked him possessed were his hands . . . and his teeth.

That was all he needed.

Ky asked, "Are you taking statements?"

"Trying to. You want to sit down? You're not looking your usual chipper self, if I may say so."

Ky's reply was a little dry. "Well, it's been a full day."

But when Trey gestured him toward the police car parked at the head of the alley, Ky shook his head. He wanted to stay within easy hearing distance of the crime scene investigators . . . and he didn't want to lose sight of the woman. Amy.

The little building and the half block surrounding it had been cordoned off with police tape, keeping back a curious crowd, although there were not as many onlookers as one might expect. In this neighborhood, people stayed as far away from the police as possible, even when the trouble the cops were investigating was someone else's.

The area was bathed with strobing blue-and-white lights, and the red counterpoint pulse of the ambulance gave the whole scene a surreal air. Flashbulbs popped from inside the building where Amy had been held as investigators gathered evidence. Ky was quite certain nothing they would find would put them any closer to catching the killer than they had been before.

Amy was sitting in the back seat of an open police car, her feet resting on the ground and her back toward the interior of the car so that she could see everything that was going on around her. Ky was dimly amused to note that she, like he, couldn't stand to be cut off from the action, although he suspected their reasons were far from the same. Amy was being interviewed by two detectives, a male and a female. Ky knew the female—he had, in fact, dated her once—but he didn't recognize the man, who appeared to be in charge of the case.

Trey said, "So what were you doing down here?"

"What do you mean, down here? It's only a few blocks from my place."

"If you don't mind getting a knife between your ribs taking the shortcut home. What are you, working a case in the neighborhood or something?"

"I was on my way out for Thai food," Ky said. "I got cut off by the parade. I cut through the alley to circle around and I heard a woman scream."

"You hear women scream every hour on the hour in this neighborhood," commented Trey. "Men, too. Go on."

"I heard a woman's scream," repeated Ky, "coming from that building. And a crash, like she was being knocked around. Well, you know my Good Samaritan instincts..."

Trey gave a grunt but did not look up from the notes he was taking.

"So I tried the door, and it was unlocked. I opened it. She was in the shadows, on the floor, I think, crying or screaming. He was wearing a black turtleneck, black boots, black gloves, black tights. A costume. Black cape. The mask was one of those full-head things, glass eyes, fur-covered, big snarl—a wolf."

"Jeez."

"Not something you want to meet in a dark alley," agreed Ky. "Which I guess was the point. He was about my height, minus the ears, and slim built. One-sixty, I'd guess. Moved fast."

An understatement, if ever there was one. No human had ever moved that fast, as Ky knew very well. But he did not feel it was necessary to go into that much descriptive detail.

"So what happened?"

"He was standing right in front of the door, I was blocking his way. We looked at each other for a few seconds..." *A lifetime,* thought Ky, feeling ill again. *The time it takes for a world to be torn apart brick by brick.* "Then he rushed me. He knocked me down but I didn't know I'd been cut until I saw the blood on my shirt. By that time he was gone. I didn't see in which direction."

"You carrying a piece?"

Ky cast him an impatient look. "Of course not."

"I had to ask."

They had reached the car where Amy was being interviewed. She was outside the car now, standing with the two detectives. Ky and Trey arrived as she was saying in a small strained voice, "He said I should ask if anything was taken from the body of Sherry Wilson, the August victim. He gave me this."

She passed the small locket on a chain to the male detective. The recognition on his face was instantaneous.

Amy said, "There's a picture of a little girl. I—I didn't know she had any children."

The detective pushed the catch and looked at the picture inside only long enough to confirm its existence. His expression was grim. "She didn't," he said. "Her friends said it was a picture of herself as a kid, used to be her mother's or something, that she never took it off. We kept that information from the press in case, well, in case the locket ever turned up."

Amy cleared her throat. "He said—he said you might find traces of her blood still on it. In case you needed more proof, I guess."

The detective nodded and turned to a uniformed officer who had just come up. "Bag this and get it to the lab," he said, handing over the necklace.

Ky asked, "Did he say why he kept it?"

Amy gasped and whirled, clearly startled to find him at her elbow. She was a lovely woman, Ky couldn't help noticing, even in disarray, even frightened, even with her hair mussed and her makeup worn off. Very few people looked as good in person as they did on television. Amy Fortenoy looked better.

"Where did you come from?" she demanded, shaken.

Trey grinned. "Don't let him rattle you, miss, he's got a bad habit of sneaking up on people. We used to call him the chameleon back on the force."

Amy's eyes widened with quick understanding. "You're a policeman?"

"Ex," Ky corrected.

Then Trey said, "Ky, you know Diane Kelsey, don't you?"

Diane's eyes lit up with genuine pleasure. "Ky. It's good to see you again."

Women liked him; they always had. And Ky liked women, in general and in particular; what he didn't like was having to hurt them when they began to expect more from him than he was able to give. He therefore made it a policy never to allow a relationship to get to that point, which left the women he dated ever-hopeful . . . and always liking him.

He said, "How've you been, Diane?" and noticed that Amy was following the exchange with interest.

Trey said, "Winston Tremont, this is Ky Londen. Ky and I worked together out of the fifteenth district a few years back."

Ky said slowly, extending his hand, "Tremont. I do know you. You're in charge of the Werewolf task force."

Tremont shook Ky's hand absently. "Good to meet you. Did we get your statement?"

"Yeah. Listen, do you mind if I—"

Tremont cut him off. "Then if we know where to find you, you can go on home. We're real busy here, as you can see."

"No," Amy said clearly.

Everyone looked at her, even the busy Detective Tremont.

She continued, "He didn't tell me why he kept the necklace, but that's a good question—one I'd like to have the answer to if no one else would. Did he take anything from any of the other victims, Detective?"

The lines around Tremont's mouth deepened, and he looked for a moment as though he might dismiss her with the same brusqueness with which he had treated Ky. Then he seemed to remember that he was dealing not only with a victim, but with a reporter—and a very powerful reporter at that.

He replied in a tense, clipped tone. "His victims lived on the street. They didn't have anything for him to take. Maybe he kept the necklace because it was the only thing Miss Wilson *did* have."

"Or maybe," Ky said, thinking out loud, "he kept it for just this moment. Because he knew he'd have to convince you—" he looked at Amy "—that he was who he said he was."

Amy went a shade paler. The reddish bruises on her lower face and throat stood out in stark contrast.

"Do you mean—" she spoke with difficulty "—that he has been planning this... since August?"

Ky wished now that he'd never brought the whole thing up, but he had to answer. "That was about the time you started calling him the Werewolf Killer, wasn't it? Maybe that singled you out in his mind."

Tremont frowned, clearly annoyed. "What do you think, Miss Fortenoy? Could there be anything to that?"

Amy touched her throat in a nervous gesture, clearly disturbed by the thought. "I don't know. He did say that he had chosen me to bring his story to the world. I told you that. Maybe... I don't know."

There was a moment's silence while everyone looked at Amy uncomfortably. Then Tremont announced abruptly, "And I don't think it matters. We can't waste time on trivialities when there's a killer on the loose."

"True enough," agreed Ky, glad to change the subject. He hadn't intended to upset Amy, who had certainly been through enough tonight, by anyone's standards. "Will you be providing Miss Fortenoy with police protection?"

Again the muscles around Tremont's face tightened, and his eyes narrowed just a fraction. He said, "We'll do what we can, of course. I wonder, Mr. Londen, if I could speak with you in private for a moment?''

Ky intercepted a look between Diane and Trey that was all too easy to read. Half pained, half exasperated, it said, *There he goes again.* Ky had never gotten along particularly well with authority figures.

He walked away with Tremont, feeling like a kid being sent to the principal's office... again.

When they were out of hearing of the others, Tremont wasted no time. "I know about you, Londen," he said. "They still talk about you on the force."

"I'm flattered."

"Trouble finds you like a magnet," he said shortly. "You're a hotshot and a boat rocker. You went through four partners in six years. You weren't happy if you weren't stirring things up. You were a certified pain in the butt."

"'Does not work or play well with others,'" agreed Ky mildly. He did not add, because he didn't have to, that he had the highest solve record of anyone in the history of the force, ever. Tremont knew that, or he wouldn't be wasting time talking to him now.

Tremont said, his gaze steady, "I don't need that kind of grief, do you understand me? This is a touchy situation that just got a lot touchier, and the last thing I need is interference from a know-it-all has-been."

Ky nodded gravely. "You mean because Amy Fortenoy can slaughter you in the press and her family can buy and sell your carcass on the open market. Not to mention forgetting any aspirations you might have for a political career if you blow this one."

Tremont's eyes grew hard. "It's a lot more complicated than you know, Londen. And for your information, I'd be just as worried whether it was Fortenoy or a waitress down at the Dunk 'N Dine who was at risk, so don't go throwing politics in my face."

Ky believed him. And he wondered what, exactly, was making the case "more complicated than he knew."

"You're not going to be able to give her protection, are you?"

Tremont looked frustrated. "We're stretched to the limit on this thing already. I've got a task force pulling overtime and officers working around the clock. Where's the staff supposed to come from?"

Ky nodded. He knew that story too well. But he also knew that the werewolf was far from finished with Amy Fortenoy. He glanced toward the building where Amy had been held. "Do you mind if I look around in there?"

He would have done it with or without Tremont's permission, but it was polite to ask. He always tried to keep a good relationship with the police, out of both respect and expediency.

Tremont looked for a moment as though he would argue, then he said impatiently, "Suit yourself. Follow procedure. And Londen . . ."

Ky glanced back.

"I mean it. I don't need you poking around in this case."

Ky answered with the simple truth. "Looks to me like you need somebody."

The room had been photographed, vacuumed, dusted and swept. The candles had been taken, as had the broken pieces of the glass that Amy had broken and the wine bottle . . . an '87 French Pinot, Ky could smell it. He knew the police would find no prints but Amy's, no fiber evidence of any significance, nothing much at all that would help them in their research.

Ky was in the building less than five minutes, and he did not have much better luck. The sensory evidence was already fading, having been trampled upon by so many different people, but in a way he was glad. The scent of the werewolf was deeply disturbing, and he couldn't be around it for long. But he forced himself to examine every nuance of what was left behind, to memorize the feel and the substance and the character of the scent, not that there was much chance he would ever forget it. Not that there was any chance at all that, should he ever come upon it again, he would mistake it for anything other than what it was.

Even before he left the building, he knew the media had arrived. He could hear the clatter and babble and see the reflection of camera lights bouncing off the damp brick walls. As he turned to leave the building, he was amazed to hear Amy Fortenoy's voice, crisp and professional, giving a report.

She must have called her own news station from the police car. Half an hour ago, she had been the victim of a crime that would have traumatized most women—and men—for months. Now she was standing before the cameras with a microphone in her hand, telling the world about it.

"Is that dedication," wondering Ky out loud, "or stupidity?"

He reached the door just as he heard her say, "—held inside this building here for approximately thirty minutes, although I can assure you, it seemed much longer…" And it was too late to turn back.

He thought he could move quickly through the shadows behind her and be out of range, but the camera lights caught him full in the face, and Amy turned.

Her hair was combed back and she had applied makeup to the bruises for the camera, but her voice was husky from the injury as she exclaimed, "And this is the man to whom I am convinced I owe my life. Ky Londen, a former New Orleans police detective, happened to be passing by when he heard my cries for help."

As she spoke, she was moving toward him and so were the cameras. It wasn't just Amy's station, but two other television cameras, a half-dozen radio microphones and several print journalists whom he recognized from his days on the force were pressing the police barrier. Ky did his best to get out of the way or, failing that, to hide his face, but it was hopeless.

Amy caught his arm. "Mr. Londen, will you tell us what exactly you saw when you opened that door?"

And someone from the barricade called, "Do we have a definite confirmation that it *was* the Werewolf Killer?"

And someone else, "Mr. Londen, do the police have an official statement—"

And Amy, gentle but persistent, "Mr. Londen, you can't deny the central role you played in this drama. Please, just a few words."

He gave her one long, hard and disbelieving look, then pulled his arm away and walked quickly out of camera range.

Tremont stepped before the cameras with his hands upraised. "I'd like to emphasize, please, that Mr. Londen is in no way connected with the police department at this time—"

"Great," muttered Ky, shoving his hands into his pockets.

Trey fell into step beside him. "Unbelievable, isn't she?"

Ky shot him a dark look. "That's one word for it."

"We tried to stop her, but you know these reporters."

Ky said nothing.

"'Course, the fact is, it all worked out pretty well for her, careerwise, that is. If it weren't for that necklace, she might even be suspected of setting this whole thing up."

Ky stopped and looked at him. He glanced back at Amy, who was still holding the microphone, pale and composed, doing her job. He said to Trey, with perhaps just a little too much emphasis, "She didn't set it up."

Trey smiled. "You like her, don't you?"

"I don't even know her."

"Yeah, but . . ." He gave Ky one of those man-to-man winks. "What's not to like, right?"

"The woman just got me knifed, put my face on camera for every psychopath in New Orleans to see, made me an enemy for life out of Tremont, and you're asking me what's not to like?"

Trey chuckled, but the mirth faded quickly. "Give me your impressions, Ky."

They had worked together too long, and knew each other too well, for Ky to dissemble. He said, "Amy Fortenoy is in trouble, more than she knows. Get her some protection."

He didn't wait for an answer; he saw it in Trey's eyes. He turned to continue down the street.

"Where're you going?"

"To feed my dog."

Trey caught up with him, turning him with a hand on his shoulder toward the police car that waited at the curb. "Let's take a ride first."

"Oh, man, don't do this to me." Ky's protest sounded annoyed but not very hopeful. "I gave you my statement."

"Now you get to give it again for the stenographer."

"I've got things to do."

"Yeah, I keep forgetting about that rollicking social life of yours. The mutt will wait."

Ky could have continued the argument, and he might even have won it, but he knew it would be faster to simply do as Trey asked. He got into the back of the cruiser and leaned his head against the seat with a long release of breath.

"The perfect ending to a hell of an evening," he grumbled.

Trey got in beside him. "Yeah, well, if it makes you feel any better, your evening has got to have been better than hers."

He nodded toward Amy, who had surrendered her microphone and was now giving Diane the same kind of argument—though a bit more energetically, Ky noticed—that Ky had given Trey about coming downtown to give an official statement. She was quite a woman. In other circumstances . . .

Ky almost smiled, then he remembered Sebastian St. Clare and fifty thousand dollars in cash, a hundred unanswered questions and a renegade werewolf with the smell of Ky's blood on his fingers. Suddenly, he was almost overwhelmed by fatigue, and the cuts on his neck throbbed like fire.

He leaned back and closed his eyes. "You want to bet?" he said heavily.

There was no humor whatsoever in his voice.

CHAPTER FIVE

They kept Ky in the interview room over an hour; it would have taken half the time if old friends hadn't kept stopping by to say hello. And on any other occasion Ky would have enjoyed visiting with them; tonight he had too much on his mind.

When he finally came out, Amy Fortenoy was waiting for him. He had known that, of course. Hers was a presence he wasn't likely to miss had they been separated by twice as many walls and concrete pillars. What he had not been able to figure out was why.

She came over to him quickly. "I thought you might like a ride home. The station sent a car for me."

He was tempted; there was no point in pretending he wasn't. "Thanks. That's kind of you. But I'll catch a ride with one of the guys."

He walked toward the door. She kept up.

"I'd really like a chance to talk to you."

"As in interview?"

"As in thank you, for heaven's sake!"

"You've thanked me, Miss Fortenoy. Good night."

He knew the lobby would be filled with reporters so he turned left, toward the back entrance. She followed.

She said, "Look, it's no trouble to drop you off, really. And there are some things I wanted to, well, ask you about..."

She was distressed, but that didn't surprise him. The uncertainty he sensed in her did.

He stopped in the hall and turned to her. "All right, ask me now, *before* we get in front of the lights and cameras."

Her tone was a little exasperated. "Look, I'm sorry if you're camera shy, but you'd better get over it. What you did tonight made you a hero, and there are going to be more cameras than mine pointed at you for the next few days. My advice to you is to learn to enjoy it."

He said, as patiently as he could manage, "Miss Fortenoy—"

"Amy, please."

"Amy," he said, keeping his tone calm, "I am not a hero. What I am is a man who spent six years undercover putting half this city's bad guys behind bars, and I'm not real crazy about having the other half see my face splashed all over the evening news, okay?"

She looked abruptly chagrined. "Oh," she said. Her voice had lost some of its power. "I hadn't thought of that. I mean, I didn't realize... The last thing I wanted was to put you in danger."

"Forget it." He started walking again.

In fact, he was a little ashamed of himself because he hadn't told her the whole truth. It wasn't the criminal element of New Orleans he had once stalked that he was worried about, but one specific madman. Not that it mattered whether or not the Werewolf Killer saw his face on television or knew his name; he had Ky's scent and could track him anytime he wanted. Knowing who he was would only make it easier.

Of course, the reverse was also true.

But Amy was quicker than he had thought, and she caught on to the implications immediately. She said, "I should have thought. He already knew who I was, but you were nothing but a face in the night to him until I announced your name and your profession—your former profession, anyway—on television. Oh, Ky, I am so sorry."

She looked up at him with such genuine fear and distress in her eyes that he couldn't be angry at her. He even managed a smile. "Look, it's okay." He wished he could mean that. "He's got no reason to come after me. Forget it."

But her eyes were filled with doubt, and Ky reminded himself not to underestimate her again.

"Listen. If you promise not to try to interview me, I'll take you up on that ride home."

She shook her head, her eyes still troubled. "No interviews. This is personal."

Ky was intrigued, but he said nothing more as they walked to the parking lot.

The car was a limousine with a privacy panel and a uniformed driver. Ky said, as he followed into the back seat, "I'm impressed."

"It's usually reserved for anchors and network executives," she said. She seemed a little nervous. "I guess I'm the celebrity of the moment."

"Looks like it."

The interior of the automobile smelled of good leather and expensive whiskey and Amy...Amy, a cornucopia of scents so complex and so intriguing that he wanted to bathe in them. Honey and cinnamon, a citrusy perfume, silk and body powder, rain-drenched cobblestones... and oh, yes, still far too distinct was the acrid smell of fear, the musty room where she had been held, traces of wine and him, the werewolf, that disturbing thread of something wrong in the midst of all that was pleasant, just enough of it to make Ky uncomfortable but not so much that he could ignore the other, more powerful effects she had on him.

And those effects were very interesting indeed.

"My place is on Rue Creche, near Canal and Rampart," he said, mostly to distract himself from how easy it was to be with her, close in the little cave of her car, wrapped in her scent.

"Do you mind if the driver drops me off first? I'm supposed to go on the air at eleven, and I need to clean up."

"No problem."

She gave the instructions to the driver, then closed the intercom and settled back in the big seat, trying to smile though she still looked nervous. "Besides, it's a longer drive to my place and that will give us more time to talk."

Ky said, trying to put her at ease, "Usually that's the kind of thing I love to hear from a woman. Why doesn't it make me happy now?"

Amy returned a smile that was a little feeble, then glanced quickly away. She was embarrassed about the car, as she always was by ostentation, but she was glad for the privacy panel. She didn't want anyone to overhear what she had to say to Ky Londen.

She was also nervous, and that was an unaccustomed sensation for her. She had her reasons, of course—not the least of which was the very sexy man sitting next to her in a car that suddenly seemed a great deal smaller than it ever had before—but still, it was an uncomfortable feeling.

She searched in her purse for a tissue to blot her damp palms, then remembered she didn't have one and closed the purse with a tiny snap that sounded like the crack of gunfire in the silence of the car. She actually jumped a little, then glanced over at Ky apologetically.

"I'm not used to being a victim," she said. "I guess I don't do it very gracefully."

"Oh, I don't know. I would say grabbing a microphone and doing a live report from the scene is a pretty graceful way of handling being victimized."

She liked the way he smiled in the dark, and the way he stretched his arm over the back seat and folded one long leg over the opposite knee, making himself comfortable in the unfamiliar limousine, looking as natural there as he had in that run-down alleyway, surrounded by cops, as natural as he had looked silhouetted in a doorway, saving her life.

She had to swallow back the tightness in her throat that inevitably recurred every time she thought of that place. She pushed the memory firmly aside. "Well," she said with forced lightness, "I'll either be drummed out of the business or I'll win an award. One thing's for sure, that's not a moment in television history that will be soon forgotten. Some might say it's television's *worst* moment, of course."

Ky said, with surprising perception, "You're not the first person who's fallen back on work to get them through a trauma. And could you help it if you were the first reporter on the scene?"

She smiled at him gratefully. He really was the most extraordinary man.

The car sailed along in smooth silence for a time, like a big ship on a calm sea. Headlights flashed and faded across the dark windows, providing brief uncertain illumination and the only reminder that they weren't, after all, the last two people in the universe.

Amy tried to find some way to collect her thoughts, but it wasn't easy. All she wanted to do was just be quiet and comfortable with him in the car...feeling safe, she realized, for the first time since they had left the studio.

"Funny," she said softly, "you never realize what it means to be safe until suddenly you're not anymore. I guess nothing will look quite the same to me again, after this."

"No," he assured her frankly, "it won't. But that's not necessarily a bad thing."

She liked the way he didn't try to placate her with false reassurances or soothing platitudes.

She said, "I asked some people at the department about you."

He had a dry, lazy half smile that turned up one corner of his lips slightly and was made even sexier by the fact that his gaze never wavered from her. "And they told you I was a troublemaker and a hard case."

"Also that you were a good cop. Why did you leave?"

"They must have told you that, too."

"They said you got shot. They made it sound pretty serious."

Ky shrugged. "Serious enough for disability pay. Seemed like a good time to retire."

Amy knew it was none of her business, but he didn't look disabled. And he didn't seem like the kind of man who would go into shell shock after a shooting incident; if he were, he never would have burst through that door tonight.

As though reading her thoughts, he volunteered, "I have amazing powers of recuperation." He added, perfectly deadpan, "Good nutrition."

She couldn't help smiling. He was as easy to talk to as he was to be with in silence. That was a good feeling. She wished the drive could last all night...or at least until she stopped being afraid to go home by herself.

"So now you're a private investigator?"

"I thought this wasn't going to be an interview," he reminded her gently.

Amy took a breath, staring down at her hands, which were knotted in her lap. "I know. I'm sorry. I—I need to talk to you about what happened in that room and it's hard . . . harder for me to think about than I thought."

His silence was neither oppressive nor encouraging. He merely waited, giving her time.

Amy drew another breath, and looked up at him. "There was something I didn't tell the police," she said.

He frowned. "You shouldn't withhold anything. Anything, no matter how insignificant it might seem to you, might be the break in the case they've been looking for."

She was glad of the flickering darkness, which allowed her to keep her gaze steady on his but protected her from what she might see there. She said, tightening her hands in her lap, "They wouldn't believe me if I told them. But you will. Because you saw it, too."

Ky was very still on the seat beside her. Faint and far-off lights played across a face so composed it might have been carved of stone.

Amy plunged on, "When you opened the door, the way he stared at you—it was as though he was *frightened* of you."

"That's good. Because he sure scared the hell out of me." Behind the dryness, his tone was stiff, almost guarded. Amy could feel the sharpness of his gaze as though it were a physical thing.

She gave a brief impatient shake of her head that was directed more at herself than at him. She was saying it all wrong. She, who made her living by choosing just the right words and asking just the right questions, could not find a single word to describe the indescribable.

"That growl," she said, her voice growing tight with the memory. "It wasn't the sound a man makes. I don't think a man is capable of making a sound like that. You heard it."

She was starting to shake inside, but she refused to give in to it. She stiffened her muscles and said determinedly, "And when he attacked you, he didn't just run, he didn't just jump at you...he was airborne. From a full stop, his feet didn't touch the ground until he was outside, and he was so fast."

He said nothing, and Amy had to stop and catch her breath, or try to. But she couldn't stop for long, because she knew if she did, she would never speak of it again. She would block it out, deliberately and completely, and she might never know the answer to the most profound mystery that would ever touch her life.

So she gathered her courage, forced as much steadiness into her voice as she could, and said, "Something happened in that room. Something happened to him. Something...not natural. You saw it, too. I know you did. I saw it in your eyes, in your posture. Just tell me—tell me what you think it was."

Wheels turned. The engine hummed. Faintly and for the first time, Amy became aware of the sound of distant traffic. The driver slowed and made a right turn into Amy's neighborhood. Ky said nothing for a long, long time.

When at last he spoke, it was only to say simply, "It was dark. You couldn't possibly have seen my eyes."

And she replied. "I can see them now."

He looked away, but not before she saw a glimpse of the truth there, quickly hidden, but the truth nonetheless.

She could tell she had caught him off guard with this confession, and she had a feeling he was not a man easily surprised. That was good. She didn't want to give him time to prepare an answer.

But his tone was neutral, his words carefully chosen. "It *was* dark in there," he said. "On my side as well as yours. And it was a highly charged situation. You were under unbelievable stress. As for me, when I opened that door and saw a six-foot-tall wolf-monster standing there— how could I trust anything I saw after that?"

"I'm a trained observer. So are you. We both make our livings by being certain of what we see," Amy said deliberately.

There was stubbornness in his silence, so she tried a different tack. "How did he cut you?"

"Switchblade."

His tone revealed even he didn't expect her to believe that, but she felt compelled to offer a reason, anyway.

"You and I both know he couldn't have concealed a weapon anywhere in that costume. It was skintight. And when you show me a knife that leaves three parallel cuts with one motion, I might start listening to you."

He said impatiently, "He scratched me, then. Is that what you want me to say?"

"He was wearing leather gloves."

The car turned left and moved slowly down a quiet side street lined with magnolias and live oaks. Ky looked out the window. "Is this your neighborhood? Nice."

Amy said, "You knew who he was. When you regained consciousness, before I told anyone about the necklace, I asked you who he was and you said, 'You know who he is.' I knew because he told me. How did you know?"

His voice was long-suffering. "I don't know, Amy. How did I know?"

Her hands clenched tighter in her lap. "Because you saw what I saw. Because you knew what I knew."

"And what was that?"

Still no commitment in his voice one way or another. It occurred to Amy that even without the mask of night to conceal his features, this man would be a master at hiding his thoughts.

But despite his reserve, or perhaps because of it, there was only so far Amy was willing to go. Rather than answer his question directly, she said, straining to see his expression in the darkness, "He told me he was a werewolf. A real one."

She didn't know what to expect from him then. Laughter, derision, contempt, pity. The moment the words were out, she knew how they sounded and she regretted having spoken them, yet she could not have stayed silent.

The car slowed in front of Amy's town house. Ky looked out the window. And then he said, after a very long time, and in a low, quite voice, "You don't want to go down that road, Amy. I promise you, you don't."

He turned to her and said, "I'll walk you to your door."

Amy's house was in a gentrified neighborhood off Esplanade. The eastern end of the community was given over to authentically restored Victorian town houses and cottages reminiscent of the French Quarter and each priced well above the half-million mark. The western end preserved the architectural integrity of the neighborhood with modern reproductions of Victorian town houses, much more affordably priced but still, Ky guessed, out of the range of the ordinary worker. The neighborhood was well landscaped and well lighted, complete with a pool and clubhouse and brick driveways. Lamps glowed yellow behind lace curtains, and all the doors of the imitation Victorians were painted different colors.

They went up the mist-shrouded walk in silence and stopped before Amy's door, which was a rich forest green. Amy took out her keys. Her hands were unsteady, but more from anxiety now than from any specific residual fear. She didn't want Ky Londen to think badly of her. She did not know why this was so very important to her, but it was.

She glanced up at him. He stood close, at a distance that was protective but not overwhelming. His hands were in his pockets and his stance was relaxed, but every muscle in his body was alert, ready to act at a moment's notice. Again she was aware of feeling safe just because he was near. Safer than she had ever felt in her life.

She didn't want to say good-night to him. There was more she wanted to say to him, more she wanted to hear from him. Surely two people couldn't go through what the two of them had experienced tonight and then simply walk away and never see each other again. The very thought left her feeling empty.

She said, "Would you like to come inside for a while? I could put on some coffee or offer you a drink if you like."

He smiled. "Thanks, but you have a show to prepare for. And I have someone waiting for me at home."

"Oh." She was crushed, and then she didn't know why she should be. Of course, a good-looking, sexy guy like him wouldn't live alone. What had she expected?

She turned away quickly to hide her embarrassment, unlocking the door.

"Well." She looked back at him, forcing a smile. "I wish I could say more. Thanks again for saving my life."

"You're welcome." He hesitated. "Listen, if you have any trouble, or need anything, Detective Sentime—you met him tonight—he's a good cop. Ask for him."

She nodded.

Still he hesitated. "And be careful, okay?"

Again she nodded. "Believe me, I will."

He turned then and started down the steps.

"Ky..."

He looked back.

She said softly, "Please don't make me think I'm crazy."

He looked at her for a long moment, his expression as unreadable in the streetlight as it had been in the depths of the car. He said, "I don't think you're crazy."

He turned and went down the walk.

Amy let herself inside the apartment, kicking the door closed and pushing the play button on the answering machine with one motion, as was her habit. She dropped her purse over a chair rail and scooped up the mail.

A disembodied voice, terrifyingly familiar, came to her out of the darkness.

"A very bad business, *chérie*, very bad indeed. Tell your friend that the last thing this world needs is another hero, and soon there will be one less. But don't be distressed, I'll never desert you. I'll be in touch soon."

Amy didn't hesitate. She ran to the door and threw it open.

"Ky!" she cried.

CHAPTER SIX

Ky felt a tug of conscience as he went down the walk toward the car. He knew Amy didn't want to be alone, and he didn't blame her. Under ordinary circumstances, he would have done the chivalrous thing and stayed a while to hold her hand.

There had of course never been more extraordinary circumstances, but for her sake as well as his own, Ky did not want Amy to grow dependent on him. And after what she had said in the car... Now more than ever he could not afford to become involved with her.

He left her reluctantly, though, half listening to the movement she made inside her empty house as he moved toward the car and indulged his own dark thoughts. When he heard that voice, so chillingly familiar as the one he had last heard inside the boarded-up building where Amy had been held captive, he did not at first realize it was on an answering machine. He spun around and by the time she flung open the door and cried his name, he was halfway up the steps.

"He called here!" she gasped. She was shaking. "The killer, the man who—he called and he left a message on my machine. Oh, Ky, it was about you!"

Ky took her shoulders gently and moved her away from the door, stepping into the house. She had not turned on any lamps but he did not need light to know that no one was lying in wait for her; no werewolf had been in this house while she was gone.

He spotted the blinking light on the answering machine. Luckily, she had saved the message, and Ky now replayed the tape. She remained pressed against the doorframe, hugging her arms tightly, her eyes enormous in a marble white face. He didn't need to hear the tape again, but he listened for her sake. As it played, he spotted a light switch and turned on the living room lights.

No wonder she had been frightened, hearing that voice coming at her from the dark like that. He felt a powerful surge of resentment for the werewolf who delighted in such cheap tricks, tormenting the innocent and making strong people hostages to fear.

"Tell your friend that the last thing the world needs is another hero, and soon there will be one less . . ."

Ky thought, *Bastard*. And out loud he said, as the message finished playing, "Well. Sounds like he intends to make this personal, doesn't it?"

"Oh, Ky." Her voice was high and tight and her eyes were filled with distress. Her fingers dug into the silk material that covered her shoulders as though sheer physical effort could keep her terror inside. "What have I done?"

Ky realized in surprise that she was frightened for *him*, not herself. He smiled in what he hoped was a reassuring way, and extended his hand to her. "Come away from the door," he suggested. "You're safe inside. We're going to call the police and have them pick up this tape. Don't worry, he's miles away from here. He won't be bothering you again tonight."

She let him take her hand, and came inside the apartment a few steps. Ky closed the door, feeling a little better when she was no longer making a target of herself in a lighted doorway. What he told her was true: the killer was

not near—at least not now, and to the best of his knowledge. But if there was one thing tonight had taught him,
it was never to be sure of anything, so he did not want to
take any chances.

Her hand was like ice, and instinctively he took her
other hand and closed his hands around hers, warming
them. She looked up at him, startled, and he felt it, too—
a quick flash of something between them, recognition or
welcome, an electric pulse of excitement that was more
than sexual, an intense and startlingly clear awareness of
each other that seemed almost visceral...and all from
nothing more than a clasping of hands.

The sensation disoriented Ky, surprising him as much
as it did her. He had never felt anything like it, but after
all he had been through tonight, he did not entirely trust
his own senses; certainly he didn't trust his logic. He released her hands and immediately regretted it.

Amy's eyes were big with wonder, searching his.
"Wow," she said softly. "What was that?"

Ky had to look away, confused. He said, "I'd better call
the police."

Trey arrived within fifteen minutes. During that time,
Amy put on a pot of coffee, called her producer and, at
Ky's suggestion, dismissed the driver who was waiting for
him. Ky looked around her apartment, letting his natural
investigator's curiosity and his always-active instincts put
together a picture of the woman who lived here.

The room was light and airy, with a mismatch of Pal-
ladian and cathedral windows, which were a part of the
Victorian theme, as the main architectural feature. The
furnishings were inventive but inexpensive—a lemon yellow sofa decorated with a silk paisley throw that might
have been found at a flea market, a low wooden cocktail

table painted with black enamel, a wicker rocking chair piled with colorful cushions.

In contrast, there were elegant pieces of Lalique and Meissen in a shadow box on the wall, and the painting over the sofa of a drifting feather and an unfolding sunflower was by a Native American artist whose latest work had been auctioned for the price of a moderate-size house.

There was a computer workstation in one corner, and a greenhouse window filled with lush tropical plants enclosed the dining area. The kitchen was separated from the dining area by a butcher-block work island whose underside was lined with bookshelves. The cookbooks there did not look as though they had ever been opened. In fact, the only thing in the spotless, state-of-the-art kitchen that looked as though it ever got much use was the microwave. Ky had to smile at that. He wasn't much of a cook himself.

The books were well read and her collection of music CDs and videotapes eclectic. Her scent permeated every surface: clean and fresh, warm and feminine, crisp and electric. Exciting. Ky tried not to think too much about her scent.

There was no sign that any man had ever lived here, and every indication that those who visited were mostly friends, not lovers. Ky found that interesting.

The locks on the doors and windows seemed adequate to deter the average intruder, and the outside lighting was good. Of course, if the Werewolf Killer decided that he wanted her, iron bars would not have kept him out.

Over and over, Ky reminded himself that this woman was none of his business, that her destiny was not his to control, that as soon as Trey got here, he would be out of her life forever. He had problems of his own, and he could not allow her to become one of them.

She served coffee from a heavy silver pot, but poured it into chunky crockery mugs. Ky liked that; a study in contrasts, like Amy herself.

She said, handing him a mug, "I talked to my producer, told her I didn't think I'd be able to make the eleven o'clock broadcast. She seemed to think that tape of me at the scene was more interesting than me on the set, anyway. I didn't say anything about the telephone call. I wasn't sure if I should or not." She frowned into her mug, still clearly upset. "I'm usually much more together than this. Damn it, I hate being a victim."

Ky did not try to offer her meaningless platitudes. He wasn't sure he knew any that applied.

He said instead, "Good coffee."

She glanced up at him and smiled gratefully, seeming to relax a little. Ky wasn't sure whether the smile was for the coffee or something else, but he was pleased he had made her smile.

Trey arrived a few minutes later and Ky was glad. He was beginning to feel a little too comfortable with her, too at home in her warmly decorated town house that smelled of good rich coffee and Amy and no lovers whatsoever.

Trey was deadpan as he listened to the tape and took Amy's statement for the second time that evening. He tried to keep his tone noncommittal so as not to worry Amy, and he even asked for a cup of coffee. Ky knew it was only an excuse to get her out of the room.

"You do get yourself into some interesting situations, my friend," Trey said when she went into the kitchen for an extra mug.

Ky shrugged. "It's not the first time I've been threatened."

"Maybe. But I'll bet it's the first time you've been threatened by a werewolf."

"Not even the first time today," Ky murmured under his breath.

"What?"

"Nothing." Ky nodded toward the tape. "So what do you think?"

"I think we get a tap on this phone and her phone at work and see what develops."

"No chance this was an isolated incident?" Ky asked, already knowing the answer.

"Not in hell. He's targeted her, and he's not going to back off until he's finished with her."

"Yeah, but targeted her for what?"

Trey hesitated. "Maybe just what he said. Maybe to be his voice to the outside world. It could be as simple as that."

"Or not," Ky said, and the two men's eyes met in grim acknowledgment of the unspoken possibilities.

Amy returned in time to hear the last. She poured coffee into another mug and handed it to Trey. Her hands, and her eyes, were steady. "So how much danger am I in, Detective?"

Trey shared another quick glance with Ky. Ky sipped his coffee.

"I don't know, Miss Fortenoy. I know quite a few people down at headquarters who'd sleep easier if you were to take a nice island vacation for a few weeks," Trey said, lacking many options.

But even as she was shaking her head, he continued, "On the other hand, you might be the best chance we have to catch this guy."

Ky looked at him, startled, and Trey explained about the wiretaps. Amy didn't look comfortable with it, and neither was Ky, but she agreed to sign the necessary papers. Trey went to make a phone call.

Amy said worriedly, "Do you really think he'll call again?"

Ky saw no reason to lie. Amy was not the kind of woman who would appreciate being protected from the truth, and Ky had never believed in doing that kind of thing, anyway. "Unless he's captured or killed first," Ky said, "he'll call back."

Amy caught her lower lip between her teeth, cradling her coffee mug. Ky saw then that she was not so much frightened as thoughtful. "He said he wanted me to bring his story to the world. But I don't think he's going to like having his conversations recorded."

Trey, returning to the room, assured her, "He'll never know. This is state-of-the-art equipment..."

Ky let him go on explaining how an extension would ring at the police station and the recordings would be made automatically. There was no point in explaining to his friend that the werewolf, with his supercharged hearing, would know immediately and precisely what was happening to his telephone calls and would allow them to be recorded only if he wanted them to be.

Then Trey said, "I've arranged to have an officer stationed outside your house tonight."

Ky shot him a grateful look, and Amy nodded absently.

Trey returned Ky's look with discomfort in his own, and said to Amy, "But, Miss Fortenoy, I'd advise you to look into a private security service first thing in the morning."

Amy looked surprised. "You mean a bodyguard?"

"More or less."

She frowned. "Do you really think that's necessary?"

"I do."

She looked at Ky. "Do you?"

Ky agreed, "You need protection."

But what human could protect her from this monster? The presence of a police car or two might deter him simply because he did not appear to like messy complications. A private bodyguard wouldn't have a chance in a real confrontation, but it was, Ky supposed, better than nothing. At least if she had someone watching her, perhaps she wouldn't take foolish chances that would make her easy prey for the killer.

Amy chewed her lip for another second, then made a decision. "Do you know a good private service?"

Trey answered mildly, and with no warning whatsoever, "Ky Londen is pretty good."

Amy looked at Ky with relief. "Would you?"

Ky looked into his coffee mug for a moment, just until he got over the urge to swear at Trey. Then he told Amy, "I don't do security work."

"I can afford your fee," she said quickly. "My family—well, I guess you know that." She seemed embarrassed.

Ky said, "It's not the money." And he thought about the satchel full of it on his coffee table at home. He also thought about Sebastian St. Clare's words when Ky had asked, "Why me?"

Who else? St. Clare had replied. Who could better track a werewolf than Ky? Who else could protect Amy from the werewolf but Ky?

He could also, of course, lead the killer right to her door.

He gave Trey an annoyed look and said shortly, "While I appreciate the detective's recommendation, it just wouldn't work out. I'm sorry."

"Why not?" Amy insisted.

Her eyes, Ky noticed, weren't particularly remarkable in and of themselves. They were a rather nondescript hazel with flecks of brown, surrounded by thick, fringed lashes and accented by delicate eyebrows. But they were the most expressive eyes he had ever seen, and when she wanted them to be, the biggest.

Those eyes were extremely difficult to resist, as she no doubt knew.

Ky said, a little more sharply than was strictly necessary, "For one thing, I have other obligations."

Trey lifted his eyebrows expressively but, very wisely, said nothing. Amy just looked at him with those big waiting eyes.

"For another," he said, not even trying to conceal his exasperation, "didn't it occur to either of you that this guy is after *me* now? Instead of protecting you, I could end up leading him right to you!"

And then he knew; he didn't even need the flash of guilt in Trey's eyes to confirm it. That was what Trey wanted; what he counted on. Two pieces of bait doubled his chances of catching the werewolf, and if one of the lures was also a trained law officer, there was even a respectable chance that at least one of them might make it out alive. And as much as he resented his friend for putting him in that position, Ky had to admire the strategy.

"Well, Trey. You can't tell the players without a program anymore, can you?"

Trey squirmed beneath the force of Ky's gaze, but he held firm. "It makes sense, Ky. You would have done the same."

"Yeah, maybe." Scowling, Ky looked at Amy, and then away. "But that doesn't change my answer."

"He's right, Detective. I've put him in enough danger. Besides...." Calmly, Amy put her coffee mug on the black enamel table and stood. "If either one of you could see past your male egos, it might occur to you that I'm not

nearly as vulnerable to this guy as Ky is. He *needs* me."
She looked at Ky. "But he hates you. The truth is," she
added with a small, meaningful lift of her eyebrow, "we
should probably be making arrangements for *me* to protect *you.*"

Ky smiled at her, but it faded when he looked at Trey.
He felt like a heel.

Headlights flashed on Amy's window and Trey glanced
in that direction. "There's the unit. The officer won't
come to the door unless you need him, but there should
be a car parked outside until morning."

Amy said, "Thanks. I don't think there'll be any more
trouble tonight though, do you?"

Trey said, "I hope not."

But she was looking at Ky and he said, "I think he's had
a pretty full night." If he had not thought so, he wouldn't
have left her.

But of course, he couldn't be sure.

Trey agreed, "Yeah, well, we all have." He glanced at
Ky as he moved toward the door. "You need a ride?"

"Yeah. I'll be right there."

With another one of those man-to-man glances that Ky
hated, Trey said good-night to Amy and left.

Ky was not sure why he lingered. He felt as though he
should make an apology, or another excuse, but everything he thought of sounded lame. And all the while, she
stood there, waiting, mesmerizing him with her scent and
her silence, making him wonder what her hair would feel
like beneath his fingers and whether she would taste like
cinnamon and honey. Finally, he fell back on the truth,
which was in itself rather feeble.

"I want you to understand," he said, "that the reason
I didn't take the job is nothing personal."

She smiled. She seemed tired, and little lines, which he had never noticed before, strained at the corners of her eyes. "Oh, I think it is," she said. "But it's okay. I understand."

"I doubt it." Ky blew out a long breath. He was fighting the edges of exhaustion, himself. "Look, the thing is, I already have a client, and there could be a conflict of interest."

Again she nodded, and again she looked unconvinced.

"If I thought you were in any immediate danger, I would stay."

She reminded him gently, "I'm not your problem."

That was exactly what he wanted to hear. That was *all* he wanted to hear. So why didn't he feel relieved?

He said, "Still, I wanted you to know."

Amy smiled. "Look, it's my fault. I put pressure on you in front of your friend, and I had no right to do that. The truth is..." And her smile deepened at one corner, forming an enchanting dimple. "I think I may have a little crush on you, something like hero worship. But don't worry, I'll get over it."

That made Ky smile. "Not too soon, I hope."

She pulled a solemn face. "Only after a suitable interval, I promise."

He stood there a moment longer, smiling at her, drinking in her scent, listening to the soothing whoosh and thud of her heartbeat that had become, since the moment he'd met her, a reflection of the rhythm of his own thoughts. And he wished . . . he wished a lot of things.

Then he said, glancing toward the door, "Trey's waiting."

She nodded. They stood a moment longer, and he could hear her heart speed a little with anticipation, or uncertainty, just as his did.

He lifted his hand, as though to touch her hair or caress her cheek, and stopped the motion in midair, remembering the electric touch they had shared earlier. He couldn't afford to be distracted by something like that now. He was confused enough as it was.

She remembered, too, and took an involuntary half step back. Her heartbeat was fast now, its rhythm definitely sexual. They both smiled awkwardly.

"Good night," he said.

"Good night, Ky." She opened the door for him. "And thanks again for saving my life."

He wanted to kiss her, even if it was nothing more than a brush of his lips across her cheek. He didn't, of course. He didn't even shake her hand. He just nodded to her, and left.

Trey was waiting in the car. Ky got into the passenger seat and slammed the door hard.

"Damn you, Trey," he said angrily.

"Hey, I do my duty as I see it." Trey put the car in gear and pulled off. He lifted his hand to the uniformed officer in the cruiser opposite Amy's house, and the officer waved back.

"This is not my problem," Ky said fiercely. "She is not my responsibility."

"Well, maybe until tonight it wasn't your problem. But from the sound of that tape, it looks like you've bought yourself a pack of trouble, whether you like it or not."

Ky was silent for a time, scowling savagely into the night as the car rolled on.

"I'm thirty-eight years old," Ky said. "I got to live that long by staying out of other people's business and looking out for number one."

"Isn't that why all the great ones become cops?"

"I'm not a cop anymore, Trey. You seem to have a real hard time remembering that."

"Don't kid yourself, my friend. You may not wear the badge anymore, but you're still out there fighting the bad guys. And you always will be."

Ky didn't say anything else, and the rest of the ride was silent. When Ky got out in front of his building though, Trey leaned across the seat.

"By the way," he said, "there are no Thai restaurants in this neighborhood. I checked."

Ky slammed the door on his friend and went up the stairs.

The scent of the werewolf still lingered in the apartment, but it was St. Clare, and not the other. This time, Ky could tell the difference. And he was far too tired to reflect upon the coincidence of going one's whole life without ever meeting a werewolf, then finding two within an hour of each other. But it did occur to him, with something like a superstitious chill, that maybe it wasn't a coincidence at all. Maybe he had passed the Werewolf Killer on the street every day, maybe the monster had been stalking his neighborhood for months, even years, but until he met St. Clare, he simply hadn't been able to recognize the scent.

Ky turned on all the lights in the apartment, which was not something he usually did.

Voodoo greeted him enthusiastically, if somewhat reproachfully for the lateness of his dinner, and nothing in the dog's behavior led Ky to believe anything unusual had occurred while he was out. The money was still on the coffee table. He opened the bag and looked at it, but was too tired to even count it.

Amy Fortenoy had a crush on him. That made him smile, but when he caught himself at it, he deliberately stopped. She had a crush on him. All the more reason to stay as far away from her as possible.

But he kept thinking about her. How could he not? Her scent was everywhere—in his hair, on his skin, on his clothes, drifting through the back of his mind. Had the essence of any woman ever stayed with him this long?

"She'll be okay." He spoke out loud, because it sounded more convincing when he did. "For now, at least. And the only way to make sure she stays okay is to catch this psychopath. I can't do that and watch her twenty-four hours a day."

Voodoo looked up with interest from his meal, licked his chops and waited politely to see if Ky had anything else to say. But Ky had turned his attention back to the bag of money and the array of sensory impressions that were left behind with it. Voodoo finished his dinner.

Ky let the dog out and went to take a shower, gingerly peeling off the bloody shirt and the dressing that covered the wound on his neck. Beneath the bandage, butterfly tape held the edges of the cuts together, and already they had begun to lose their ragged, puffy appearance. But despite the rapid healing rate—which was one of the few advantages of his heritage to weigh against the many, many disadvantages—the cuts were still distinguishable for what they were. They were claw marks. Anyone could see that.

Ky turned away from the mirror. What if it had been Amy the werewolf had struck instead of him?

She was still on him, everywhere. The silk of her blouse, the tang of her perfume, the aroma of coffee, the leather of the limo, the sunshine of her hair—each layer of scent held a new dimension of memories of her, and underscoring them all was the simple, pure essence of her, and that in itself was indescribable. He washed his hair, but it was still there. He lathered his body, but she clung to every pore. He stood beneath the steamy water until St. Clare was gone and even the memory of the monster was washed away, but she remained.

Ky let the dog in, then, naked, he collapsed on the bed, too exhausted to even get beneath the covers. Voodoo curled at his feet and fell asleep immediately, but Ky lay in the dark, staring down sleeplessness, and tried to get her out of his mind.

It was almost 2:00 a.m. when he called Trey. His friend answered groggily and Ky took a childish satisfaction in knowing that he wasn't the only one who was losing sleep tonight.

"Listen," he said abruptly, "if I'm going to do this thing, I can't have any interference."

"Ky?" Trey was coming around foggily. "Is that you?"

"I'm running this show, and I don't have any time to waste on bureaucracy."

"When did you ever?" Trey was awake now, and cautious enthusiasm was beginning to underscore his voice.

"I need you to get them to hold off on the wiretap. I have a feeling the subject is going to change her mind about giving permission."

"I can do that."

"What about the FBI?"

"They're in my hip pocket," Trey assured him confidently.

"Well, they'd better be closer than that or we're both going to end up in jail. I might need some things expedited."

"I know just the man."

"And Tremont. Keep him off my back, will you?"

"You got it. Anything else?"

"Yeah," Ky said grimly. "If you know any prayers, you might start saying them. We've only got a week till the next full moon."

CHAPTER SEVEN

"**Y**our family must be going bonkers with all this publicity," Janice said. "I hope you've let them know you're all right."

"I doubt they've noticed," Amy replied absently, checking her notes for the story she was writing. "Mother and Father are in Paris, I think, and if the story didn't make the *New York Times,* none of my brothers or sisters will hear about it. Besides, except for weddings and funerals, we pretty much stay out of one another's lives."

Janice frowned, clearly not understanding, and disapproving of what she did understand. "Well, let's just hope this doesn't turn out to involve the latter, shall we?"

She sat on the edge of Amy's desk and pushed her big tortoiseshell-rimmed glasses up into her hair. Despite the casual posture, her demeanor changed from that of concerned friend to professional authority, and Amy caught the signal. She saved her work and pushed back from the computer.

"I've talked to the news director," Janice said, "the station manager and—yes, you're that important—a representative from the network. First, I'm supposed to tell you what a bang-up job you're doing, how proud we all are of you here, blah, blah, blah . . ."

Amy nodded and made a bored, speed-up motion with her hand. "I'll bet you were also supposed to tell me this over drinks or an expensive meal, right?"

"Hey, what's a few drinks between friends?"

"A few more you owe me."

"Anyway, the upshot of it all is..." The way Janice avoided her eyes made Amy suspect this was not entirely good news. "We've, that is to say, *they've* made a decision regarding your involvement in the Werewolf Killer story."

Amy lifted an eyebrow, careful to betray none of the anxiety she was feeling. "I just love it when other people make policies regarding my life."

Janice shot her a quelling look. "You almost lost that life last night," she reminded Amy sharply. "That's the kind of thing we generally do not like to encourage at Action News."

"Except of course when ratings go through the roof, like they do every time you run that tape."

"Which brings me to Part A of our policy. You are not—repeat not—free to accept any interviews for any print or broadcast organization outside this network, or to contribute in any way to any stories they might want to run on you."

Amy made a face. "Like my phone hasn't been ringing off the hook all day? Like I haven't turned down every one of them? Come on, Janice, I know the rules."

"I told them you had more class than that, but you know managerial types. They want everything in words of one syllable and signed in triplicate. Which brings me to Part B—no more dramatics. I was asked to remind you that we at WLAK like to avoid the 'tabloid mentality' whenever possible."

Again Amy's lips turned down wryly, but in fact she was embarrassed, and a little worried. Her ambition was to become a recognized broadcast journalist in the classic tradition, not to have her own talk show, or to end up a guest on one. Last night's appearance before the cameras, while it was certainly great television, was not the most professional thing she had ever done.

It had, on the other hand, been picked up by affiliates all over the country, aired twice on the "Morning" show, and was scheduled for a four-minute segment on the national evening news. It was bringing her to the attention of some very important people in television. How bad could that be?

"Part C," Janice said, and took a breath. "We're taking you off the air."

Amy was out of her chair in an instant, outrage and disbelief flooding every cell. "Are you insane? What are you saying? You can't do that! You—"

Head were turning and Janice made urgent shushing motions with her hands. "Not permanently, you dolt!"

"Not even for a day! You—"

"Will you just sit down and listen? Can you do that, please?"

Glaring, ready to spring and fight at a moment's notice, Amy sank reluctantly into her seat.

"First of all," Janice with with an exaggerated show of patience, "we're not doing this just for the sake of the show. We'd like to make as little a target as possible out of our reporters, if that's okay with you."

Amy opened her mouth to protest, but Janice overrode her.

"Second, you're not being punished, you're being *featured*. We want you to prepare a documentary special on the werewolf killings to air in prime time with a possible network pickup. I'll take my apology now."

Amy was, for once in her life, speechless. A prime-time documentary. Possible network. Seasoned anchors didn't get that much exposure, and she had only been with WLAK four years.

"Wow," she said. Her tone, and her expression, were a little dazed. "That's almost worth being kidnapped for."

Janice's expression sobered. "Don't even joke about that."

Amy's head was reeling with questions and possibilities, ideas and demands, all of which she knew would be answered by the news director as soon as she began firing off the memos. What size crew, what kind of shooting schedule, what kind of budget...

But one thing was of more immediate concern. "What about in the meantime?" she asked. "We've been doing updates on this story three times a week. What if there's a development?"

Janice's gaze was steady, although not entirely happy. "We expect," she said, "that there will be. And we anticipate, judging from what this guy has told you, that you'll be at the center of it."

She paused, giving Amy a moment to digest that, and to anticipate the direction in which the plan was moving.

"When that happens," Janice said, "you'll be interviewed, either by remote or at the desk, by Steve."

Steve Randall was their senior anchor, an award-winning journalist and perhaps the most respected newsman in the city. Amy was impressed. The station was definitely doing this thing right.

Steve Randall would not, for example, file a story that had anything to do with inhuman growls or air that became electrically charged or creatures launching themselves six feet off the ground...or men turning into wolves. Any more than Amy would.

"Amy? You with me?"

Amy shook away her distraction and focused on Janice again. "Sorry. I guess I'm a little excited. What about tonight's report?"

"Give your notes to Steve. He'll interview you at six. Then—" Janice grinned at her as she stood "—you're free to go celebrate. You're a star."

"Yeah," Amy said, and returned her friend's grin, although a little more slowly. "I guess I am."

By 10:00 a.m., Ky had signed a six-month lease on the house across the street from Amy's. There were three of them for rent in her neighborhood; and he had made note of them all the night before. He was a private investigator, after all, and trained to notice such things.

By noon, he had moved into the house, set up his computer to begin an automatic data-base search on St. Clare and to download the police records on the werewolf case, and arranged his surveillance equipment in the upstairs bedroom. From there, he could see directly into Amy's bedroom—she had not made her bed that morning, and a pair of panty hose dangled from the bedpost with wanton allure—part of her bathroom and most of her living room downstairs.

After a quick check for nosy neighbors, Ky let himself discreetly into Amy's house and began his work on her telephone system. His modifications were much less likely to be detected by the werewolf than those the police might have made, consisting only of a mild amplifying device and an intercom. His hearing was extraordinary, and he was confident that if anything untoward should happen at Amy's house, he would know it without the aid of listening devices. But even he would not be able to decipher her telephone conversations from that far away without the amplifier.

He had never liked being in other people's houses without their knowledge, and he felt particularly odd because it was Amy whose privacy he was invading. It was, however, a necessary part of the job, and when he finished the electronics work, he moved quickly through the rooms, familiarizing himself with the layout, the entrances and exits, obstacles and pitfalls far more thoroughly than he had been able to do the night before. He never knew when he would need to be inside her house or get her out of it in a hurry, and he had to be prepared.

He moved through the kitchen, with its lingering scents of toast and coffee and the orange-juice stain on the counter—double dead-bolt and leaded-glass window above the sink—the bathroom where she had spilled a dusting of spring-scented bath powder on an emerald green rug—no egress—and into her bedroom where the sleepy-musky scent of her was thick and intoxicating. He couldn't stay long in that room before anticipation began to knot in his stomach and a hunger that was deeply sexual prickled the roof of his mouth.

The second bedroom she used as a guest room. Like the main bedroom, it had French doors that opened onto a wrought-iron balcony just large enough for one person to stand on, and overlooked a small walled garden with a miniature bubbling fountain. For the ordinary burglar, access might be difficult, but for a werewolf. .for a werewolf, very little was impossible.

There were, of course, only so many precautions Ky could take. Until the killer made his next move, the most anyone could do was be alert and prepared, and that was all Ky was trying to do. He left Amy's house as discreetly as he had come, the only sign that he had ever been there his lingering scent, and that would be detectable to no one...except a werewolf.

At two o'clock, his rental furniture was delivered; just the essentials. He didn't intend to give up his old apartment and wouldn't be here long enough to make the move worthwhile, at any rate. Besides, St. Clare's money had to be put to some use. In another half hour, he even had cable television so he would be able to watch Amy on the news that evening. It did pay to have contacts.

In the afternoon, he took Voodoo for a walk. To any passing observer, they looked like nothing more than a man and dog out for a leisurely stroll on a beautiful spring day. They were, in fact, working, each in his own way using his unique senses to scan the area, making a memory map of the neighborhood by imprinting the sights, sounds, textures and scents onto their subconscious minds. There was no indication that a werewolf had passed through these streets, not since the last rain, anyway.

Amy's neighborhood was designed for the rich and the soon-to-be rich. Just off the upper end of Esplanade, it catered to young professionals like Amy who wanted the convenience of Midcity living and the prestige of a historic address, as well as the more established monied gentry whose historic homes had been either inherited or purchased for more money than the average cop made in his lifetime.

It was quiet, tree-lined, charming. The air smelled thick and humid, redolent of bougainvillea and white azalea and the effusive, ever-present scent of green and growing things. Just across the St. John Bayou was busy City Park, and one block over on Esplanade were the array of bars, restaurants, shops and businesses that provided all the necessities of life.

Within easy reach—by werewolf standards, at least—were also the high-crime districts along Tulane Avenue and the massive, sprawling cemeteries at the tip of Canal. In between were a hundred, a thousand, small alleyways and dark niches, shadow pits and hedgerows in which danger could hide, from which it could spring, into which it could drag its quarry.

One lived in New Orleans with the reminder of death a constant companion. There were jokes about the cities of the dead—the above-ground cemeteries—being more elaborate than many cities for the living. The Grim Reaper was one of the most popular figures on Carnival floats. Dixieland bands stopped traffic to herald the newly deceased to their appointed destination. It was all part of the charm of living in this place of legends and dark magic, as endemic as the stifling heat or the swarming mosquitoes and just as inevitable. But until that day, until he walked those still quiet streets with senses straining for some sign of that darkest magic of all, Ky had never been quite so aware of the specter that hovered in his shadow, grinning, waiting for him to make a mistake.

He was glad to get off the streets.

When he returned home, he settled down to examine the results of the computer's work. Modern technology made it possible for ninety percent of an investigator's work to be done from his armchair, and Ky had long ago learned to refine that technology to suit his own needs. But even he could not find someone who did not want to be found and who knew how to prevent it, particularly if that someone was a werewolf.

No Sebastian St. Clare had flown in or out of New Orleans on a commercial or chartered plane within the past week. No Sebastian St. Clare had rented a limousine or a private car. No Sebastian St. Clare had stayed in any of the city's hotels, motels, bed-and-breakfasts or private host homes, at least not under his own name. None of this surprised Ky.

There were approximately seven thousand St. Clares living in the United States and Canada. Eight of them were named Sebastian, and none of them fit the age profile. None of them owned private planes. There was even a St. Clare Corporation, with offices in New York and Montreal, and, according to the computer, several dozen subsidiaries. Ky made a note to research those further, though he didn't expect to find anything helpful.

St. Clare was obviously an underworld figure, and such men spared no effort when it came to maintaining their privacy...even the human ones. Ky had hoped it would be easier, but he was not discouraged. He would just have to look harder.

He spent the rest of the day studying the printout of the police files on the Werewolf Killer. He was not happy with what he saw. "He's laughing at them, Voodoo," he said in disgust, absently rubbing the dog's ears. "He's tossing them crumbs and laying down false trails and then sitting back to watch them fall all over themselves trying to catch him. Laughing."

At six o'clock, he turned on the news and was once again treated to the sight of his face staring straight into the camera with the identifying tag running underneath: Ky Londen, Former New Orleans Police Officer. Amy in the foreground, looking tousled but composed as she gave her report, the run-down alley in the background and a reporter who was not Amy doing a voice-over capsulization of what had happened the night before. When it was over, Amy was sitting at the news desk with the male anchor, her hands folded atop the desk, her expression pleasant and composed.

Ky turned up the volume.

The anchor said, "First of all, Amy, we want to welcome you back after your harrowing experience last night, and to express our relief that you weren't hurt in any way."

Amy smiled. "Thank you, Steve. I do appreciate all the calls and faxes from our viewers, and I want to assure everyone again that I'm doing just fine."

"I understand that police have now confirmed that the man who abducted you last night was, in all likelihood, the man we all know as the Werewolf Killer."

"Yes, Steve, that's right. I was able to obtain evidence from my captor, which the police have determined links him to the killing of Sherry Wilson, who was found dead in August of last year..."

The report went on in this vein for some time, and all the while, Ky was half listening for Amy's phone to ring across the street, for the answering machine to pick up, for a killer's voice to speak. The monster was watching her now, Ky was sure of it, approving or disapproving of what she said. And if he disapproved? What would happen the first time Amy did something to disappoint or annoy the killer?

Damn it, Amy, Ky thought with sudden, unreasonable anxiety. *Get out of the spotlight. Be quiet. Come home.*

And then the camera narrowed in on the anchor who said, "Amy Fortenoy will be on special assignment for the next few weeks, but she will be joining us as the situation warrants with updates on this most compelling and bizarre case."

And then Amy's phone began to ring.

The only bad thing about being single—or one of the bad things, anyway—was that there wasn't anyone to celebrate with. Paul surprised her with a bottle of champagne as congratulations on the documentary, but when Amy invited him to share it, he told her he and Cindy had theater tickets. Janice had to work until eleven-thirty, as did everyone on the news desk. She thought about breaking open the bottle, anyway, and pouring it into paper cups for the crew, but somehow that seemed an insult to Paul's gift.

"I have got to find some friends with better working hours," she muttered to herself as she trudged across the street to catch the trolley, champagne bottle under her arm.

She got off at the corner of Esplanade and ducked into the market for a couple of rib eyes—everything was packaged for two, she noticed sourly—and fresh vegetables. The walk home took four and a half minutes.

It was a walk she had taken dozens of times, in twilight and dawn, full dark and bright sun. She was alert and careful. The route was well lighted. She wore her purse across her body and held a canister of pepper spray in her hand. These were the normal precautions any woman who walked alone at night should take to feel reasonably safe, and they had always been a matter of routine to Amy.

But tonight she was absolutely terrified.

The click of her pumps echoed like gunfire on the mist-shrouded sidewalk. The yellow haze of street lamps looked like ghosts bobbing and weaving in the distance. The air tasted cool and wet, and when a breeze lifted a strand of her hair across her cheek, it felt like cold fingers stroking her face. She kept imagining hooked claws reaching through the bars of the wrought-iron fences she passed, and narrow yellow eyes watching her from behind the drapery of Spanish moss in the sprawling live oaks. And was that someone behind her, or merely the echoing of her own footsteps? Continually, she cast quick furtive looks over her shoulder, but all she saw was shadows, and anything could be hiding in those shadows.

She knew it was nothing but a natural reaction to the trauma of the night before, but that didn't make it any easier to deal with. Her heart was not just pounding, it was thundering in her chest so painfully, she could hardly take a breath by the time the familiar sight of her own home came into view. She quickened her steps until she was almost running, which of course only made her chest hurt more. *Stupid, stupid,* she chided herself furiously. Mardi Gras was over. She should have taken her car. What had she been thinking of, walking to work after what had happened last night? Had she forgotten she would have to walk home afterward?

She hated herself for her cowardice, and hated the man—or monster—who had reduced her to this.

The security lights spread their welcome glow over the tiny front lawn when she reached the walk that led to her front steps, and Amy breathed a sigh of relief, relaxing her shoulders. She juggled the grocery bag to her other arm and began to search in her purse for her keys, and then a figure stepped out of the shadows and blocked her path.

"Hi," he said.

CHAPTER EIGHT

The sound that escaped Amy's throat was somewhere between a gasp and a scream. She stumbled backward and almost lost her hold on the grocery bag. He stepped forward quickly to save it and she dropped the pepper spray.

They both went to retrieve the canister at the same time, but Ky was quicker. He straightened slowly, regarding the little leather-encased bottle for a moment with contempt, then turned that wry violet blue gaze on her.

"First," he said, holding up the canister between the thumb and forefinger of his long, slender hand, "this wouldn't stop him. Second, it won't stop anybody if you can't hold on to it. Be more careful next time."

Amy snatched the pepper spray from him irritably. "Damn it, how do you keep sneaking up on people like that? What are you doing here, anyway?"

That was not, of course, how she wanted to greet him. It bore no resemblance to the manner in which she had planned to renew their acquaintance the dozen or so times she had imagined the scenario since they had parted last night. But in none of those daydreams had he materialized from the shadows of her own front yard, scaring her witless and leaving her feeling fortunate to be able to say anything at all, much less anything civil.

Ky answered, "I've decided to take the job, and just in the nick of time, I see. Could we talk about it inside?"

Amy scowled at him for a moment, feeling resentful and put out and awkward and oddly, ridiculously, excited, like a teenager on her first date. What was it about him that did that to her? The silky black hair that was finger-combed back from his face and fell raggedly over his collar could have benefited from the talents of a good stylist. His face was too narrow, and he always looked as though he needed a shave. Those eyes... well, the eyes were undoubtedly his best feature, and for a blue that deep and a gaze that piercing a woman might forgive a great many other faults.

He was wearing a Tulane sweatshirt and faded scuffed jeans with cowboy boots that would have been rejected by a thrift store, and the clothes fit him so naturally, she almost could not imagine him wearing anything else. Amy generally preferred men who were built a little more substantially, but he was lean and dangerous and he radiated sexuality like a low-level electric hum and that, Amy supposed, was something no one could explain or rationalize.

After a moment, she gave an uncomfortable shrug and a toss of her head, and she led the way up the steps. Ky took the bag of groceries from her while she found her keys, and when she opened the door, he turned on the lamp and carried the groceries to the kitchen with a familiarity she could not say she entirely liked.

"Check your messages," he commanded over his shoulder, and Amy didn't like the brusque authority in his tone, either. What had happened to the gentle charmer she had met last night?

"Now, wait just a minute—"

He cut her off, his tone tense and his expression impatient. "Just do it. Fast-forward to the last one, 6:27 p.m."

Slowly, Amy began to understand, and a chill crept into her stomach. She did as he ordered.

Ky left the groceries on the dividing bar and came to stand beside her as she fast-forwarded through six previous messages—concerned friends and colleagues, no doubt, who had seen the tape of last night's adventures and who couldn't get through to her at work. She stopped at number seven, the last message. The voice was musical and familiar and with the first syllable it made her throat go dry.

"Now, *chérie,* you disappoint me. How are you going to bring my story to the world if you go away on special assignment? And how can I bear the evening news, I wonder, without your lovely face to sustain me, bringing the tale of my exploits to all and sundry? We must talk about this, truly we must. This is the last tape I will leave for the police to study, by the way. While doing so no doubt keeps them happily occupied and out of my way, the things I have to say to you in the future should be for your ears only. You will kindly answer your phone from now on."

The disconnect tone sounded.

Amy hadn't realized that she was still standing there, motionless and staring at the machine, until Ky reached forward and pushed the rewind button. Amy shivered and took a quick step backward.

"Well," she managed to say a moment later. "It could have been worse."

Ky said, "I want you to call Detective Tremont and tell him you've changed your mind about having taps put on your phones. Use this tape as an excuse if you want. They can override your decision, of course, but you probably know enough lawyers to keep the police too busy to do anything about it for a while."

Amy focused on him slowly. As the horror of that invading voice began to fade, other things started to occur to her. "Wait a minute. That message—how did you know about it? If the police didn't tap my phones—"

"I did," he said shortly. "It's simpler that way, believe me."

"What?" she exclaimed. "That's illegal! You can't just—"

"You may as well know I broke into your house today, too," he went on, his tone and his expression oblivious to her shock.

"You did *what?*"

"And I've set up surveillance equipment that can observe and record your movements from just about any room in this house, so if you have any scruples about privacy, I suggest you get over them. Now, I want to explain the operation of the electronics to you, and then we need to discuss your schedule."

"Wait a minute, just wait a minute!" Amy thrust her fingers through her hair and then knotted them there, staring at him in a mixture of outrage, frustration and utter disbelief. "What the hell do you *mean*, thinking you can just walk in here and take over—breaking into my *house*, putting wiretaps on my phones, setting up surveillance equipment? Who do you think you are, anyway? Are you completely insane? I ought to call the police right now and turn you in! You could lose your license for this, do you know that? You *deserve* to lose your license. I can't believe the arrogance—"

He smiled. "Getting over your crush on me, are you?"

It was such a ridiculous thing to say. His smile was so unexpected and sexy and charming, that for a moment Amy could do nothing but gape at him. Then she scowled and, straightening her tousled hair with a few more angry brushes of her fingers, she assured him darkly, "By the minute."

"That's good," he said, and once again his manner was neutral and businesslike. "Because from now on, neither one of us is going to have much time for flirting. Now, what I need from you is—"

"All right, that's it." Amy flung up both hands in a gesture of defiance and defeat, and spun on her heel toward the door. She covered the distance in three angry strides and threw open the door. "I don't need this. Get out. You're fired."

Ky made no move to obey. Amy stood there with her arm indicating the open door, her nostrils flared and her eyes snapping, and he merely looked at her with a mixture of annoyance and impatience.

"The first thing they teach us in bodyguard school," he said, "is that it's real hard to protect someone who insists on standing in open doorways."

He walked forward and closed the door. "I don't work for you, Amy," he told her. "You can't fire me."

"Damn it!" she cried. She felt like stamping her foot in frustration. He put out a hand as though to guide her back into the living room, but she jerked away from his potential touch and turned on him defiantly. "Who the hell are you, anyway, to come in here and start throwing out orders? What do you mean you don't work for me? Just who do you work for?"

Ky hesitated, then said, "You don't need to know who I'm working for. As for who I am..." His expression was controlled, his eyes distant. But the coolness in his tone sent a shiver down Amy's spine. "I might be the only thing standing between you and a psychotic killer. But don't let me boss you around, by any means."

Amy folded her arms over her chest, glaring at him, trying to control both her anger and the sudden prickle of fear his words had brought. *Calm,* she commanded herself. *Just be calm.* And in a moment she managed to inquire levelly, "Will you tell me what's going on?"

Ky hesitated, and Amy saw—or thought she saw—the first hint of a crack in his taciturn demeanor. Then he gave a short nod of his head toward the counter where the groceries were, and said, "You're expecting company and I've got things to do. I'd rather just show you how the phones work."

Without waiting for an answer, he went over to the telephone stand by the door and picked up the receiver. "There's a device in every phone that will allow me to hear your conversations. It's virtually undetectable by sight or sound, so I don't think your caller will object. You can talk about me all you want, just be aware I'm listening."

He replaced the receiver and lifted the instrument off the table, turning it over to display a small black box that Amy was almost certain was not part of the original equipment. "This is an intercom," he said, "that connects you directly to me. It's voice-activated so all you have to do is call out from anywhere in the house and I'll be able to hear. It also responds to sudden loud noises like breaking glass or..."

He didn't finish that sentence; he must have seen Amy shiver. He put down the telephone.

"When you've finished speaking," he continued, "you disconnect the intercom by pushing the pound button on your telephone. You don't have to have a dial tone to do it. I have a similar device on my telephone, of course, so I can speak to you without dialing your number."

Amy frowned, still holding her arms. "I don't see what good any of this does. Why would I want to talk to you? Why wouldn't I just call the police in case of trouble?"

"Because I'm just across the street, and the police are across town."

Amy's eyes widened. "You're *where?*"

"The house with the yellow door, to be precise."

"But... I thought you lived in the Quarter."

"I couldn't do much good from there, now, could I?"

Amy was chagrined. She still didn't like the idea of him entering her house while she was away and setting up surveillance equipment, and she wasn't at *all* sure she liked the idea of him listening in on her telephone conversations. She was certain she didn't like much about his attitude at all. But he had pulled up stakes and moved across town just so he could protect her; he had put his own life on hold and disrupted his business because she had, for whatever reason, become top priority. For that, the man at least deserved her courtesy, if not her cooperation.

"I'm not expecting company."

He frowned, looking distracted. "What?"

She gestured toward the grocery sack. "A friend gave me the champagne to celebrate my new assignment. Only I couldn't find anybody to celebrate with, so I decided to make myself a nice dinner and celebrate alone."

Nothing in his expression gave any indication that he found her explanation even interesting, much less pleasing. He looked at her for a moment as though waiting to see whether or not she had anything else irrelevant to say, then he went on, "I really shouldn't have to tell you not to walk home alone anymore. There's a car in your garage. Why don't you drive it?"

"I do. I mean, I will. That is, it doesn't really matter anymore because I'll be working mostly at home for the next few weeks."

Now a flicker of interest crossed his eyes. "Well, that'll make things a little easier, anyway."

Amy said, "Have you had dinner?"

He looked startled. "No."

Amy was a little startled, herself. She hadn't meant to say that and couldn't imagine what had possessed her, but having spoken, there was nothing to do now except blunder on. Gesturing rather lamely toward the grocery sack, she explained, "Because there's enough for two, and we could..." She felt embarrassed color rising and tried to hide it with a shrug. "Never mind. I guess that would be too much like flirting, wouldn't it?"

Then to her absolute astonishment, he smiled. "Is that a real blush?" he inquired.

Amy crossed her arms and knitted her eyebrows, as though either gesture could force down the escalating pinkness in her cheeks. "The curse of being a blonde." Then she darted a cautious, almost defiant look at him. "So what do you say? If you're not going to eat with me, I'll put the other steak in the freezer. But make up your mind because I'm starved."

His eyes were smooth and blue and completely unreadable, yet she imagined she saw debate there, and perhaps even the faintest flicker of regret as he said, "Thanks, but I have—"

"Someone waiting for you at home. I forgot," supplied Amy quickly. "Forget it."

The color in her cheeks began to recede, and she was actually a little relieved. He was right, neither of them had time for flirting, and heaven knew, the last thing she needed with everything else that was going on in her life was to become involved with her bodyguard. She did not have to exercise much imagination to realize how very, very easy that would be to do.

In a deliberately dismissing movement, she went to the kitchen and started unpacking the groceries. He watched her for a moment, frowning, obviously unused to anyone walking away from him in the middle of a lecture. Amy felt a small satisfaction for having disconcerted him.

He said, "What time do you get up in the morning?"

She shrugged, opening the freezer and noisily removing ice trays. "I don't know. I don't have a schedule. Maybe I'll sleep late. Maybe I'll get up early and go to the library."

"Amy..." Impatience tinged his tone.

She dumped ice into an ice bucket and stuck the champagne bottle inside. She didn't think she'd open it tonight, after all, but she wanted him to think she would.

"I run at seven-thirty," she told him grudgingly.

He gave a short nod. "I'll run with you."

"I won't wait for you."

"You won't have to."

He was almost to the door. She turned. "Just tell me," she said. She hated the eagerness that lurked just beneath her solar plexus, mostly because she suspected it showed in her face. "Was it my father who hired you? Was he worried about me?"

Ky looked surprised. "Your father? No. I've never spoken to him."

Amy turned away, but not in time, she was afraid, to hide the thread of disappointment she felt. It was a foolish emotion, and she was embarrassed. She tried to shrug it away as she took out the steaks. "Probably the station, then."

His silence neither confirmed nor denied.

"But if they think I'm going to be a prisoner in my own home," she said, dumping vegetables into a salad bowl.

"You're not a prisoner."

"I'm not going to be *your* prisoner, either."

"The last thing I want, believe me."

She *definitely* did not like the way that sounded. She turned on him, scowling, and he was fighting back a grin.

"Good night, Amy," he said. "Enjoy your dinner."

"I will," she assured him, but he was already gone, the door closing gently behind him.

CHAPTER NINE

Ky did not even make it down the steps before remorse struck him. A lot of things rattled around in his mind. A beautiful woman like Amy, having no one to celebrate with. That hopeful, hesitant expression in her eyes when she'd asked if it had been her father who'd hired him, the hurt she had tried so quickly to hide. That way she had of crossing her arms when she was trying to hide her emotions, as she had done so many times in the short time he had been with her tonight. The courage in her eyes as she'd listened to the message on her answering machine, and the smell of terror on her skin.

"Damn it," he muttered out loud to Voodoo, who had materialized at his side like a shadow. Because it was his own behavior that most distressed him, and the fact that he had not even once come close to telling her the whole truth.

He was using Amy. And as long as he could do that without a twinge of conscience, he was no better than the spawn of the devil who had sired him. Ky had spent a lifetime trying to be better than that.

Ky stopped at the end of the walk and looked back at the house. From this angle, he couldn't see into her kitchen, but he could hear her, chopping vegetables on the board. It was a lonely sound.

"Damn it," he said again, but this time it was more of a sigh than a curse.

He looked down at Voodoo with a wry expression. "Well, what are you waiting for?" he said. "Let's go. And put on your best cute-dog face, will you? I have a feeling I'm going to need all the help I can get."

He was glad to see that Amy checked through the peephole before she opened the door. Still, her expression was not particularly welcoming until her eyes fell on Voodoo, who was sitting at Ky's side grinning and looking—in Ky's opinion, anyway—extremely cute.

"Meet my roommate," Ky said.

Amy slanted her gaze up to him, then back to the dog. "This is who was waiting for you at home?"

"He worries if I'm late," Ky explained, deadpan.

Amy's lips compressed at the corners. To hide a smile, Ky hoped. She inquired, "What's his name?"

"Voodoo."

Amy bent from the waist and addressed the dog politely. "It's a pleasure to make your acquaintance, Voodoo. As it happens, I have an extra rib eye ready for the pan. I don't suppose you'd care to join me for dinner?"

Voodoo looked as though he would like that very much indeed, but then, he had always been a fool for a pretty face. Ky spoke up quickly. "Actually, I just realized I don't have any pots and pans at home. Forgot to pack them. So, if the invitation still holds..."

Amy looked at him skeptically. "You remembered to pack spy cameras and bugging devices, but you forgot to pack pots and pans? I don't know. Sounds to me like you deserve to go hungry."

"You're probably right," he agreed, "but I'd rather not. And I was raised to believe it's extremely bad manners to allow a lady to dine alone."

The look she gave him now was of puzzled amusement, and she stepped back from the door. "It sounds as though someone raised you very well. Come in," she invited. "And bring your friend."

Ky came inside, with Voodoo at his side, and she closed the door. "The truth is," he said, "there are a couple of things I wanted to tell you."

She turned back toward the kitchen. "Am I still going to want to eat with you after you do?"

"I'm not sure."

"Then open the champagne while you tell me."

"It hasn't chilled long enough."

"I know. But it's the only thing I have in the house that's alcoholic and I've had a really hard day."

She tossed him a dish towel, and Ky went to work on the champagne bottle.

He said, "First, I'm sorry if I was short with you. Sometimes I forget to be charming."

Her tone was dry. "I can't believe that."

He looked up from the champagne bottle, his expression sober. "It's very, very important that you let me be in charge here, Amy. I know you don't think so, but it is. I can't have you questioning everything I say. When I tell you to do something, I've got to know that you'll do it without arguing. If that means I have to be a little cold with you, then that's what I'll be."

"How do you like your steak, Voodoo?"

The dog licked his chops and looked at her with bright expectant eyes.

The champagne cork released with a muted pop. "Amy, this is serious."

"No, Ky, this is not serious." She turned suddenly, her hands braced against the counter behind her. Her voice was tense and her shoulders rigid; her eyes glittered with repressed emotion.

"What's serious," she said, "is being kidnapped off the street by a madman. Being almost choked to death..." Her hand went unconsciously to her throat where the makeup was wearing away in places to reveal pale purple bruises. "Being carried to a warehouse and thrown on a mattress that smelled like—like...and he—" A gasp that sounded like a sob was torn from her throat. "He put his hands on me! Those cold leather gloves, inhuman hands—he touched me!"

Ky took a swift step toward her, his heart rushing with anger and distress, but she flung up a quick harsh hand to stop him. She turned her face away and drew in several slow calming breaths.

Ky asked, very quietly and as calmly as he could, "Were you sexually assaulted, Amy? Because last night you told me you weren't, and if that's not true, I need to know."

She shook her head adamantly, as though the very thought revolted her, as well it might.

"No," she whispered. And then, more strongly, "No." She turned back to him. "I was *mentally* assaulted, don't you understand that? Mentally and emotionally, and what happened afterward—what you *saw* happen afterward— that was the worst assault of all. It was an assault on my sanity."

Ky turned back to the work island where he had left the champagne.

"You betray me when you pretend it didn't happen."

The words pelted him like small sharp stones. It was all he could do to keep from flinching. He said, without turning, "I'm trying to save your life."

She cried, "And you can't do that if you admit the truth?"

He turned and looked at her, his jaw tightening. "No," he said sharply. "Because if what you say is true, if this monster does have superhuman powers—then we can't stop him. We don't have a chance. And you don't want to believe that, do you? You sure as hell don't want me to believe it."

Amy swallowed hard, the movement of her throat muscles visible across the room. Voodoo sat in the middle of the kitchen, looking anxiously from one to the other of them, clearly not liking the tone of their conversation.

Amy turned abruptly and opened a cabinet, taking out two champagne flutes. "Pour," she commanded hoarsely, thrusting the glasses to him.

After a moment, Ky took the glasses and returned to the counter. He filled one and handed it to her. "I don't drink champagne," he said, trying to lighten the atmosphere between them. "So enjoy yourself."

She held the glass in both hands. But she, too, tried to keep her voice light. "Does it make you sick?"

"Makes me talk too much," he admitted.

She smiled. "Drink," she suggested. "You look like a man who has an awful lot to say."

"Maybe," he agreed with a wry twist of his lips. "But most of it would be better left unheard."

Nonetheless, he filled a glass for himself, and lifted it to her in a salute. "Shall we toast your special assignment?"

Amy hesitated, looking into her glass. Then she said, "Let's toast..." She lifted her glass to him, and held his gaze. "Staying alive."

"That I will drink to."

They did.

Amy said, "I guess I don't have to tell you what the special assignment is."

"Something to do with the Werewolf Killer, I'd guess."

She nodded. "A prime-time special. It's an enormous career break for me."

"Congratulations."

"Thanks."

But she didn't look very happy.

Ky took another sip of the champagne. He would have rather had beer. He said, looking at Amy, "Yesterday afternoon a man came to my apartment. He offered me a hundred thousand dollars to catch the Werewolf Killer. Half of it was paid up front, in cash."

Amy's eyes widened. "Who was he?"

Ky shook his head. "He said his name was St. Clare. Sebastian St. Clare. My guess is he's some kind of mob figure." He saw no reason to elaborate on exactly what kind of mob.

Amy's eyes, if possible, grew even bigger. "Good heavens," she said. She did not sip so much as gulp her champagne. "And he—you—"

Ky nodded. "I took his money. So you see, I wasn't entirely honest with you. I'm working for him, and he doesn't even know you exist—or if he does, he doesn't care whether you live or die. My job is to catch this guy, Amy. And, frankly... you're the bait."

She looked at him, eyes unblinking, for a long time. It was so silent in the room, Ky could hear the slow hiss of expanding metal as the heating elements on the stove warmed. And her heartbeat, of course. And her breathing, slow and soft.

Then she said, "Is that what you do, then? You work for the mob if they offer you enough money?"

Ky dropped his eyes to his glass. He drank some more. He said, "It would be easier to let you think that, I guess, but I promised myself I wouldn't lie to you any more than

I had to. It wasn't just the money. He had something I wanted more.''

Amy raised a questioning eyebrow, waiting for him to finish. When he didn't, she insisted sharply, "Well? What was it? Sex, power, drugs? A forty-foot yacht? Come on, Ky, we've gone this far.''

Ky's lips tightened. He almost didn't answer. He told himself he didn't have to answer. But in the end, he knew that silence would cost him more than anything he might say, so he answered as best he could. It wasn't easy.

"I never knew my father,'' he said. "I've spent most of my life looking for him. One of the reasons I left the police department was so that I could spend more time looking. I'd started to look at it like one of those mythical quests, you know, something that's never-ending . . . until I met St. Clare.''

He paused, then looked at her. "He says he knows who my father is. He said he'd bargain the information. I thought I could turn it down, but I can't. Even if it hadn't been for you, and my own encounter with the killer, I'm not sure I could have.''

Amy nodded, silent for a moment. Then she inquired, quite sensibly, "You believe St. Clare?''

Ky answered, "Yes.'' And the firmness of his tone, the steadiness of his gaze, warned her not to ask why.

Somewhat to his surprise, she took the hint. She said instead, speculating out loud, "Maybe it's not the mob at all. Maybe he's just an eccentric millionaire with a sense of social responsibility.''

Ky shrugged, drinking again. "Maybe.''

He put down the glass, more than ready to put an end to the subject, and nodded toward the steaks on the counter. "Do you know how to cook those things?''

She accepted his change of subject gracefully. "The only way I know how to cook anything is to cover it with Cajun spice and panfry it."

He grinned. "Just the way I like it."

She turned and opened a cabinet, stretching overhead for the jar of spice. Ky followed the graceful lines of her arm in profile, the thrust of her breast and the curve of her buttocks where the nubby, light pink wool skirt was pulled taut against them.

Without thinking about it at all, he stepped forward to help her, enclosing her in his personal space as he lifted his arm to the level of hers, closing his fingers around the spice jar a second before she did. She had no choice except to drop her hand, and to half turn in the space that was formed between his body and the counter to look at him.

Ky did not have to touch her to experience the pleasure of her. That close, her body heat seeped into his pores like a sauna, her scent made him dry-mouthed. That close, the beat of her heart echoed in the pit of his stomach and tightened in his loins with a singular, intensely pleasurable sensation. Her own unique, syrupy sensuality was as thick as fog around him; he breathed it in like an illicit drug.

Had it been another woman, of course, such caution would not have been necessary. They would have let their instincts lead them where they may, they would have enjoyed each other; they would have parted friends. But Amy was different. Amy was dangerous.

This then was his secret: He could take his pleasure from her without ever touching her; he could fulfill his needs without risk to himself or to her; and she would never know...or she shouldn't have to. Because just then, looking into her eyes that were bright with sudden awareness, tasting the breath that flowed through her parted lips, listening to the rush of blood through her veins and smelling the subtle pleasured invitation on her skin, it was as though Amy felt it, too, this invisible caress of heightened senses. It was as though she took from him just as he took from her, and that of course was impossible.

He never should have had that champagne.

Amy said softly, her lips so close they almost brushed his, "Rare?"

"What?" His voice was hoarse. He had been so involved in the rhythm of her heartbeat that he had not until that moment noticed his own, which was hard and harsh and far too fast.

"Your steak," she said. "Rare?"

"Oh. Yes."

He took a step backward, handing the jar of spice to her. She smiled.

Ky watched her heat a big iron skillet and smother the steaks with spice, and when she turned from the stove, her face was flushed with heat from the skillet and her eyes were diamond bright and Ky had to glance away.

He asked, "Is there anything else to drink?"

"Sorry."

He poured more champagne for her and for himself. She stir-fried vegetables with garlic and pepper while he put plates and cutlery on the table in front of the big bay window, then tossed the steaks into the skillet to an eruption of spicy black smoke. There was a candle in a glass globe in the center of the table, and Ky lit it. Amy smiled as she came over with the platter of steak and vegetables, Voodoo following devotedly at her heels. Ky suspected she had been sneaking the dog treats while he wasn't looking.

"You're very useful to have around the house, aren't you?"

"Like you said, I was raised right." He turned a severe look on his dog, who was panting happily at Amy's feet. "All right, Voodoo, you made your point. That's enough cuteness for one evening. Go lie down somewhere." He gestured toward the living room. "Go on."

Voodoo looked downcast, hesitated for a moment to see if Ky would change his mind, then left the dining area with a great show of reluctance.

"And stay off the sofa," Ky called after him. "You're not at home."

Amy grinned. "Great dog."

"He thinks so." Ky held her chair for her.

"My goodness. His master has manners, too."

"Occasionally."

He sat across from her and they served their plates.

"Were you born in New Orleans?" Amy inquired.

"That's right."

She cut her steak. "Did you go to Tulane?"

Ky looked confused and she gestured to his sweatshirt. "Oh," he answered. "No."

He tasted his steak. It was so spicy it made his eyes water. "Perfect," he assured her, though a trifle huskily. He reached for his champagne glass.

Amy grinned and took a much smaller bite of her own steak. When she had swallowed, and taken a healthy gulp of champagne, she said, "Ky. That's an unusual name."

"Hmm. Irish, I think."

"Were your folks Irish?"

"No."

"Would you like me to stop asking you personal questions?"

He put down his knife and fork and looked at her for a moment. Then he said ruefully, "I think we'd get on a lot better if you did."

"A man of mystery, huh? I can deal with that."

She sipped her champagne, eyes bright above the glass. It occurred to Ky that she had had even more to drink than he had, but he didn't begrudge her. She needed to relax.

He, on the other hand, needed to be careful.

"Then let me ask you a professional question. Why don't you just move in with me?"

Ky almost choked on the peppery steak. It was a moment before he could answer. "What?"

"That's what bodyguards do, don't they?" she continued innocently. "They stay at the subject's side twenty-four hours a day?"

He answered guardedly, "Sometimes."

"So, aside from the obvious danger of my almost irresistible sex appeal . . ."

Ky smiled. "Aside from that."

"Why don't you?"

Ky said, "I think you'd better eat something."

"I'm not getting drunk."

"Well, I am."

"That," she observed, "should be interesting." She cut her steak. "Anyway, I know the answer."

Ky didn't encourage her.

Her tone was matter-of-fact as she concluded, "Because I'm not the real bait in the trap, I'm just the smoke screen. It's you he's after, and if we're both under one roof, our chances of survival are roughly cut in half."

"Amy, darlin', you're a pretty fair Cajun cook, and really nice to look at in the candlelight. But you talk too much. Eat."

After a moment, she smiled at him, and complied.

They were clearing the table before she brought up the subject again. "So," she said, taking a clean plate from the cupboard. "What's the plan?"

"I think I'll help you with the dishes, then go across the street and go to bed. I didn't get much sleep last night."

He started to scrape the plate into the disposal but she snatched it from him. "Wait."

She transferred the meat scraps and leftover vegetables onto the clean plate. "For Voodoo. Do you mind?"

"He'll be your slave for life," Ky assured her.

He whistled for the dog and Voodoo came running, his claws skidding when he hit the tile of the kitchen floor. Ky started to place the plate on the floor but Amy held up a staying hand. She rummaged around in the refrigerator for a moment and came up with a sprig of parsley, which she arranged artfully on the plate.

"Presentation is everything," she said, and placed the plate on the floor for the dog.

Ky watched indulgently as Voodoo dived into the leftovers, then he observed, "The way to a man's heart is not through his stomach. It's through his dog's."

"Ah," said Amy, smiling, "so my plan is working." She turned to put the dishes in the dishwasher. "Speaking of plans..."

Ky poured the last of the champagne into their two glasses. "I don't suppose you want to hear that I don't have one?"

"I'd rather hear that than that you have a plan, but you don't want to tell me."

Ky hesitated. That was closer to the truth than he liked to admit, but the main reason he didn't want to tell her about his plan was that he wasn't at all sure yet that it would work.

"We have to wait for him to make the next move. I'd like for you to stick close to the house the next couple of days. He'll call again, and when he does, just follow his lead. The most important thing you can do right now is make him feel comfortable, and get him to tell you as much as you can."

Ky handed Amy her champagne glass and they went into the living room. Voodoo remained behind, trying to lick the pattern off his plate.

Amy sipped her champagne. "Do you think he'll come here?"

She kept her voice deliberately nonchalant but anxiety clung to her skin. Ky's heart clenched in sympathy for her. He said, "I'll know he's coming before he gets within a hundred yards of you."

She looked up at him with big hopeful eyes. "How?"

Ky's smile was just a fraction slow in coming. "I can't give away all my trade secrets."

Amy took another sip of champagne. So did he. She sat down in one of the wing chairs in front of the marble fireplace, curling her feet beneath her. Ky took the other.

Amy said, without looking up, "He knew you were there before you opened the door yesterday. He started yelling at me. He thought I had brought you somehow—all before you opened the door."

"Amy, don't keep going over it in your mind. All that's going to do is give you nightmares. I'm here now, and I'm going to protect you. Think about that."

Amy smiled, though a little wistfully. "First," she said, "I'm not the kind of woman who puts much faith in the magical powers of men. Second, I certainly know better than to depend upon the promises of a stranger. Still, it sounds kind of nice, to hear you say that. Maybe I will think about it."

"Good." Ky put the glass aside and got to his feet.

Amy stood, too, looking disappointed and, perhaps, a little alarmed. "Are you going?"

He gave her what he hoped was a casual and reassuring smile. "I'm tired," he said. "And I still have some spy equipment to unpack. Are you nervous about staying alone?"

"I stayed alone last night."

"Because I can leave Voodoo with you."

She smiled, and he knew she thought he had been about to volunteer a service of quite a different sort. He was amused, and predictably tantalized by the possibilities.

She said, "Thanks, but I've had just enough champagne to make sure I sleep tonight. And I couldn't take your dog."

"All right then." He slapped his thigh lightly and Voodoo came from the kitchen. "But don't worry, okay? He's not going to bother you again tonight."

She nodded, and he could tell she was trying to convince herself. "You're probably right. Although in a way I almost wish he'd call. The suspense is the worst part."

Ky nodded sympathetically, but what he was thinking was, *No, it's not the worst part. You can't even imagine the worst part...*

"Thanks for supper, Amy," he said. "Good night."

Instinctively he stepped forward and took her shoulders, meaning to kiss her on the cheek as he would any other young woman to whom he was saying a pleasant good-night. He had momentarily forgotten about what had happened the last time they touched, and the champagne had dulled his warning system.

It started with a tingling in his skin, a tightening in his stomach, and he could tell by the catch of her heart, the quick surprised widening of her eyes, that she felt it, too.

He might have stepped away then, but she lifted her hand and rested it lightly, experimentally, against his chest. Wonder touched her eyes.

"Do you feel that?" she whispered.

Ky could only nod. Pleasure unfolded like a sweet hot flush from his solar plexus outward. Where she touched, electricity throbbed.

Curiosity, instinct, or perhaps mere weakness made him move closer to her, made his hands drift from her arms to her waist, then gently explore the shape of her back. She drew in a sharp breath of pleasure with his touch, her breasts rising to brush his chest.

Instinct. He should have guarded against it.

She lifted her hands to his face, enclosing him in her heat and softness, dizzying him with her scent. Her eyes were moon bright, the gateway to wonder. Her fingers pushed into his hair. caressed the back of his neck, being careful near the bandage, and shaped his shoulders.

"I think," he murmured, trying without much success to keep his breathing even, "it's pheromones."

Of their own volition his hands moved down to stroke her thighs, and though he knew he shouldn't, he dipped his face close to her neck, where her scent was the strongest, and he drew it in. Then he couldn't help himself. He had to taste her.

She gasped with pleasure at the pressure of his mouth on her neck, the caress of his tongue. She arched herself into his touch. "Pheromones?" she repeated somewhat breathlessly.

"Pheromones." He buried his face briefly in her hair. It was like drowning in sunshine. "A chemical secretion undetectable by humans except on a primal level ..."

"I know what it is."

Her hands found the waistband of his sweatshirt and slipped beneath, stroking bare flesh. Ky groaned out loud. *This has got to stop,* he thought. *I've got to stop this.* But he made no move to do so. Instead, he took her earlobe into her mouth, savoring it, caressing.

Her heartbeat and his mingled together and sounded like crashing surf in his ears. But he heard her whisper, as her hands slid up his sides and over his ribs and created an almost mind-stripping sensation of magnetic pleasure, "But I don't think that's what it is. It feels ..."

"Better," he managed to whisper against her throat. His hands cupped her buttocks, pressing her close. Her heat infused him, making him weak. Making him strong. "—than that. More ... intense than that. It feels like ..."

And then he saw her eyes, fever bright, filled with wonder and query and he knew the questions; he just didn't know the answers. She whispered, "I wonder what would happen if you kissed me?"

His heart was roaring, but so was hers. Their breaths, short and choppy, blended and her eyes were enormous, filling him. His lips were so close they almost brushed hers when he whispered, "I don't think I should."

"Probably not."

Her breath flowed into his and her hands slid around to his back, electric touch on naked skin; heat and scent and essence, all mingling together and seeping into him. Becoming a part of him. And with her lips so close, her eyes so hypnotic, it was all too easy to let his tongue sweep out, tasting her, caressing the soft inner flesh of her parted lips, pushing his hands into her hair, cradling her, feeling her melt against him ...

The sound, when it came, was less of a shock than a distant disturbance; the alarm clock heard from the depths of a pleasant dream, gradually dragging one from slumber. Ky was not certain how many times the phone had rung before they shook off the soporific heaviness that had locked them in the depths of each other's gaze, before they realized, as one, what the sound might mean.

Ky felt the realization strike Amy like a cold wave; she stiffened in his arms and her eyes grew dark with alarm. Her heartbeat raced, not with pleasure now, but painfully, jarringly; he could feel it in his own chest. Her hands left him, she cast her eyes fearfully toward the telephone.

Ky held her arms for a moment, just to steady her. The return to reality hurt, aching in his muscles like the onset of an illness, or the aftermath of a battle. He said calmly, holding her eyes and giving her his strength. "It's okay. Answer it."

He followed her to the phone. She snatched the receiver from its cradle as though it were a deadly thing that might bite if given the chance. Her voice was tentative. "Hello?"

She held the receiver a little from her ear so he could hear. She did not have to do that, but he leaned in close, anyway.

"It is an abomination in itself," said the cultured, female voice on the other end of the phone, "when human beings are required to conduct conversations with machines. However, when the owners of those machines fail to perform the common courtesy of returning one's telephone call..."

"Grandmama!" exclaimed Amy. Her shoulders sagged and she closed her eyes in a demonstration of relief.

Ky smiled and moved away from the telephone.

"I'm sorry, Grandmama, I haven't listened to my messages today. It's been rather hectic..."

"So I've gathered," returned the other woman crisply. "Jasmine informs me you've had a bit of difficulty." Jasmine was Grandmama Fortenoy's maid of thirty-two years; she *did* watch television.

"But having spoken to you," the older woman went on, "I can assure myself, and anyone else who might inquire, of course, of your well-being." Without giving Amy a chance to reply, she added, "You will kindly come to tea on Sunday week. Bring a young man if you have one."

"Oh, I . . ." Amy seemed momentarily disconcerted. "Thank you, yes, I'll be there."

"Of course you will. Goodbye."

Amy hung up the phone slowly, looking a little dazed. She cleared her throat and raised her eyes to Ky. "Um, that was my grandmother."

He smiled. "So I gathered."

She gestured rather awkwardly to the machine, where the message light still blinked. High sexual color still stained her cheeks, although her face had lost some of its former animation. She said, "I probably should listen to the other messages."

"Yes," agreed Ky. "The police will want the tape. And don't forget to tell them you've changed your mind about the wiretaps."

She nodded, looking back at the telephone. Then she raised eyes to him that were confused and uncertain . . . and looking to him for answers. "Ky, what just happened?"

"We've both had too much to drink," he said firmly. "It's okay. Forget it."

But Amy, so steady, so honest, was not that easily distracted. She held his gaze and she inquired without a blink, "Can you?"

Ky said, his voice still firm and reasonable, "I'm leaving Voodoo with you. He's a good watchdog, and you'll feel better with company. Just let him out when you get up in the morning, he'll come home for breakfast. And I'm meeting you at seven-thirty to run, okay?"

She looked at him, eyes big and still and filled with waiting. Then she swallowed, and nodded, and lowered her gaze.

"Good night, Amy."

Then, to prove the point to himself if nothing else, Ky leaned forward and kissed her cheek gently. He felt it, oh, yes, he did, that wave of awareness, that stab of need, that pull of unity. But he ignored it, and stepped away.

"Voodoo." His voice sounded hoarse as he addressed the dog. "Stay here."

The dog pressed against Amy's knee and looked only too pleased to comply. Amy dropped her hand to his head.

"Good night," she said. "Thanks...for the dog, I mean."

He nodded, and left while he still could.

From his own darkened bedroom window, Ky watched until Amy came upstairs, followed closely by Voodoo, who was performing his duties admirably. She switched on the bedroom lamp and went into the bathroom, unbuttoning her shirt. Ky transferred his attention for a moment to the front door, checking the locks out of habit. He knew better than anyone how worthless locks would be against the enemy they were waiting for.

When he looked back, Amy had returned from the bathroom, wearing only a lacy bra and the pink skirt. She grabbed the wayward pair of panty hose from the bedpost and balled them up, tossing them toward a trash can in the corner of the room. Ky smiled, suffused with the pleasure of simply watching her.

She reached behind her and unfastened the skirt button, then lowered the zipper. She turned to say something to Voodoo, who lifted his ears alertly. Then she stepped out of the skirt and tossed it toward the closet. She started to tug down her panty hose.

Ky leaned forward and pushed the intercom button. "Amy," he said, "close the curtains."

She spun toward the window, snatching the discarded skirt to cover herself. Her eyes were glittering, her color high. Ky was glad to see it.

"You couldn't have said something *before* I undressed?" she cried angrily.

Ky answered, "No." Chuckling, he pushed the disconnect button and went into his own bathroom to shower.

When he returned with a towel wrapped around his waist, air-drying his hair with his fingers, he wasn't particularly surprised to hear the intercom hiss.

"Ky," she said sweetly, "close the curtains."

He looked across the darkened street into the gentle honey-colored light of her bedroom. She was wearing a flower-print nightshirt and knee socks, sitting on her bed crossed-legged with books and papers spread around her. A pair of wire-framed glasses rested low on her nose.

Ky grinned. "I've got an extra pair of binoculars if you'd like to borrow them."

"Not unless you intend to do something more interesting with that towel than wear it."

Ky leaned forward and turned off the lamp. "Good night, Amy."

"Good night, Ky." A pause, then, "Keep watching for a while, will you? Just till I go to sleep."

He pulled up a chair before the window, and watched.

CHAPTER TEN

To: afortenoy@news6.com
From: amsc@postnet.edu
Subject: Anatomy of a Werewolf—Lesson One

First, to dispel the illusions. Werewolves are not part of a cultural myth; they are not imaginary monsters; they are not mentally ill humans nor, in fact, human at all. They are an entirely separate species, as different from you and I as the dolphin or the bird. They spend part of their time in human form and part of their time in wolf form. In human form they are exceptionally attractive specimens, with particularly striking eyes and hair. The hair of the males is almost always worn below their shoulders; the females usually have thick, lustrous locks that fall to their waists or lower. They are usually tall and rather lean. Their eye and hair color, along with any scars or other distinguishing characteristics, always transfer with them to wolf form.

As you've no doubt already determined, the werewolf you are looking for has black hair.

The werewolf senses of hearing and smell are approximately five hundred times more acute than humans'. They have excellent night vision. They are particularly adept technologically—you would be surprised how many advances in the computer and telecommunications industries originated in some werewolf's laboratory—and are very quick at learning any skill in which they have an interest. Their reflexes and physical stamina are extraordinary. No human, in any contest they could devise, would have a chance against a werewolf.

Forget silver bullets, by the way. Werewolves, although they do have some accelerated healing capabilities, die of the same causes humans do. The difficulty lies in finding them. Their enhanced senses and superintelligence make it easy for them to conceal themselves from anyone except another werewolf—and sometimes even from other werewolves.

Werewolves do not in their natural state kill humans. They have a strict moral code and a much more refined degree of civilization than do humans. Violence, while certainly not unknown to them, is never directed at the weak. Werewolves do not use weapons. They are forbidden, by ethical and practical codes, to attack in human form.

The creature you have encountered is a deviant, a monster in the same manner as any human killer is monstrous. He has been cast off from werewolf society and seeks revenge by preying upon yours. He is diseased, and must be put down.

Over the next few weeks, you will be receiving a lot of information about werewolves. Consider the source. Some of what he will tell you may be true, but everything he says will serve his own purpose. As for what I tell you, use it as you see fit, but we naturally hope you'll exercise good judgment, for your sake as well as ours.

One more thing. Male werewolves are very sexy. Some human women find them almost irresistible.

Ky sat in Amy's living room, glancing through the volumes she had accumulated on werewolves with a mixture of amusement and disgust. Elongated teeth, gnarled joints and hair sprouting from unlikely places seemed to be the unifying theme in the illustrations. He wondered what on earth Amy intended to do with such references.

It was the second morning. Ky was waiting while Amy collected her e-mail from work before they went running. Two days and nothing had happened. No telephone calls, no contact of any kind. Amy's nerves were beginning to show signs of strain, and even Ky was growing restless. The countdown until the full moon was growing shorter by the day and he was no closer to catching the Werewolf Killer than the police were.

Then he heard Amy say in an odd, strained voice, "Ky?"

He tossed aside the book he was scanning and went quickly around the corner to Amy's computer station. She was staring at the screen in a sort of fixed fascination, and she was so tense that Ky could see the tendons strain at the back of her neck. He leaned over shoulder and scrolled to the top of the message.

Amy cleared her throat, forcefully relaxing her shoulders. "Do you think it's from him?"

No expression at all registered on Ky's face as he read through the message. Amy could see the vein on the side of his neck become engorged as a dull flush crept upward from the collar of his T-shirt, but his lips were white. When he reached the last paragraph of the message, his eyes narrowed, just the slightest bit. It was amazing—and a little frightening—how hard his face could look with such a small change.

Amy persisted. "Is it him?"

Ky didn't answer. Instead, he took her shoulders and moved her, not particularly gently, out of the chair. His fingers were flying over the keyboard before he even sat down. He selected "reply" and typed, "We're curious about where you get your information. What is your interest in this situation? Please reply this address only: 6664698@datacom.com. I'd like to continue this correspondence.''

As soon as that message was sent, he accessed another computer and began a ''Who is'' search. Amy waited anxiously, watching over his shoulder, for the few minutes it took before the computer responded with, ''Unable to locate mailing address for amsc@postnet.edu.''

''Damn,'' Ky said. He sat back in the chair and drummed his fingers absently on the desktop for a moment, staring at the monitor. ''It doesn't mean anything,'' he explained to Amy. ''Not everyone is on the list I just checked. I've got some access software at home that should be able to get us some more information on this character, but it might take a couple of days.''

He returned to the original message and selected ''print.'' The printer began to whir and Amy read the message again as it came out of the machine.

''One characteristic of werewolves he didn't mention,'' muttered Ky, ''is that they're obsessively secretive.''

''Wouldn't you be?'' Amy asked without looking up from the printout.

''What?''

''If you were a werewolf, wouldn't you be secretive?''

Ky looked startled, and something else. It was a subtle thing, a mere flicker in his eyes, a tightening in the muscles of his jaw, but it made Amy's senses sharpen, and her curious instincts were alerted. But before she could even form a question, the look was gone.

Ky frowned as he turned back to the keyboard. ''Are you ready to log off?''

Amy hesitated, then shrugged, deciding to let it go. She looked back at the paper in her hand.

"This is amazing stuff," Amy murmured, taking the sheet of paper over to the rocking chair where she had left her notepad and pen from the night before. "I mean, it all sounds so... credible. Do you think it's him? The killer, I mean."

"Actually, I don't." He exited the program and came back into the living room. "It's probably someone who picked up on your coverage of the killings and decided to have a little fun. But it doesn't hurt to check it out."

Amy agreed thoughtfully. "I don't think it's him, either. It just doesn't sound like him, if you know what I mean. Not his style. But I don't think it's a practical joke, either."

Ky's laugh sounded forced. "So what do you think, it's from some professor of werewolfology who's just trying to help you out?"

Amy glanced up at him. The color had returned to his lips, but she noticed the vein in his neck was still throbbing. The gashes made by the Werewolf Killer had almost healed into three parallel, angry red scars that disappeared into the neck of his shirt.

She said coolly, "Maybe." And then she shrugged. "Anyway, I'm going to follow it up. This thing about the black hair—do you think that could be anything?"

He shrugged. "It's pretty obvious. Black animal hair was found at the scenes. Naturally, the werewolf must have black hair."

Again, something tickled her reporter's instincts, and she looked at him hard, trying to determine whether or not he was joking.

At her look, he added, perfectly deadpan, "According to the theory, of course."

"Of course," Amy murmured.

He stood before her. "Are we running, or what?"

He was wearing a loose gray police academy sweatshirt and faded red-and-black shorts. His running shoes were scarred and well used, his hair pushed back with a red bandanna sweatband. Below the shorts his legs were long and muscled and covered with dark hair; it was difficult to concentrate on anything else when his legs were so close, in her direct line of vision.

Running with him yesterday had been an experience beyond anything Amy had expected. He was a superb athlete, obviously slowing his pace to hers and running five miles without even breathing hard, or breaking a sweat. Amy had pushed herself to keep up, but running with him—simply *watching* him run—was such a pleasure, she hadn't wanted to stop. Those lean, strong legs pushing aside ground, the effortless strides, the serenity of intense pleasure that was in his face... Sexy, she decided. That's what it was, running with him.

But then, doing almost anything with him was sexy.

She glanced again at the paper. "Um, yes. Let's go. I can do this later."

She got up and stuffed her ponytailed hair beneath a baseball cap as Ky whistled for Voodoo. The phone rang.

They both reacted with a quick glance at each other, a simultaneous tightening of nerves. Amy wondered if the sound of a phone ringing would ever give her pleasure again.

She answered it cautiously.

"Miss Fortenoy, this is Detective Trey Sentime. I'm sorry to bother you so early, but I'm looking for Ky Londen."

"He's right here." Not even trying to disguise her curiosity, she handed the phone to Ky.

As always, nothing was evident on Ky's face during the brief conversation. When he hung up, he turned to her, a small frown forming a line between his eyebrows. "Some kind of accident at my place—my old place," he said. "I have to go check it out."

"I'll come with you." She snatched up her purse.

For a moment he looked as though he might object, then nodded. "You're right. It could be some kind of trick to separate us. Come on."

"Looks like somebody was trying to get my attention," Ky commented, kicking aside the charred bits of rubble that were the remains of his apartment.

The incinerated second story had collapsed onto the brick first floor, wrecking part of the foundation and spilling the giant trash heap of what once had been Ky's dwelling place into the street. The ashes were still smoldering. Radios crackled in the background as fire fighters rewound their hoses and repacked their equipment. The scent of the werewolf was everywhere, overpowering the odor of smoke and ruination, so strong at times that Ky had to fight back the gag reflex.

Trey said, "They think it was an incendiary bomb through the window. Hot, whatever it was. The place was gone before the fire department even got here."

Ky nodded. "Napalm."

"What? Are you kidding me?"

"The homemade variety. He used soap as a thickener."

Trey looked a little skeptical, but he had known Ky to be right too many times to seriously question his judgment. "Oh, yeah? How can you—"

"I can smell it," Ky replied briefly, and then he had to walk away a few steps in search of clean air.

Amy, ever the reporter, was talking to the fire chief, and Voodoo was at her side. When they first arrived, the dog had been eager to explore, sniffing the charred remains with the innocent enthusiasm that only a dog can display for the unusual. Then he had caught the werewolf scent, and he could not be coaxed back to the site again.

Ky supposed the killer must have tracked him down by scent and lain in wait for him to come home. Perhaps that was why Amy had heard nothing from him since the message two days ago. Finally realizing Ky was not going to return, the killer had torched the place out of spite or frustration or simply as a grand gesture, a demonstration of power.

Of course the fire would have destroyed his scent, and he wanted to make certain Ky knew he had been there. So he left his mark on the street outside, on the bricks that wouldn't burn, on the very ashes themselves.

"So," Trey said, standing beside him again, "you make some pretty talented enemies. Got any thoughts?"

Ky jammed his hands into the pockets of his shorts. "Could be anybody."

"Sure could. An undercover cop gets his picture on television—"

"*Ex*-undercover cop," Ky corrected.

"Right. So who do you think it was?"

Ky barely hesitated. "It was him. The Werewolf Killer."

"You got any evidence to prove that?"

Ky's lips twisted in a bitter imitation of a smile. "None that would stand up in court."

"Yeah, me neither. But for what it's worth, I think you're right."

Trey closed his notebook and the sympathy in his tone was genuine. "I'm sorry about your place, man."

Ky shrugged. "It was time I redecorated, anyway."

Amy arrived to hear the last part. She touched his arm lightly and Ky could feel her distress; it was much greater than his own.

But all she said was, "The arson squad will have to make it official, but the fire chief said it looked to him like some kind of napalm. They can tell by the burn patterns or something."

Trey lifted his eyebrows at Ky. Ky said, "It's a gift."

Trey smiled. "Listen, I gotta get going. I'll keep you informed. You do the same for us sometime, okay?"

"You bet."

Trey clapped him on the shoulder. "You need anything..."

"I won't."

"You never do."

Ky and Amy walked slowly back to the car, silent until they were out of sight of the burned building. It wasn't until then that Ky felt he could take a deep breath.

Then Amy said quietly, "Ky, I am so very sorry. This is all my fault."

She was trembling inside, Ky could feel it. Her distress surprised him because he had never known anyone who felt that strongly for another's pain before. Certainly he never did.

"He hates you because you rescued me," she went on in a slightly unsteady voice. "Then I had to show your face on television so he could find you. Now you've lost everything—" Her voice caught, and she stopped to clear her throat. "And sorry doesn't seem like enough."

He shook his head, touched and amazed by her concern. "Amy, it's not your fault. I knew he'd come here. That's why I left."

"But he wouldn't have come looking for you if—"

"Besides," he interrupted firmly, "I didn't lose anything. Some junk furniture, old magazines..."

"Pots and pans?" she suggested, bravely trying to smile.

"Right."

Without thinking about it, he slipped his arm around her shoulders and squeezed gently. The thrill that pulled at him was low and lovely, like the musical sound a summer breeze makes as it rustles through grasses. She seemed to sink into him, melting against him in a way that was so natural and right it seemed she had always belonged there, in the circle of his touch. Even now, in the midst of this horror, with the scent of fire and werewolf still clinging to his hair and clothes, the comfort of her nearness made everything else seem insignificant.

This was puzzling, troubling, and, most alarming of all, completely out of his control. Ky made himself drop his arm, and Amy looked at him questioningly.

They had to talk about this, he knew. But he couldn't do it now.

He said, "I'm going to take the causeway going home. Any stops you want to make on that side of town?"

The look Amy gave him was one of absolute bafflement. "You want to drive across Lake Ponchatrain to get back to Midcity? Kind of taking the long way home, aren't you?"

"Maybe," he said. He looked back over his shoulder, unable to resist giving his surroundings one last quick scan as he took out his car keys. "But I feel like driving over water."

It was close to noon by the time they arrived home and Amy wanted to make him lunch. Ky refused. She thought it was because he was more upset about the fire than he admitted, and he let her think that. Better that than the truth, which was simply that he was not prepared to deal with the tangle of emotions being near her aroused, if emotions were what they could be called.

Pheromones, he had told her before. A mere chemical reaction between two physical substances. But if that was all that was going on between them, someone should write a paper for a scientific journal. It would certainly be worth a multimillion-dollar study or two.

Ky Londen had not led an uneventful life. He had been a child of mysterious origins, left to discover the sometimes terrifying, sometimes magical truths of his life with a mother who very often knew less about the answers than he did. Nonetheless, she had inspired in him a dedication to the search and a firm, unshakable moral center. All these years of searching, encountering on the way adventures sometimes exalted, sometimes banal, finding friends and sometimes lovers but never touched by any of them, always searching . . .

And then, on a single day all paths had intersected, all the pieces started to fall together in a crazy-quilt design of incredible possibilities; a lifetime of searching was within mere moments of reaching a conclusion. All at once, St. Clare, the Werewolf Killer and Amy, all related somehow, each of them in his or her own way holding an essential part of the puzzle that was his life.

Was it any wonder he was overwhelmed? Disoriented, wary, distrustful even of his own judgment? All his instincts warned him to take it slowly, but that was difficult to do when he knew he was running out of time.

Ky had known many women. He had been fond of most of them, even had had sex with some of them. None of them had affected him the way Amy did. No one had even come close.

The burning question that kept driving him was, *Why?* What was it about Amy, about him, that made them react as they did? Had any two people ever had this effect on each other before? Was it real or was it simply fantasy, the hopeful longing of two people drawn together in crisis and captivated by lust?

Or was this, the inexplicable and almost overpowering attraction he felt for a woman who, until two days ago had been a stranger to him, only another part of his secret heritage he would never understand? Perhaps even the most important part...

He should have been thinking about deranged killers and powerful, mysterious werewolves who appeared out of nowhere to enjoin him in a "business proposition." He should have been thinking about the "others"—*others!*—to whom Sebastian St. Clare had alluded, about the improbable missive from the bizarre correspondent on the Internet and all it implied. Lives hung in the balance, his entire future was about to unfold before him, mysteries of universal import stood poised on the eve of revolution... and all he could think about was a woman.

Among werewolves and humans, the motives were often much the same.

He settled down at the computer and initiated a more extensive search for the identity of the mysterious Internet correspondent, then spent a few moments redefining the search parameters on Sebastian St. Clare. He wondered if the most efficient way to find St. Clare might be to do nothing at all; the man would eventually have to contact him, if for no other reason than to find out what had become of his money. Unfortunately, with Amy's life at stake, Ky could not afford to do nothing. Besides, he didn't like surprises.

Finally, he checked his e-mail. He was shocked to find two messages waiting.

The first one was addressed directly to him, from amsc@postnet.edu. It said:

Ky

I'm sorry, I can't help. We don't know you; in my position you'd be cautious, too. I'll cc my messages to Amy. You'd probably see them, anyway. It's the best I can do. A piece of advice: Don't waste time trying to track down the St. Clares, you don't have enough of it to waste. Do your job, the rest will take care of itself. Good luck.

He stared at the message for a long time. *Ky.* That was the first thing he noticed. The writer had called him by his first name, but he had given only a numerical address. That meant that either the operator on the other computer had access to technology even more sophisticated than his—unlikely—or that the writer already knew who he was.

Which meant the mysterious correspondent was a werewolf.

His heart began to pound with excitement, which he tried hard to contain. The second thing he noticed was the tone of the message. It seemed to be helpful, even sympathetic. *I'm sorry,* it said. *Good luck,* it said. St. Clare? He didn't think so. From what he knew of the man, this definitely wasn't his style. Then this could only mean there was someone else, someone who was on his side but didn't quite trust him, someone who wished him well ...

Others, Ky thought. A cautious surge of wonder ached briefly in his chest. *Others* ...

He called up the second message.

To: afortenoy@news6.com
From: amsc@postnet.edu

cc:664698@datacom.com
Subject: Anatomy of a Werewolf—Lesson Two

Just then, Amy's phone rang.

Amy was standing before the window, gazing in a
brooding fashion across the street, when the phone rang.
She went to answer it almost absently.

"Hi, sweetie. How you holding up?"

"Cindy, hi." Belatedly, Amy realized that the voice on
the other end was Paul's wife, Cindy, friend not foe, and
she experienced relief without ever having felt the anxiety. She supposed that constant dread was a self-limiting
state, and after so much time had passed with no word
from the killer, she had stopped expecting anything.

Or perhaps her mind was simply occupied elsewhere.
With a pair of long strong legs, perhaps, that had left her
at the door and crossed the street . . .

"You're a hard lady to get hold of," Cindy was saying. "I guess that's what comes of being a celebrity, huh?
So tell me the truth and I'll know if you're lying. Are you
doing okay or not? How are you handling this thing?"

Amy smiled, sinking into the chair beside the telephone table and drawing her legs up beneath her. The past
few days had taken her out of her comfortable, familiar
world and plunged her into the land of the improbable,
the fantastic, the terrifying. It was good to hear a familiar voice. Good to be connected once again with what any
sane person would call the real world.

"Pretty good, actually," she told her friend. "I'm
holding up pretty good."

"On a scale of one to ten?"

"Where ten is running naked down the street with a
butcher knife screaming at the top of my lungs? Maybe
four."

"Not bad," conceded Cindy. "Listen, Paul said something about you having a bodyguard?"

"Well, yes, as a matter of fact. It's the same guy who rescued me."

"No kidding. I saw him on TV. He's cute. Is he any good?"

"He makes me feel...safe," admitted Amy cautiously. And she thought, *He makes me feel so much more than that....*

But either Amy was utterly transparent, or Cindy was an extraordinarily perceptive woman. She exclaimed, "Oh, jeez, Amy, you've got to be kidding me. You've got a thing for your bodyguard. Oh, this is too precious! Just like something out of the movies."

Amy scowled. "You're a horrible person, Cindy, and I don't know why I'm friends with you. First your husband tries to fix me up with his tennis partner—"

"Ray? Oh, forget him. He's a total jerk. Now, this bodyguard—"

"Then you start casting aspersions on my personal life—"

"Are you going to tell me or not?"

"Are you going to listen or not?"

"Listening."

Amy took a breath. "Imagine," she said in a low, secretive voice, "the best sex you've ever had. Then double it. It's like that every time he touches me. All he has to do is look at me and I get a fever. The things he can do with his tongue..."

"My God," murmured Cindy. "Please don't go on. No, do."

"And that's before we even get our clothes off. The man has got a body like a Greek god. I mean, he could have posed for Michelangelo. And you want to talk about athletic prowess..."

"Amy, I'm shocked! More, more."

"Well, I would," Amy agreed modestly, "but he's listening to every word I say."

There was a stunned silence. Then, "Amy, you imp! Is he there?"

"No," answered Amy, grinning, "but he's got my phones bugged, and all my calls go through him first. I hope I just gave him a thrill. He's a nice guy and he deserves it."

"You rat!" exclaimed Cindy. "You—I can't even think of anything bad enough to call you! He must be a *really* nice guy to put up with that warped sense of humor of yours."

"Paul said you were going to invite me to dinner this week. I'll bring him along and you can see for yourself."

"Not a chance. I'm too humiliated. You're never coming to my house again." Then, "How's next Friday?"

"I'll check my calendar and get back to you. Wait a minute, I've got another call."

"No, I've got to go, anyway. I'll expect you Friday at seven. And bring a nice red wine, will you?"

"Thanks, Cindy. 'Bye."

She connected the other call, fully expecting it to be Ky with some dry remarks of his own related to her sense of humor.

When she heard the voice, she was so disoriented she almost didn't recognize it for what it was.

"Hello, *chérie,*" said the smooth male voice on the other end of the line. "It's been too long."

CHAPTER ELEVEN

Amy sat up straight, her feet on the floor, every muscle in her body going tense and alert. She wanted to go to the window, to signal Ky somehow in case he wasn't listening, but the phone cord wouldn't reach. She was on her own.

She said, amazed at the steadiness in her voice, "I thought you'd grown tired of waiting for me."

"Never, *chérie*." The voice was musical, seductive, deceptively charming. "I merely had other things to attend to."

"Like blowing up apartment houses?" She didn't know where the words came from, couldn't believe she spoke them out loud.

He chuckled. "Ah, you noticed that, did you? I hope you won't think badly of me, pyrotechnics is a mere hobby of mine. As for the esteemed Mr. Londen... Please inform him, should you happen to see him, how very disappointed I am that I missed him when I came to call."

Amy's throat was dry. It was an effort to make her voice sound natural. "I won't see him. I don't even know him. Inform him yourself."

"Hmm." It was impossible to tell from his tone whether she had said the right thing or not. "Perhaps I will."

Anxious to get him off the subject of Ky, she said, "I thought you were going to tell me about yourself. You know that I've been assigned to do a television special on you, don't you? This would be the perfect opportunity to bring your story before the world."

"Indeed? How delightful. And how fortunate for you that I can be of service."

"Yes." Giving up on her attempt to reach the window, Amy sat back down on the edge of the chair, winding the telephone cord tensely around her fist. "It is. I couldn't do it without you, really."

"No doubt. Well, where to begin, where to begin?"

"How about with your name?" Amy picked up a pen and notepad, and as soon as it was in her hand found herself slipping into reporter mode. "I don't even know what to call you."

"You may call me..." He was thoughtful for a second. "Etienne."

"Is that your name?"

"No. But that is what you may call me."

"All right, Etienne. What would you like me to tell the world about you?"

"You may tell them," said Etienne, "that I am not alone."

Amy's hand, which had been moving across the pad in a series of mostly aimless doodles, went very still. "What?"

He laughed. "Surely this can't come as a surprise to you, *chérie!* Do you mean he hasn't told you?"

Amy thought of the Internet message. She said carefully, "It's hard to know who to believe sometimes. Especially about something like this."

"I won't argue with that."

"How, um, how many of you are there?"

"Oh, thousands," he said carelessly. "Hundreds of thousands, perhaps, all over the world."

"I assume you mean werewolves."

"Don't be deliberately dense, *chérie*, my patience is not unlimited. Of course I mean werewolves. If you have one of those electronic tracking devices on your telephone, by the way, I assume it has already shown you that this call is coming from somewhere in the Gobi Desert. Before the local gendarmes send out the helicopters, may I assure you that is *not* where I am."

Amy said, "You don't have to play those games with me. There aren't any tracking devices on this phone."

"You wouldn't lie to me, would you, *chérie?*"

"My only interest in you is to hear your story. I don't want to try to trap you or capture you. I'm not working with the police. I just want to hear what you have to say."

"Hmm. Perhaps. But allow me to entertain myself with my electronic games, anyway. It's another hobby of mine."

"Tell me about the others," Amy said. "Are they like you?"

"No one is like me!"

"I know," soothed Amy quickly.

"How could you know?" he snapped. "You know nothing except what I tell you!"

"Then tell me," Amy insisted, her hand tightening on the pen. "Tell me how you are different from the others."

"They are fools." Contempt was heavy in his voice. "So proud of their so-called civilization. They hang human artwork on their walls. They patronize theaters that feature human actors and listen to music composed by humans, and *this* they call civilization! They are no better than humans, pathetic, weak mewling creatures whose only measure of worth is the amount of *human* wealth they can accumulate. Once we ruled the earth, and now look at us! We have forgotten our natures, we have betrayed our very selves.''

Amy's head was spinning. Her hand raced across the page, jotting notes, and she was not even aware of what she was writing. She said, ''What is your nature?''

''To kill,'' he returned promptly. ''To hunt, to spring, to rip and tear. To taste hot blood as it gushes from the wound, to crush the bones, to feast on the power. To dominate and to rule, to spread fear wherever we go. We are werewolves, the most perfect and ancient creatures ever to evolve on this planet. This is our nature. Tell them that.''

Suddenly a sheet of paper was thrust before her. Amy barely suppressed a gasp in time. It was Ky, standing close beside her, and how he had gotten there or how long he had been there she could not say.

With her heart pounding so hard it felt as though it might actually jump out of her skin, she focused on the message Ky had written. In strong black strokes it said, *Ask for a meeting!*

Amy looked up at him in alarm, but the ferocity of his expression brooked no argument. His eyes were so dark they were almost navy, and ablaze with the low hot fire of determination. The shadow of his beard seemed slightly more pronounced, making his face look leaner, hungrier. His lips were compressed tightly, and they were as pale as they had been that morning, when he'd read the message on the computer.

Amy shivered a little, just looking at him, and she didn't entirely understand why.

She made herself focus again on the man at the other end of the phone. ''I want to, Etienne. But it's hard for me to do this over the phone. There are so many things we need to talk about. Do you suppose…is there any way we could meet somewhere?"

"You disappoint me, *chérie*, with your pointless shallow tricks. Is it worth dying for, this need you have to see my face?"

"I don't have to see your face," Amy said quickly, looking up at Ky for reassurance. His own face was so dark and intense, it was far from reassuring. "You could wear a mask or—"

"Mardi Gras is over, *chérie*. That won't work twice."

"Then it can be someplace dark—"

"And how will your hidden video cameras work in the dark?"

"I don't want to film you. I just want to sit down with you, and talk…"

"Quite impossible, I'm afraid."

"Will you at least think about it?" she insisted a little desperately.

"Perhaps," he agreed. "Perhaps one day I will surprise you, and come to your house, and we'll have a nice long chat, eh?"

Amy went cold inside. "I'm not sure that would be appropriate."

He chuckled. "You may be right. But now I must go. I'll call again soon."

"But you can't hang up yet. I wanted to ask you—"

She was listening to a dial tone.

Amy took a deep breath and released it shakily. She replaced the receiver with both hands, very carefully. Then she just sat there in a silence so heavy it actually seemed to pin her to her seat, trying to catch her breath.

Ky reached down and pulled her gently to her feet. "You did fine," he told her. "Just fine."

She turned to him, and then she was in his arms, her face against the soft worn fabric of his T-shirt, against the hard muscles and certain heat of his chest. His arms embracing her, his hands tangled in her hair, he murmured again, "It's okay, you did fine. It's okay."

"I know," she whispered. "Hold me anyway."

She tightened her arms around him; he dropped a kiss to her hair. She felt his strength seep into her, his comfort and certainty. He held her, and it was as though he wrapped a physical blanket of serenity and security around her and with a whisk of his magic cloak transported them both to another place. She could even feel the atmosphere around them change, like a popping in her ears, and the heat that grew between them was as lulling as a tropical sun. She thought, *I can grow drunk on you without even tasting you...*

She lifted her face, and looked up at him. Those eyes. That extraordinary blue, so beautiful it was almost not a natural color.

"What a strange thing. Since I met you... I've started to believe in magic," she said softly.

Ky lowered his lashes, stiffening his muscles in preparation for stepping away. He didn't want to leave her, and she didn't want him to. A faint smile softened his lips. He said, with forced flippancy that did not quite ring true, "I've been told I have that effect on people."

Deliberately, he dropped his hands from her, and stepped back.

Amy turned away, thrusting her fingers through her hair and holding them there for the few seconds it took to compose herself. Then she drew in a deep breath, forcefully relaxing her shoulders, and said, "Okay. This is what struck me. A remarkable similarity between what he said and what the 'werewolfology professor' said on the Internet. Maybe we should reconsider the theory that they're the same person. Maybe he's a multiple personality, or maybe he just has an extremely bizarre sense of humor."

Ky agreed reluctantly, "Maybe. The investigator in me says anything is possible. But my instincts tell me no, not this time. They're two different people."

Amy turned to look at him. "Which do you usually listen to? Your instincts or the investigator?"

"My instincts," he replied immediately.

"And how often are you wrong?"

He thought about that for a moment. "In the past ten years . . . maybe once." Then he looked at her, his expression rueful. "Of course, that one time was when I got shot."

Amy chewed her lip. "Not a very comforting thought." Then she said, "You didn't really think he would agree to a meeting, did you?"

Ky's expression grew opaque. "He will," he answered. "His ego is too big to allow him to resist."

"And when he does . . . ?"

"Then we've got him," Ky replied simply.

"You mean," Amy specified carefully, "the police have got him."

Ky looked away. "You should check your e-mail again."

Amy studied him silently for a moment. "You're a very honest man, aren't you, Ky?"

"No," he said, meeting her eyes and holding them. It was almost like a warning. "I'm not."

Amy went to the computer and logged on.

Anatomy of a Werewolf—Lesson Two

Werewolves are superfast, superstrong, superintelligent . . . but they're also some of the most playful creatures on the planet. Their senses of humor are delightful, and it's rare to find a werewolf who can't eventually find something amusing or ironic in even the most gloomy situation. Werewolves are supreme egoists—not without some justification, I admit—and highly competitive. It goes without saying that any or all of these traits can be used against them, although until now I don't think anyone—certainly not I—ever imagined wanting or needing to do so.

Why am I telling you this? Perhaps something in the information I share will help save a life, but I don't flatter myself into thinking my role in this whole affair is that important. I'm telling you because I want you to know the truth, and up until now you've had a very one-sided picture. As for why you, specifically... If you don't know the answer to that already, you will very soon. And then you'll thank me. Or perhaps you won't...

"Fascinating," murmured Amy, pacing the floor with the printout in her hand. "The whole thing is just . . . fascinating. I mean, what they're saying—the guy on the Internet and the Werewolf Killer—is that there's a whole subculture out there, no, an entire superhuman species—living among us, working with us, sharing this planet with us and going about their daily affairs and we never even noticed!"

She had changed from her early-morning jogging clothes to a pale pink terry warm-up suit. Her hair was piled atop her head and caught with a pink ribbon, her face was adorned by the oversize glasses as she studied the paper in her hand. The way the soft material of her outfit clung to her petite, firm shape as she marched back and forth was very distracting, and Ky frowned as he looked up from the computer.

"I don't think they're saying that," he mumbled.

She turned on him. "What? That there's a werewolf subculture out there? Of course that's what they're saying!"

"That these so-called werewolves are superhuman," explained Ky impatiently, his attention focused on the scrolling screen. He was using Amy's computer to access his own—a foolish endeavor, of course, since he could have done a much more efficient job by simply walking across the street. But after the events of a very crowded morning, he didn't feel entirely comfortable about letting her out of his sight, even for a few minutes.

The truth was, he was never comfortable when she was out of his sight, and the reasons went beyond a fear for her safety.

Amy was in an argumentative mood. "How can you say that? Superstrong, superagile, superintelligent—senses more acute than any other creature on the planet!—what would you call them, if not superhuman!"

Again Ky scowled, trying to concentrate. "Manipulative, for one thing."

"What?"

"Come on, Amy, these guys have got you charmed out of everything but your socks. Are you forgetting the corpses that your telephone buddy has left littering the streets? Have you forgotten how they died? And you want to call this *super*human?"

Amy grew subdued. "Of course not. I haven't forgotten he's a killer. And don't *you* forget I'm the one he kidnapped, okay? What you call 'charming' I call terrifying. But..." And once again her tone grew animated. "Even he—Etienne, or whoever he is—admits he's not like the others. He vilifies everything they hold sacred and vice versa! And listen to this..." She scrambled among her papers for the printout of the first message. "Listen to this. 'They have a strict moral code and a much more refined degree of civilization than do humans. Violence . . . is never directed at the weak. Werewolves do not use weapons . . .' For heaven's sake, Ky, how could anyone object to that?"

"Right," he muttered absently, working the keyboard. "They don't use weapons because their teeth kill more efficiently. Sounds to me like this refined degree of civilization of theirs is open to interpretation."

Amy gazed at him for a long thoughtful moment, too long and too thoughtful. Ky felt it on the back of his neck and looked up, disturbed by the speculation in her eyes. It was an odd thing, but sometimes he could almost feel what she was thinking . . . and he was afraid of what she was thinking now.

He said, just a little too abruptly, "This is a very strange conversation we're having." And turned back to the keyboard.

Amy murmured, "Maybe. On the other hand . . ."

"Gotcha!" Ky exclaimed softly. He spun in his chair away from the computer and reached for the telephone.

Amy came over to him quickly. "What?"

"The werewolfologist on the Internet," Ky said, punching out numbers on the telephone. "The 'edu' designation on the address had nothing at all to do with a university. It's from the *Seattle Post*."

Amy waited anxiously while the connection was made. Ky said, "A. McDonald, please." A pause, and he repeated, "McDonald, first initial A."

Another pause, and he said, "Connect me to Personnel."

He looked up at Amy. "They say there's no such person there. Could be this guy used to work there and still uses the same Internet address. The switchboard doesn't always keep up with hirings and firings."

He spoke into the phone again. "Yes, ma'am, this is Ky Londen from the Credit Bureau in Tacoma." Amy lifted an eyebrow at the facile lie and utterly charming way in which he'd uttered it. "I just need to verify employment on one of our clients, please. McDonald. First initial A."

Amy watched as Ky frowned and picked up a pencil. "Six McDonalds, huh? None of them with the first initial A? What about as a middle initial?" Another pause. "I see. Let me ask you this. Does your department handle everyone associated with the paper, or does the payroll for certain departments—staff reporters, for example, or maybe accounting—come off another budget?"

Ky listened for a moment, then said, "I understand. Thank you for your time." Soberly, he replaced the receiver.

Ky was thoughtful for a moment, tapping his pencil against the desk absently. "Well, that wasn't particularly helpful. I'm beginning to think our friend might be playing a little trick on us, after all."

Amy frowned. "A newspaper? This guy works on a newspaper?"

"Maybe," said Ky. "Maybe he just wants us to think he does. Maybe he got access to the newspaper's address with a false name. Maybe..." And he looked at her. "Maybe anyone who can make a phone call in New Orleans look like it was coming from the Gobi Desert wouldn't have any trouble at all covering his tracks on the Internet."

"Technologically advanced," murmured Amy. "He said they were technologically advanced."

Ky leaned back in his chair and threw up his hands in a gesture of helplessness. "Amy, will you listen to yourself? You're building up this whole insane mystique about something that—''

"If you say 'doesn't exist,'" she interrupted sharply, rattling the papers at him, "our conversation is over. There's something here, Ky, you know there is."

The determination in her eyes was penetrating, and she might have said more if he had given her the chance. He deliberately did not.

Ky pressed his head against the high back of the chair and closed his eyes. "Only in New Orleans," he muttered. Then, "Look, say you're right. Say all of this information you've been getting is perfectly on the level. Will you please tell me what's so enchanting about it? A race of part humans keeping themselves secret for centuries, feeding off the hard work and accomplishments of humans—sometimes feeding off humans themselves— what's noble or magical about that? These creatures are liars and parasites at best, genuinely evil at worst. Why would you want to glorify that? Why would you want to *believe* it?"

A small sharp line appeared between Amy's eyebrows and she looked uncomfortable. "All right," she muttered, "maybe there are two sides to the story. But," she added more strongly, "I wouldn't be so quick to believe it if I hadn't seen him for myself, if I hadn't *felt* what happened in that room, if I hadn't seen what his claws did to you even through leather gloves. And I'm admitting that there may be other explanations, some of them even more bizarre than simply believing he is what he says he is."

She shrugged, tossing the papers aside and sinking onto the sofa, drawing up one knee to rest beneath her chin. "Maybe I'm losing my professional edge. Maybe I'm losing my mind. Maybe I've been trampling through the seamy underside of life for so long that I just have to believe in something. Something magical, something better than this, or maybe just something bigger."

Ky said quietly, "I'm not convinced that your theory represents any of those things. But if it did, and if it were true, what difference does it make? What would you do with the information?"

Amy shrugged again, one corner of her mouth turning down wryly. "Well, that's the thing, isn't it? What could I do with the information except ruin my career? I mean, here I am, this hotshot reporter, on to the story of my life and thinking this is it, the one that could put me over the top—and the story behind the story turns out to be tabloid material. And if you think *that* would be my first choice for how this whole thing would turn out, you're very much mistaken."

Ky smiled sympathetically. She looked so vulnerable sitting there, her chin resting on her upraised knee, that he wanted to come over and put his arm around her. And this time he didn't want to stop, either. He wanted to let the mysterious something that was generated by their touch take them where it would, catch them up and let them soar...

Magic. That was what she called it. Everywhere Ky turned he was surrounded by it, some dark, some glorious. He wasn't sure he could fight it much longer. He wasn't sure he wanted to.

Ky said, "Your job is to report the facts on a serial killer. Just the facts. As long as you do that, you don't have anything to worry about with your career."

"I guess you're right." And then she chuckled, although the humor sounded a bit dry. "You know the worst part? I was so excited to get this assignment, and when the story started unfolding the way it did—I mean,

I was picked up all over the country, and on the network more than once—I thought, Finally! Something I've done that will impress my family!"

She glanced at him, a little shyly, a little uncomfortably, and explained, "You'd really have to know them to understand. They're all such intellectual snobs, and I'm the black sheep of the family, not bright enough to do anything but work in television. I've had to compete with them all my life, and I guess maybe the only way you survive in a family like that is to convince yourself you're even better than they are. So ever since I was a little girl, I've had this fantasy—a secret conviction, really—that I was meant for something really special, something more spectacular than anything any of them have ever done. Maybe..." Her cheeks were pink as she looked at him again, her eyes anxious for his understanding. "That's why I'm so swept up in this werewolf 'mystique,' as you call it. Because it makes me feel special.

"Not that I'm putting any of them down," she assured Ky quickly. "I mean, my father is an important person. He can't be expected to notice every little thing that goes on in his daughter's life, especially when that life is, well, not very interesting to him, I guess. But I really thought this might be something he could be proud of..." Again the wry face. "And instead I'm probably going to end up on morning talk shows with women who've been impregnated by aliens."

The wistfulness in her voice when she spoke of her father, the way she rushed to the defense of a family who ignored and belittled her, clutched at Ky's heart. He murmured, "I guess there are worse things than not having any family at all."

Amy said quickly, "I didn't mean to be insensitive. I know that my complaints probably sound shallow to you."

He smiled. "Nothing about you sounds shallow to me."

Amy's expression was gentle and curious. "Do you mind if I ask about your mother?"

"She was a wonderful lady, and I admired her more than anyone I've ever known. She died about seventeen years ago."

"And she never told you anything about your father?"

Ky hesitated. "Some." And his voice hardened. "Enough to make me decide he wasn't someone I particularly wanted to know."

Amy looked confused, and Ky was compelled to explain, "Not that my mother ever said anything derogatory about him. She had too much class for that. Besides, she was devoted to him, even after all those years without a word from him. She never could admit to herself that he was a heartless, amoral son of a bitch who used her, lied to her and deserted her."

"Deserted you both," Amy said with gentle perception.

Ky shot her a sharp look, a little uncomfortable at having inadvertently revealed more of himself than he'd intended. "Right."

"But I don't understand. If you hate him so much, why is it so important for you to find him?"

Ky had to think about that a moment himself, searching for the right words. "It's complicated. I want answers, I guess. A lot of answers. And maybe... I don't know. Maybe I just want to find a way to forgive him."

Amy reached across the distance between them and covered his hand with hers. The thrill was intense and mesmerizing. The temptation to give in to it was almost overwhelming.

Ky pulled his hand away and stood up. "I'm going back across the street to work on this some more. You're not going to leave the house, are you?"

She looked unhappy with his sudden change of subject. And with the just as deliberate change of mood between them. Ky was unhappy, too. But intimacy was an insidious thing. She was already far too close to the truth about him than she had any right to be...and he was far too close to not caring. He had to be more careful.

"I might go to the library later," she said.

"I'll drive you."

"You're not my chauffeur."

"You drive, then. But you're not leaving the house without me."

She scowled, but without real rancor. "This could get old real soon."

He grinned, on easier ground with her now. "Not much like the movies, after all, is it?"

A reluctant smile curved Amy's lips, and her eyes dropped, rather deliberately, he thought, to his legs, which were naked below the running shorts. "That all depends on how you look at it."

That made his pulse speed. It was foolish. He turned toward the door. "Call if you need anything."

"Maybe he's a she," Amy said.

He turned. "What?"

"Your A. McDonald," she explained. "Women get married, you know, change their names. Maybe that's why she's not listed at the switchboard under McDonald."

He lifted an eyebrow. "I'm impressed."

"I've done a bit of research in my time," she admitted with pretend modesty.

"Then I won't point out that it doesn't do much good to know she's changed her name unless we know what she's changed it to."

Amy shrugged. "Hey, I can't do everything for you."

He grinned again and turned for the door.

"Ky."

Patiently he turned back.

She said, very gently, "Someday you're going to tell me the whole truth, aren't you?"

Ky didn't answer for a moment. He opened the door, and could not look at her as he said, "For your sake, I hope not."

Amy woke with a gasp from a dream that left her heart pounding and her nightgown damp with sweat. It was the old being-chased-by-a-monster dream, hardly unusual under the circumstances. The monster wore a wolf suit and full-head mask like the one the Werewolf Killer had worn when he kidnapped her—also not particularly obscure, for a dream. And when he caught her, she'd struggled wildly, ripped off the wolf mask... and looked straight into the violet blue eyes of Ky Londen.

And then—this was the worst part, the most bizarre part—he had pressed her close, tight against his hard body, and kissed her. She'd thrust her hands into his silky black hair and kissed him back, sinking into him, drowning in him ...

The bed covers made a crinkling sound when she shifted, and she realized that she had fallen asleep while reading, surrounded by the printouts of her Internet messages, notes of her conversation with the killer and research materials. The lamp was still on, and the sound of male snoring came from Voodoo, who was sound asleep at the foot of her bed.

She remembered wondering, just before she fell asleep, why it was that Ky seemed to know more about this case than he was telling her, and how much, exactly, he was keeping from her. Why did he continue to scoff at the possibility—no, the probability—that something genuinely unknown, if not actually supernatural, was involved here when it was clear he did not believe his own denials? He was like a man whistling past a graveyard while denying that he even noticed the tombstones.

Amy groaned out loud and stretched forward to stroke the dog whose heavy weight warmed her feet. "So, Voodoo," she murmured. "What do you think?"

The dog opened one sleepy eye to gaze at her.

"Is your daddy keeping secrets from me? And if he is, why? And if he's not, what *is* he doing? Or is your friend Amy slowly losing her mind?"

"Amy?" Ky's voice over the intercom sounded a little husky, but otherwise quick and alert. "You okay?"

Amy smiled and settled back against the pillows, brushing black dog hair off her hands. "Fine. I just had an erotic dream about you."

A moment's pause. "Oh, is that all?"

"Sorry I woke you."

"Part of the job."

"Ky..." She turned on her side and bunched the pillow under her cheek, gazing at the telephone intercom beside her bed. "Who are you?"

Another pause then he said, "A Greek god? A model for Michelangelo?"

She smothered a grin in the folds of the pillow. "Very funny." Then, "It was true, you know. The things I said to Cindy about the way you make me feel, all true." She heard the words come out of her mouth, but she couldn't believe she'd said them. Perhaps it was the lateness of the hour, or the safety barrier provided by the intercom. Two disembodied voices in the night who could say almost anything to each other...

The pause was longer now, and his voice, when he spoke, much huskier. "Pretty late at night for that kind of talk, darlin'."

"Or maybe just pretty late in our relationship. We have to talk about it sometime."

He didn't answer.

Amy closed her eyes with a sigh. "Or maybe not."

Again he was silent. Except for this distant static through the open line, she might have thought he had disconnected.

Then he said, "Amy?"

"Yes."

His voice was somber now, heavy. "There are things about me you don't know. Don't... speculate, okay?"

Speculate. Another word for "fantasize." "No deal," she answered. "Speculate is what we reporters do when we can't get a straight answer. You should know that by now."

"Maybe you're better off, sometimes, not knowing the answers."

"Maybe I have a right to decide that for myself."

The silence was longer this time. Then, "It's been a long day, Amy. Good night."

"Good night," she said.

She was the one who disconnected first, but Ky couldn't go back to sleep. He got up, paced around the house for a while, and finally went outside where he could see the moon, just above the top of the live oak in his neighbor's yard, from his small back patio. A waxing moon, almost full, cold and white yet subtly alive, almost pulsing with power in the black, black night.

The sight of it filled him with a strange excitement, and a shiver of dread.

He thought about secrets.

Finally, he went back inside, dressed and made coffee. In the past, he had done some of his best work in the wee hours of the morning. He hoped that would prove to be the case now.

He studied the Internet messages again, savoring every word, reading between the lines, allowing himself to feel the emotions it wasn't possible to show in Amy's presence. And then he remembered what she had said about the writer being a woman, possibly married.

It made sense. He noticed for the first time the letters in her sender designation. AMSC. They might be initials. If the first two were her maiden name—A. McDonald— then the last one might be a married name. Or the last two...

He looked at a clock. Someone would be on duty all night at a paper the size of the *Seattle Post*. He dialed the number, which was locked in his memory along with most figures and all facts he had ever read, with an amazingly steady hand.

A brusque voice answered, "City Desk."

Ky said, very calmly, "I'm trying to get in touch with Ms. St. Clare."

Barely a pause. "Aggie St. Clare?"

"Would that be—Aggie McDonald St. Clare?"

"Yeah, that's who you want, isn't it? She's not here. Do you want me to take a message?"

Ky hung up the phone very slowly, and stared at it for a long, long time.

CHAPTER TWELVE

To: afortenoy@news6.com
From: amsc@postnet.edu
Subject: Anatomy of a Werewolf—Lesson Three: In Love with a Werewolf

Werewolves mate for life. Although they are extremely sensuous creatures and have a much more relaxed attitude toward physical pleasure than humans do, the actual act of mating is an almost sacred experience to them, resulting in an intense empathic and telepathic bond between the mated couple that lasts for the rest of their lives. Under most circumstances, werewolves mate only in the wolf form. In some extremely rare cases, however, it is possible for certain werewolves to mate while in human form, therefore allowing them to love and join with a human.

These "mixed marriages," if you will, are so unusual that werewolf history barely records them, werewolf memory barely admits the possibility. It is easy to love a werewolf, but to be loved by one in return is rare indeed. The human who is lucky enough to know this kind of love will never be the same again.

An essential part of the werewolf's nature—in fact *the* essential part—is the Change, which is a werewolf euphemism for the ability to transform from human to wolf form and back again. Werewolves are born with this ability, although it sometimes doesn't become fully functional until they are a year or two old. Werewolves can change at will, or the Change can be triggered by any intense or primal emotion—rage, fear, or sexual arousal, for example.

I've touched on this before, but to witness the Change is the single most transcendental experience a human being can have. The beauty of it is so intense, so penetrating and awe-inspiring, that there is actually a hypnotic quality to it. Again, very few humans have been allowed the privilege of witnessing this miracle.

It is important to remember that for all their exceptional characteristics, werewolves are creatures of nature, just as humans are. They feel disappointments just as keenly, desires just as intensely, and frustrations just as sharply as we do. They are often impatient, sometimes abrupt. They are slow to anger, but their tempers can be ferocious. To love them is to love them for all that they are, and this is much, much easier than it might seem . . .

Castle St. Clare, Alaska

"Damn it, Michael," said Noel Duprey angrily, "what I fail to understand is why you can't control your wife!"

Michael St. Clare, older by a few months and, in many ways the wiser of the two werewolves, did not exert himself to take offense at his cousin's outburst. There were three females in the room, after all, who would do a much better job at that than he. So Michael merely raised his eyebrows and replied mildly, "She's not mine to control."

Clarice St. Clare, mother to Michael, wife to the ruler pro tem and symbolic mother to their entire race—in other words, the most powerful female werewolf living—gave

Noel a withering look. "I do certainly hope," she told him coolly, "that you intend to rephrase that."

And Noel's own newly mated bride, Victoria, regarded him through half-narrowed eyes and added sweetly, "Perhaps you would care to give him lessons on controlling one's wife, my love."

Aggie, Michael's wife and the subject of the dispute, ignored Noel altogether and addressed Victoria. "He needs a little taming, I see," she said matter-of-factly. "But I'm sure you're up to the job."

Victoria grinned, and Noel scowled at both women. One of the biggest irritants of his recent life was that his bride and Aggie McDonald St. Clare had become fast friends.

It was his fault, of course, for inviting Aggie to his mating ceremony, which had taken place here at Castle St. Clare less than ten days ago. But he could not invite Michael without including Michael's wife, and to fail to invite Michael would have meant an open breach between the two branches of the family, which Noel would not tolerate. He needed Michael and valued his friendship and his counsel; if he had to put up with Michael's human wife for the sake of both, so be it.

He should have known, however, that Victoria would take an instant liking to the woman. His bride had always had a weakness for human companions.

They were gathered, for this most secret of meetings, in the private living quarters of Castle St. Clare. A fire danced happily in the grate, tea was steeping in the pot, the smell of cinnamon biscuits was sweet in the air. Victoria and Aggie were comfortable on the sofa before the big-screen television set, Michael had staked out the best chair before the fire and Clarice and Sebastian St. Clare had positioned themselves, as mere observers to the proceedings, a little separate from the group, near the window and its view of the snowy woods. Noel was standing in the center of the room and thinking, with a stab of wistfulness, that but for the infernal interference of Aggie St. Clare, he would be in the South Pacific right now, on his honeymoon.

Noel turned to Clarice St. Clare and said, in a reluctantly subdued tone, "Grand-mère, I apologize. What I meant to do, of course, was express my concern over the fact that a human—" he gave the word particular emphasis and cast a contemptuous look at Aggie "—should be allowed to publish our most intimate secrets before the eyes of perfect strangers. It's treacherous and unseemly and frankly, more than a little dangerous. Why am I the only one who's upset about this?"

"A good question," murmured Michael.

Aggie said sharply, "In the first place, I'm not *publishing* your secrets at all. Did I put them in my column? Did I write a book? And if I did, who would believe it? All I did was pass on some very important information to someone with a very personal interest in what it is, exactly, she's dealing with! Of course, I realize I'm a mere human and I have no right to interfere, but my interference wouldn't be necessary if you people would police your own!"

"You know nothing about this," Noel retorted.

But almost before the words were out of his mouth, Aggie cried, "Neither do you, damn it, and that's what infuriates me the most! This maniac has been on a slaughtering rampage for years, and you didn't even know about it. Even over the past year since he's gone public, practically *trying* to get caught, it took you this long to even look at it. Do you know what I wonder?" Her face was flushed now, and her tone tight. "I wonder how many others there have been like him. How many random killings, how many serial murderers that were never caught, how many children have died at the hands of something that wasn't human!''

The silence that followed her outburst was so thick it throbbed. No one looked at her, or at one another. It was Michael who spoke at last, quietly.

''Aggie,'' he said, ''I don't think you have the right to criticize the way we govern ourselves, considering the rather glaring inefficiencies in the human justice system. We do our best. We've done so throughout history. We succeed more often than we fail. That should be enough.''

Aggie lowered her eyes, ashamed. She said, ''I know. I'm sorry.'' When she spoke, she looked at the elder St. Clares, Sebastian and Clarice, not at Noel. ''I understand these things with my mind. But in my heart—it's hard sometimes.''

Clarice St. Clare gave the smallest of gracious nods, forgiving her. Sebastian St. Clare spoke up for the first time. ''I don't think any purpose will be served from sniping at one another, at any rate. I'm sure the young lady has her reasons for doing what she has done, which we'll hear in due course. For the moment, we might address ourselves to the question of what, if any, damage has been done?''

Aggie cast the elder werewolf a grateful and respectful look. Aggie McDonald, a human woman, had come into this family of werewolves less than a year ago. To say she was warmly welcomed by all would be a vast overstatement. She had stolen from them Michael St. Clare, the heir apparent of the entire empire. She had triggered a battle for succession between Noel and Michael, which had resulted in Noel's becoming the ruler of an empire which, until very recently, he had not been at all sure he wanted. She had caused Michael, one of the wealthiest and most powerful werewolves in the pack, to turn his back on his heritage and his status in order to live with her in the world of humans.

Yet werewolves were an eminently practical species and over the months, simply by observing in Aggie the same characteristics that had caused Michael to fall in love with her in the first place, they had gradually grown more accepting of her—even Noel, who enjoyed his ongoing feud with her far too much to ever admit that she might, in fact, be a worthy mate for his cousin Michael.

Aggie would not have jeopardized her standing with Michael's family for a capricious reason. Her husband understood that. She could only hope the others would, too.

Victoria said, "Is that him?" She paused the frame of the videotape and leaned toward the projection-screen television set, which was now mostly taken up with Ky Londen's face. "He's good-looking, isn't he?"

Noel cast her a sharp look and came around to see for himself. "Do you think so?"

"Don't you?"

Noel frowned. "His face is too long. His hair is unkempt. He dresses badly."

Michael and Aggie exchanged a smile across the room for no particular reason at all. It was Michael who said with no more than a glance at the screen, "He has the St Clare eyes."

Again the silence fell, thoughtful this time. It was Noel who spoke first, noncommittally. "It's hard to tell, at this angle."

But Sebastian said, "I've seen him for myself. There is some resemblance."

When Aggie spoke, the anger was gone, and there was nothing in her face except curiosity...and wonder. "How could you not know about him?"

Sebastian said, "That is a complex subject best left to the historians to explain. It is of course pure arrogance to put forth the assumption that all our strain has its ties to Castle St. Clare, and I think what we mean when we say that is that all of us of any importance originated here. There was a group that settled in New Orleans early on, but found it virtually uninhabitable and moved on. Perhaps some remnants survived, perhaps some returned, I don't know. Our background search is still not complete."

Noel asked, "Do we know who his father is?"

Sebastian hesitated. "Yes. We're now trying to find out what happened to him."

Aggie said, staring at the shadowed figure frozen on the screen, "Will he be safe?"

Noel muttered, "Safer than any of us would be."

Once again Aggie turned on him. "How can you say that? You don't know that. What if he comes up against this killer and loses? How can you take such a chance? Do you know what this man could mean to you—to us? He's a genetic miracle! What I don't understand is how you can take such chances with him at all, why you didn't bring him back here immediately and start testing him—"

"And how do you suppose we should have done that?" retorted Noel. "With a collar and a leash?"

Aggie glared at him. "You had no scruples about bringing *me* here against my will once upon a time, if I recall."

Noel groaned and thrust his hands into his long blond hair, turning away. "Woman, will you ever let me forget that?"

Victoria explained, more reasonably, "Noel is right, Aggie. We have no right to interfere in the life of this man, not unless he asks us to. It wouldn't be ethical. Besides..." And she glanced uncertainly at her husband, as though seeking help for clarification.

Noel was glad to step in. "We still don't know who he is, or *what*, exactly, or whose side he's on," he said brusquely. "He has yet to prove himself of any value to us at all."

Aggie's mouth fell open; the familiar stubborn outrage filled her eyes. "Value!" she exclaimed. "What is he, a negotiable bond? What the hell do you mean, *value?*"

"Aggie, listen," Michael said patiently. "Ky Londen is a loose cannon, a rogue element. How are we supposed to know anything about him except what he tells us, and how can we know if any of that is the truth? Maybe *he* doesn't know the truth, did you ever think of that? He could be just as mad as this other one, or he could simply be misinformed."

Aggie said, frowning uncertainly, "You don't trust anyone who lives outside the pack, do you?"

Michael said, "It's not natural to live away from the pack. That's reason enough in itself to distrust anyone who does it."

Aggie only spoke out loud what everyone was thinking. "You live outside the pack, Michael."

And Michael answered simply, "It's hard. Without you, I couldn't do it."

Without another word, Aggie left her place beside Victoria on the sofa and crossed the room to where her husband sat alone. She sank onto his lap and placed her face against his heart. Michael wrapped his arms around her, enfolding her in his embrace. The others simply watched, understanding.

Victoria said, "Noel, Aggie is right. What if he goes up against this creature—because we asked him to, mind you—and he dies?"

Noel frowned, clearly uncomfortable. "He deserves the right to meet his own challenges. Survival of the strongest has always been the rule."

"Perhaps," agreed Victoria, "for a werewolf. But this man lives in a different world. And if he dies, will we ever know what we've lost?"

Noel frowned, clearly disturbed. After a moment he looked to Sebastian, but the elder man's silence was implicit. In June, Sebastian would step down and an official coronation ceremony would name Noel ruler of all their people. It was time he started making his own decisions.

He said, after a moment, and with obvious determination, "We can't have it both ways. If one of us tries to track this killer, he'll be on us in an instant. Ky Londen is the only one who has a chance to go undetected by him long enough to get close. We can only hope that he's enough like us—that he has that much from his heritage—to see the battle through."

His eyes were bleak as they looked around the group. "We have no choice."

Victoria reached up and took her husband's hand, pressing it against her cheek, and with the gesture offering comfort, offering strength. Then she said softly, "Darling, don't you see? That was what Aggie was trying to do with her messages. Give him the benefit of his heritage, and the courage to follow it through."

Noel looked at his wife, his eyes wide with question and disbelief. "But she was writing to the human woman!"

"The human woman," Victoria argued, "whose life is on the line because of us. The human woman who is in love with Ky Londen."

Noel looked sharply from the werewolf he loved to Aggie St. Clare. Feeling his gaze, Aggie turned her face from her husband's chest to meet it.

Noel said, "This can't be true. In love with him? And if she were, how could you possibly know that?"

Aggie replied simply, "She's met him. She's touched him. How could she not love him?"

Once again Noel thrust his fingers through his hair, letting his head fall back, and he said on a pushed-out breath to no one in particular, "Tell me this isn't happening."

Then he turned an accusing gaze on Aggie, as though she were responsible for it all. "The last thing we need," he told her, "is another mixed-breed marriage."

Michael overrode Aggie's tart response with, "Maybe it's the one thing we *do* need."

Noel was silent for a while, obviously struggling to phrase his thoughts. Finally he said, in a tone much calmer than anyone might have expected, "Michael, I know what Londen means to you—what his very existence could mean..." Reluctantly, he included Aggie. "For both of you. But you've got to understand, the chances that he is healthy, functional, even sane—well, they've got to be less than even."

"But the chance is there," said Aggie.

And Victoria said, at the same moment, "At least we should find out."

Noel looked from one woman to the other in exasperation. "You are both disgusting romantics."

Michael smiled at Aggie. Victoria smiled at Noel.

Noel glanced at Sebastian St. Clare, who said nothing. Then he looked at his bride. "Well," he said with a sigh, "we did promise him news of his father. And I suppose New Orleans could be considered to be on the way to the South Pacific. How soon can you be packed?"

"Come on in," Ky called, as soon as Amy's feet touched the front steps, and she burst through his front door without knocking, waving the latest e-mail printout in her hand.

Her color was high and her voice breathless and excited as she exclaimed triumphantly, "I know who she is!"

"Me, too." It was seven o'clock in the morning and Ky was sitting at his computer surrounded by open file folders, scattered papers, empty food wrappers, soft-drink cans and coffee cups. He barely glanced around when Amy came in.

"The thing is," Amy went on, oblivious to his reply, "I thought that name sounded familiar—McDonald, *Seattle Post*—and when I started thinking the person sending the messages might be a woman... well, it all fell into place. She won an award a few years back—Women in Journalism or something—for her column, 'Single in Seattle.' So I called her paper and guess what?"

"She got married," replied Ky, typing out commands.

Amy was only slightly taken aback. "Right. And guess what her last name is *now*?"

"St. Clare."

Amy frowned, disappointed. "You already knew."

"Let's just say I reached some of the same conclusions you did."

After a moment, Amy shrugged philosophically and concluded, "Anyway, the paper said she's out of town for the rest of the week, so we won't be able to talk to her except through e-mail."

"What would you say to her?" asked Ky practically.

Amy hesitated. "Well, I don't know. Lots of things. Like why she's doing this, where she's getting her information, who the hell she's trying to fool... Ky, this is a respected journalist. I know that all the time you've been thinking it's some gifted practical joker or cyberspace delusional, but this woman is serious. She didn't go to any particular trouble to hide her identity, she went through her paper's computer, she had to know we'd track her down. This puts a whole new spin on everything. And the man she married—St. Clare. Could that be the same man who hired you? It almost has to be, doesn't it?"

"Her husband," agreed Ky. "Or an in-law. And that of course explains her interest in this case. Did you feed Voodoo?"

"He's in your kitchen now, rummaging around for leftovers." She made a face as she looked around the room with its clutter of junk-food remnants and computer printouts. She had never been in his house before. "Is this how you live?"

"Only when I've been working all night. I thought I'd try to track down the St. Clare connection while the trail was still fresh—fresh in mind, anyway."

Amy moved farther into the room, absently straightening scattered files and picking up fallen papers. "Did you read the latest message?"

"It wasn't very helpful."

"I don't know. I thought it was kind of interesting."

"You would."

"What's that supposed to mean?"

"Come on, Amy, let's not go through that again. This whole werewolf fantasy of yours is starting to affect your judgment."

But Amy was no longer listening. She was examining part of a file she had found half scattered over the sofa. The pages she had in her hand were investigating officers' and pathology reports on the last three of the Werewolf Killer's victims.

She looked up at Ky slowly. "You son of a—" she started.

Ky turned away from the computer to look at her. He saw what she had found but his face registered no expression, neither shame nor regret nor alarm.

"You've had this all the time." Her voice was a mixture of incredulity, astonishment and outrage. "I practically begged you for validation. You let me spill my guts to you last night. You let me feel like a sentimental *fool!* And all the time you had the truth right here!"

She shook the papers at him, crumpling them in the tightness of her grip. Ky got slowly to his feet.

"Fantasy? How's *this* for fantasy?" She read from the pathologist's report. "'Sample DNA from hair taken at scene not consistent with human or known zoological specimens. Suggest samples be forwarded to cryptozoologist for evaluation.' And what about this from the FBI crime lab? 'Evidence suggests the possibility of genetic tampering by an agent or agents unknown. Imperative subject be taken alive so that studies can be initiated.' Damn you, Ky!" She was shaking now, with excitement, or rage, or a combination of both. "How could you not tell me about this? How *could* you?"

"Amy..."

She flung up her hands as though to physically throw back at him any words he might utter. With a last look of betrayal and hurt and fury so intense that it seemed to rob her of words, she spun on her heel and walked away, the papers still clutched in her hands.

Ky gave her fifteen minutes to calm down. He spent that time pacing in front of the window, cursing himself, tugging at his hair and trying to determine whether he had ever had any options... or if he had, at what point he should have exercised them.

He didn't expect her to do what she did next. He should have anticipated it, and the fact that he didn't shocked and infuriated him so much, he lost even more precious seconds to absolute disbelief.

He heard her car door slam and the engine start but it was a moment before he realized the significance. He rushed to the front door just in time to see her car turn the corner and disappear down the street.

By the time he reached that corner himself, she was gone.

It was dark by the time he found her.

In truth, he had caught up with her several times that day, only to lose her again. The longest—and most terrifying—time had been when he stood on the dock of the riverboat, which she had just boarded, and watched it chug away without him. When she came down the ramp again four hours later, he might have strangled her if he could have gotten to her through the crowd.

Ky's record for keeping a subject under surveillance was generally much better than that. But generally the subject in question did not evoke so many tangled emotions within him, and those emotions were constantly interfering with his judgment, confusing his senses, distracting him from the task at hand.

He kept thinking, *What if I'm not the only one following her? What if he's stalking her, what if he takes her while I'm out of range, what if I lose her?*

What if I lose her? The hollow fear that formed in the pit of his stomach with that thought was for more than the consequences of losing sight of her in a crowd. What if he lost her? What if he lost her without ever having known what magic she might have held for him, what part she might have held to the broken puzzle of his life? What if he *lost* her?

He was four minutes behind her when he followed her home. He parked in the street in front of her house with a screech of tires, slammed the car door hard as he got out and stalked around to the back patio where she was sitting in a redwood deck chair with club soda in a highball glass. She had lit the citronella torches that surrounded the small patio, and in their wavery, smoky light her expression was solemn and contemplative.

"Don't you ever," Ky said in a low voice, stopping at the edge of the patio with his fists clenched, "do that to me again."

She looked startled to see him there. Then she deliberately smoothed her expression into a mask of detachment and replied, "You don't have to worry. I didn't rush down to the nearest tabloid with the police report, or even to my own television station, for that matter. Your secrets, for what they're worth, are safe with me."

Ky ignored the speech, advancing on her darkly. "Damn you, do you know what a chance you took? Do you have any idea how many times today he might have grabbed you? On the street, in the park, on the trolley, getting off that damn boat—"

She looked both surprised and indignant. "You were following me? All day long you were right behind me, spying on me?"

"That's what I do, remember? Just be glad I was the only one!"

Good sense and self-control told him to leave it at that and go before his temper got the better of him. With one sharply indrawn breath and a thrust of his fingers through his hair, Ky actually turned to do just that when a new surge of frustration and anger gripped him and he spun back.

"Damn it, Amy, how could you do such a thing?" he demanded furiously. "I thought we were in this together!"

"So did I!" she cried. She put the glass aside sloppily, almost overturning it, and got to her feet, her eyes glittering with hurt and anger. "What a fool I was. I'm supposed to trust you with my life and you can't even trust me with the truth! What kind of teamwork is that?"

Ky said painfully, "I couldn't tell you the truth."

"I don't want to hear that!"

"Amy, I got those police files illegally. You're a reporter, trying to get a story—"

"For God's sake, do you think I would have jeopardized a police investigation for the sake of a story? You know that's not what this is about."

"Nothing that you read today necessarily means—"

"Stop it, just stop it." She clapped her hands to her ears in one fierce and final gesture of denial. "You're still trying to lie to me. Why are you doing that? Half truths, denials, excuses. I won't listen to any more of it, I don't have to. Because believe me, Ky, I've already given you every excuse in the book today and none of them, *none* of them are any good!"

Her words pierced the night and pelted him like small arrows, and the silence that followed still seemed to ring with things yet unsaid. She stood across from him with her fists clenched and her eyes bright with unshed tears, and the swaying orange light from the torches cast harsh black shadows on the ground between them.

"You're right," Ky said at last, quietly. "There is no excuse."

He turned to go.

"I thought you cared about me," whispered Amy brokenly.

He stopped. He didn't want to. He wanted to keep moving until he was out of range of her hurtful, accusatory and all-too-true words, until he was out of range of her scent and the pulse of her heart and the quick soft catches of her breath that pulled at him like caressing hands, drawing him toward her.

He did not turn around, but he couldn't stop the words any more than he could stop the swift rush of breath on which they escaped. "I do care about you," he said. "Until today, I didn't even know how much."

He did not have to look at her to know her distress, to feel her confused longing. "Then why wouldn't you tell me the truth? Why couldn't you trust me to do the responsible thing with what I learned, or if you couldn't, to at least let it be my decision? You know what this meant to me. You knew it was more than just a story, and that's what hurts most. You knew, and still you let me go on thinking I was crazy, or worse, all alone."

Ky turned slowly to face her. The night was redolent with jungle splendor—jasmine and green ivy and camellias and azalea and rich, dark grass. And Amy. Tropical humidity and wet paving stones and smoky citronella. And Amy. A neighbor's dinner and hot oil from a res-

taurant three blocks over and automobile exhaust from
Esplanade and Amy, always Amy. She was in his head, in
his pores, in the very air he breathed, and did he really
think that, no matter how far he walked, he could ever get
away from her?

He said quietly, "Amy, you don't know what it is to be
alone. That's why I didn't tell you the truth. Because I
didn't want you to know."

Her eyes were so big in the torchlight, misted with hurt
and confusion and need. She stood still, waiting, at the
mercy of whatever he might say . . . or not say.

How could he leave her like that? Yet how could he begin to tell her the truth she would never be ready to hear?

He took a breath. "I made some mistakes. I'm sorry.
But this is a new game to me, and I don't know all the
rules yet. You see, until a week ago, I'd never met a werewolf before."

CHAPTER THIRTEEN

Amy sank slowly to her chair. With peculiar detachment she observed how odd it was that, even though she had half expected him to say those or similar words—in fact, she had practically begged him to—when she heard them, the first thing she wanted to cry was, "That's impossible!"

And at the same time, with an even more distant part of her mind, she wondered why it should be that despite police reports and forensic evidence, despite the testimony of her own eyes and despite the validation of an award-winning journalist, nothing should be real, or completely believable until this man declared it to be.

Yet, once he said it, there would never be room for doubt again. Maybe he was right. Maybe she didn't want to know the truth in all its harsh exclusionary light. Maybe she would be happier with her comfortable illusions about what was true and what was not.

And maybe, if it had been anyone but Ky, she wouldn't have asked.

"You knew," she said softly, "before you ever opened the door that night. You knew what he was." Her heart was beating so fast, her breath was coming so quickly, it was hard to even get the words out. "How did you know?"

Ky hesitated. Amy was not sure whether that signified hesitation, or the simple courtesy of giving her a chance to change her mind.

But when she waited, hands pressed tightly together in her lap, he answered. "St. Clare told me."

That was not what she had expected. For a moment she couldn't make sense of it. "What? How did he know?"

"He was the first. He was the first werewolf I met that day," Ky said simply.

"Oh . . . my . . . God."

She wasn't certain whether she said the words out loud or merely thought them. Her head was whirling, thoughts colliding, possibilities and impossibilities melding and interweaving to form a kaleidoscope of the wonderful and the horrifying. "Then it's true . . . what Aggie McDonald wrote. An entire subculture. No, an entire species, working and playing and *living* among us . . ."

"We don't know if any of that is true," Ky said a little sharply. "We don't know who this woman is or what her motives might be for saying these things. All we do know—all *I* know, is that of the two werewolves—" the word seemed difficult for him to say "—that I've met, one is a psychotic killer, and the other one carries around satchels full of cash for the purpose of hiring assassins."

"Assassins." She repeated the word a little numbly. Of all the incredible things she had learned this day, she could not begin to say why that one word stuck out in her mind, seeming to hold more significance than any other. She looked up at him slowly. "Is that what you are then?"

Even in the uncertain light, she could see his jaw tighten. "I guess that remains to be seen, doesn't it?"

An urgency tightened in the pit of her stomach and she got to her feet. "The police want him alive."

And Ky returned shortly, "This isn't a police matter anymore, is it?"

"Ky, you can't mean—think about what you're saying! This incredible creature, this unknown species... this may be our last best chance to know anything about them. How can you destroy it?"

In a very tight, controlled voice, he said, "With as little conscience as he used when he tore out the throats of fifteen helpless victims—and those are just the ones we know about. Are you forgetting who hired me? Even his own kind want him dead."

Amy said softly, "You sound as though you would enjoy doing it."

He looked away. His profile was harsh in the torchlight. "Maybe I would."

She took a step toward him, curious, uncertain. "You've never killed anyone before, have you? All those years on the police force, and you never had to kill in the line of duty. But now someone offers you money to do it and you snatch it up. Why?"

Still he wouldn't look at her. "There's a difference between killing a human being and taking out a rabid animal. These creatures are evil, monstrous, completely amoral. They deserve no mercy."

Amy said carefully, "They? But surely you don't mean Aggie St. Clare, and her family. The ones she writes about—"

"She could be lying." Now he turned on her, his expression dark and tumultuous. "Why shouldn't she lie? We don't know what St. Clare has done to her. We don't even know if she's human. For all I know, they all may be using me for some kind of internal warfare or revenge or—hell, I don't know. I just know that none of them are to be trusted."

"Oh, Ky." She looked at him helplessly, her heart aching for him. "What happened to you to make you so cynical? Why can't you believe in something wonderful when you see it with your own eyes?"

Now his look was disbelieving. "You think that monster is wonderful? Is that what you're telling me?"

"Of course not, you know that's not what I mean!" she cried. "But I think that his existence is wonderful. That something like him could be. Yes, that's wonderful. It's miraculous. And you must believe that, too, or else..." And here her breath caught, and she took another step toward him. "Or else you wouldn't be trying so hard to convince yourself otherwise."

She did not have to be close enough to see his face in the shadows to sense the struggle there, to feel the tightness that radiated in waves from his bunched muscles. He said in a low and carefully restrained voice, "I didn't ask for this. I never wanted to have to make this choice. But it's out of my hands. When he started killing, when St. Clare told me about him, it was already out of my hands."

He took a breath and now the light shifted; she could see his eyes. They were tormented, dark with pain. "If I were still on the force, I'd do the same thing. You've got to understand that, Amy. There are certain things that are just out of my hands."

She didn't understand. All of a sudden she felt as though she didn't understand anything, as though she were poised on the brink of knowing but some essential piece of information was missing... as though when she did understand, a miracle would unfold. Whether the miracle would be terrifying or awe-inspiring or perhaps both she did not know, and the frustration was so intense she almost cried.

Amy stepped forward and touched his arm. The thrill played across her skin, skipped through her pulse, wound its way around her heart. A breeze rustled the leaves of a tree with a dry, papery sound, and in the background the fountain bubbled and splashed like music. The moon was just beginning to show itself overhead. "Ky," she said softly.

She did not know what she was asking for as she looked up at him, breath suspended, aching and heartsick. But as she stood there, so close she could feel his breath fluttering across her cheek and feel the power of his gaze delving into her soul, with awareness and expectation flowing between them like a low-voltage current, she knew that the answer, when it came, would change her life.

The phone rang.

The sliding patio door was open to the kitchen, and the sound was clear and sharp. But for a moment, it seemed to have nothing to do with her; for a moment, she almost didn't recognize it for what it was.

Ky said quietly, "Answer it."

There was no surprise at all when she heard the voice on the other end of the line. It almost seemed predestined.

"*Chérie*. How good to find you at home."

What was surprising was how calm her heartbeat was, how steady her voice. For the first time, she was wholly and incontrovertibly certain that she was speaking to a supernatural being; there were no more doubts to fall back on, no more reserves to hide behind—not even Ky's. This should have been a shocking thing, or at least an exciting one. Instead, it seemed completely ordinary.

"I was just thinking about you," Amy said.

"I'm flattered."

Ky came and stood at the entrance to the kitchen, leaning one shoulder against the frame of the patio door. His face was in shadows.

Amy said, "It's hard to think of anything else. After all, I have a deadline, and you still haven't told me enough about yourself to make a convincing story. For example..." Deliberately, she turned her back to Ky. "Tell me about this—change. When you turn from human to wolf. Is that why there's never any sign of struggle from your victims? Because you hypnotize them with the Change?"

Silence. Amy did not have to look at Ky to feel him tense. She knew he was wondering what else she would say, how far she would taunt the werewolf...or how much she would reveal to him.

"So, little one." The voice on the other end of the phone, when it came, was smooth and soft. "You have been doing your research, like a clever reporter. I am impressed. Who, I wonder, could be telling you such interesting things about me?"

Now her heartbeat started to speed, just a little. "Does it matter?"

"No," he replied. His tone was cavalier. "Particularly since I already know."

"I'd like to see the Change for myself," Amy said.

Ky took a quick harsh step into the room, as though to snatch the words from her before they were spoken. The movement was so abrupt, it startled Amy and she whirled to look at him. He stood still, frozen in place, barely breathing though his nostrils were flared with emotion and his eyes were dark with warning.

The voice on the other end chuckled softly. "My dear, what an enchanting notion. And how very persistent you are. Very well. I think I'll grant your wish."

Amy's heart stopped beating. "You will?"

"Well, your first wish, anyway. To meet with me. I believe you said something about an interview? Perhaps we'll try that and see how matters progress from there."

"That would be...good." Her voice was almost steady. "When?"

"The sooner the better I should say."

Amy's heart was beating so loudly now it was difficult to hear. "When?"

"Shall we say moonrise, tomorrow?"

Amy said, "Where?"

He laughed. "Where else, *chérie?* St. Louis Number One."

"The cemetery, of course." Her voice sounded just a little hoarse. "It's a big place. How shall I find you?"

"Never fear, *chérie.* I'll find you."

He hung up the phone.

And almost before the first buzz of the dial tone sounded, Ky was beside her, snatching the phone from her, his eyes ablaze. "Are you insane?"

The intensity of his anger caught her off guard. She took a purely instinctive step backward, crossing her arms over her chest. "I thought you wanted for me to arrange a meeting."

"You told him you knew about the Change. He didn't tell you that! Now he knows you've been in contact with—"

He didn't finish the sentence, but Amy didn't give him the chance. "What difference does it make? He already knew about Aggie, he told me so." The words sounded hollow and frail, raindrops in a barrel. She knew he was right, and already she regretted the recklessness with which she'd acted. But how could she have done differently?

Ky's eyes narrowed just a bit. Still, the fire within them was hot enough to leap out and lick her skin. "He agreed to let you see him change. Don't you know what that means? He just promised to kill you, Amy."

She felt her cheeks lose a little color, but she kept her chin high, her gaze steady on his. Her arms, still hugging her chest, tightened only slightly. "You thought I was going to warn him, didn't you? You actually thought I was going to tell him that there was a contract out on his life, put there by werewolves."

Some of the harshness of Ky's expression faded. "You could have."

"And endanger you? Do you really think I would do that?"

"Ah, Amy, I don't know." In a gesture that spoke of weariness and frustration, he pushed both hands through his long dark hair, combing through the strands and letting them fall again. "I don't know anything anymore."

Amy said distinctly, "I wouldn't do that. No matter what my personal feelings are on the subject, I would never put you in danger. You have to know that."

He gave one swift sharp shake of his head. "It's not me I'm worried about. I can't believe you agreed to meet with him—"

"He's not going to hurt me, either," she said firmly, and with far, far more conviction than she felt. "By the time he gets there, the place will be surrounded by police—"

"He's a werewolf!" cried Ky. "If the police could have stopped him, they would have done it before now."

Amy shook her head adamantly, but it was more to convince herself than him. "Aggie said it had nothing to do with silver bullets. He can be stopped just like anyone else, all we had to do was find him. Well, now we've found him. I'll show up for our rendezvous but the police will already be there, waiting for him—''

"Damn it, Amy, will you listen to yourself?" He grabbed her shoulders, his face intent with frustration. "Can you really be so naive? He's setting you up. He's calling the shots, he has been from the beginning. For God's sake, why can't you—''

He broke off abruptly, looking angry enough to shake her. His fingers were like iron on her upper arms, his face dark with anger. He must have seen the fear in her eyes as she tried to wrench away, but it was not fear of him; it was fear of the truth he spoke.

Ky closed his eyes slowly, the anger draining from his face like a receding tide. And instead of shaking her, he slipped his arms around her and drew her against his chest.

Amy sank against him, letting the strong warm essence of him wrap itself around her and hold her tight. "Oh, Ky," she said brokenly. "I had to, don't you see that? I couldn't stand it any longer. I had to have it over with. I know it was foolish, but I couldn't go on waiting for him to come after me—or you.''

"Amy." He stroked her hair, and the touch of his fingers against her scalp was magical and intoxicating, like stardust floating through her mind. "There's so much you don't know..."

His chest expanded with a breath and she felt the pulse of his heart against her ear and it was as though, in some strange way, her own wonder at being held by him was being played back to him, surprising and distracting and filling him with pleasure. Amy sank into the sensation, needing it, needing him, as much as she needed air to breathe, more.

"I don't care," she whispered. She lifted her face and placed her lips against the firm coarse skin of his neck, parted them, breathed in the taste and the scent and the power of him. She felt his muscles stiffen, his fingers harden on her back, pressing her closer. And she felt the thrill that went through him with her touch, a weakness, almost a dizziness when she swept her tongue across his skin, tasting him.

A simple taste, tongue against flesh, and the sensations that bombarded her were almost too intense to be absorbed. Salty, musky, feral and male, yet as smooth as molasses, as rich as pralines . . . this was the taste of him. But just as a drop of sweat can contain the entire genetic code, that taste unfolded inside her the entire richness and complexity that was Ky. A kaleidoscope of colors and emotions and thoughts and desires, too brief and too intense to be absorbed at once, it swirled inside her head and took her breath away and left her gasping for more.

His body was hard against hers, his breath quick and hot. When she looked up at him, his eyes were as deep and bright as a moonlit sky and just as compelling, just as hypnotic. There was struggle in those eyes, uncertainty and warning, but more powerful than that was the need, the hunger that matched her own.

He said huskily, "Amy, you don't know what you're—"

And then their open mouths met as one, tasting and drawing and drowning in each other. Amy thought, *This is it, then. The miracle.* For there was no magic more intense than this, no surprise more all-encompassing, no power greater. This kiss, this pressing of mouths and mating of tongues, this infusion of heat and intoxicating taste, this straining of muscles and faintness of breath— human beings came together in just such a way thousands upon thousands of times every day around the world to share passion and affection or simple communion. But never had it been like this. And in a single moment of blinding clarity, Amy understood why they had both postponed this moment for so long. Despite the attraction that drew them, despite the mystical electrochemical magic that flared between them with each touch, drawing them ever closer, despite the dreams and the fantasies and the wakeful nights, they had never, until this moment, kissed. They must have known on some deep and unrecognized level the power it would have. They must have known that from that point, there would be no turning back.

She was on fire with his heat and hers, her head was spinning with the influx of sensations almost too intense to be absorbed. Her hands moved over his body, feeling the shape of his thighs and the hard muscles of his buttocks, the lean tendons of his back and the breadth of his shoulders. His hands were beneath her shirt, molding naked flesh, caressing softness, exploring, tasting; both of them growing drunk on each other, dazed with the intensity of what they shared, greedy for more.

She slipped her hands between their bodies, unsnapping his jeans. With a moan that was smothered deep within his throat, he moved his mouth away from hers, though with an effort she could feel and no more than a fraction of an inch, such a small space that his lips still brushed hers as he spoke, breathless and hoarse, into her mouth. "Amy..."

They must have known, each of them from the beginning, that the passion that flared so quickly and intensely between them was generated in part by fear, by the knowledge of what lay ahead and the near certainty that before sunrise they might be torn apart forever. Neither of them wanted to say it, or even admit it to themselves, but it was there. The fear, the desperation, the need to take strength from each other and to do it now, while they still had strength to give.

Amy's vision was so blurred with desire that she could barely see him, just the moon over his shoulder and the fire in his eyes. Her hands were on his face, his heat burning into her palms, his beard stubble sharp against her supersensitive flesh. She was aching inside, feverish and hurting; she was desperate for him, as he was for her. She was terrified of the power of what they discovered, just as he was. And there was that moment when they might have backed away, where the choice was still theirs to make...and yet Amy knew, just as he had known from the moment they first touched, what the choice would be.

Searching his eyes, she whispered, "It's—okay. I have protection."

The long sweep of his breath was like an ocean breeze across her burning cheeks, thrilling, exotic, soothing. "Amy, love." He gathered her close again, cradling her with his arms and legs and the strong graceful curve of his body. "That's the least of the things you should worry about protecting yourself from."

And then he kissed her again, and their minds and their spirits and their wills seemed to flow into one another, becoming mingled and mixed until even awareness itself was swallowed in the blend. She was swept up into his arms, surrounded by him. They were on the staircase. They were moving across a moonlit room, tumbling together onto the soft embrace of her bed, and how had they gotten there? She couldn't say. Her mind was too full of him to allow room for details, her senses too overloaded with every touch, every fluctuation of temperature, every heartbeat and every breath to permit the intrusion of irrelevancies.

Their clothes were gone, their bodies full against each other in a symphony of sensation, tumultuous, cascading waves of awareness. They were swept along on a compulsion that went beyond the normal passions of men and women, just as the pleasures they knew and the wonder that unfolded between them went beyond what had ever been known before.

Before them, no one had ever loved. Before them, no man had ever touched a woman and opened up her soul. Before them, no woman had ever kissed a man and drawn his life's essence inside. When Ky entered her, it was more than the simple joining of bodies. The final barrier was pushed aside and Amy thought with sudden, wondrous clarity, *Ah. This then is the miracle . . .*

She was the air that flowed through his lungs and the blood that surged through his veins, she was the sound of his throbbing heart and the heat that radiated from his skin. She was every molecule and fiber and every thought he had ever had, and he lived inside her skin, he was the air she breathed and the pulse of her heart. This was what it had meant. This was the magic that had quivered so invitingly between them, this was the power they had longed for and feared. This was what they had almost missed.

This was what, after tonight, they might never know again.

Afterward, they lay trembling in each other's arms, exhausted and overwhelmed by the depths of what they had discovered together, dazed by its power. They simply held each other for a very long time, no longer two people but one.

The moon was high in the sky.

"Do you need to sleep?" Ky whispered.

Amy shook her head, stroking his cheek, delighting in its roughness against her palm, the feel of his long lean body wrapped around hers, the slickness of the perspiration-cooled skin—all the things in which lovers revel at such times. The scent of him, the heat of him, the simple presence of him, all of these were hers now, and because of them she would never be the same.

Yet she could feel him retreating into himself even as his arms tightened around her, even as he buried his face in her neck for one last, long, intoxicating breath of her. His hair was like silk between her fingers. They have, she recalled, exceptionally beautiful hair. And eyes.

Ky released her, slowly, and with an inner struggle she could feel. He sat up, his back to her. He said quietly, "I need to tell you some things."

The air from the open window was a little cool and Amy could see his skin prickle in the moonlight. But the sound of the fountain in the courtyard below was soothing, and the scent of jasmine floated on the evening breeze.

Amy sat up against the pillows, wrapping the sheet around her because without him she was cold.

Ky did not turn around to look at her. He spoke into the night, his eyes fixed upon the moonlit window.

"My mother was a schoolteacher," he said. "At least she was until she got pregnant with me. Back then, unmarried mothers weren't considered suitable role models for young people—probably not now, either. Anyway, after I was born, she was a waitress, and that's the only job she ever did for the rest of her life. I don't know, the tips were probably better than teaching, but she wasn't cut out for that kind of life. The irony of it is, we could have moved somewhere else, she could have claimed to be a widow and gotten a job teaching again with any school board in the country, but she wouldn't leave New Orleans. I think she was waiting for him to come back, and she wanted to be here when he did.

"My father," he said with absolutely no change of inflection at all, "was a werewolf."

Heartbeats, slow and heavy, counted off the seconds. There was no other sound. Amy did not move or shift her weight or alter her breathing. She just waited.

"She never called him that," he went on in a matter-of-fact way. "I don't know why, or how she thought about him in her own mind, except that she was infatuated with him, of course. After all he did to her, she never stopped being enchanted by him. Didn't Aggie St. Clare say something about how charming they are?"

Again he paused. It was almost as though he was giving her a chance to cry out a denial, to strike at him or to run away. Amy did none of those things.

"Anyway, like I told you, I've spent most of my life trying to find out who this creature was who was my father. And that's why I was willing to believe St. Clare when he told me he could find my father. St. Clare was a werewolf, he recognized me for what I was just as I recognized him. I thought, at the time, that there couldn't be that many of us..." His voice trailed off a little. "Anyway, about that, I trusted him. Maybe it was stupid. Probably it was. But I was desperate.

"My mother never really told me anything until I was about six. I thought it was normal to be able to hear conversations in apartments two buildings away or tell who had been in a room an hour earlier simply by the smell of their laundry soap. That's to her credit, I guess, that she always made me feel normal, even though it must have been hard for her sometimes.

"She picked me up from the baby-sitter's one night, and we were walking home about three blocks away, when this goon jumped out from a doorway and tried to grab her purse. I almost killed him with my bare hands. I wasn't even in first grade. I guess that was the first time I knew there was something different about me. And that was the first time my mother knew, I think, just how different I was.

"She told me about my father—the man who'd charmed her, impregnated her and left her—and his extraordinary abilities. That's what she called them. Extraordinary. She always made me feel blessed, instead of cursed, to be what I was, and if there's anything healthy or well adjusted about me today, it's because of her.

"But she was a human woman. She could only tell me what she knew, and she only knew what he had told her. Where was Aggie St. Clare then, I wonder, with all her romantic tales? Where was the old man with his sacks of money and his claims of pack loyalty? They left a mother and a child of their own out in the cold to starve or go mad or turn into a psychotic killer like—like the elusive Werewolf Killer. And these are the creatures you so admire? This is the highly moral, superintelligent culture that you find so enchanting?"

Until this point, he had almost managed to keep the bitterness out of his voice. Now he no longer bothered.

"The first time I . . . changed . . ." His voice grew tight, and so did his shoulders. "It was at puberty, hormone-related, I guess, and you know how crazy adolescence can be, anyway. That's what I thought, that I was going crazy. It was terrifying. There's nothing beautiful or wondrous about it, that's just another lie they tell to make themselves sound exalted. It's violent and aggressive and destructive, and I had to go through it by myself, with no one to explain it to me or help me. My mother—God, what she must have gone through. But she couldn't help me. She was human, and I was out of control. I think in a way she must have been afraid of me. I've never forgiven myself for what that must have done to her, that she should have to live to see the day she would be afraid of her own son. And I've never forgiven him.

"Finally, I ran off into the bayou and I lived there like a wolf for months. I don't know how long. I don't remember the things I did there and it's probably better I don't. I might have died then. I might have just given up on whatever humanity was left within me and lived like an animal for whatever life I had left. I might have turned into a killer like the one we're after now, because the line, you see, is very thin in that state. Very thin.

"But what happened was that I made a decision. I realized I was better than that. Because I was half human, I had a choice. I didn't have to be like the monster who'd sired me, I could *control* the monstrousness. I could be good and decent and honest and everything he wasn't. After that, I never took the wolf form again. It's hard sometimes not to, but I haven't. From the time I walked out of the bayou, I've spent every waking moment trying to be as different from him as I possibly could. Until now, I thought I'd done a pretty good job."

His voice fell. "I never wanted to hurt you, Amy. I never wanted to lie to you. But I guess it's just in my nature."

Amy sat forward and linked her arms around his waist, laying her head against his back.

Ky turned in her arms, confusion darkening his eyes. "What are you doing? Why don't you hate me?"

She smiled gently, loving him. "Oh, Ky. You didn't lie to me. You didn't even shock me. I've suspected from the beginning, surely you knew that. And when you were inside me—I knew. And I think..." Now her voice softened, becoming more contemplative. "I think I must have known the truth, on some level, even before that. Because I've loved you for a long time."

Ky didn't answer. For the first time since their union, Amy couldn't even hear him breathing. He just looked at her with those hypnotically blue, still as unreadable, infinitely beloved eyes, until she thought her heart would break.

Then he enfolded her in his arms and together they sank to the pillows.

CHAPTER FOURTEEN

"Do you remember when I told you," Amy asked softly in the dark, "how I used to believe there was something really special waiting for me? This was it. You. And I never, ever imagined just how special it would be."

Ky propped himself up on one elbow, looking down at her, stroking her cheek with his index finger. It was that darkest hour just before dawn, and his face was deeply shadowed. His eyes shone with the gentle light of the purest jewels.

Had they slept? Neither could remember. Had they talked out loud with words, anytime before this? Perhaps. The night was a tangle of memories and sensations, of discovery and longing, joy and sadness and need and wonder. At times it seemed as though it had lasted only the span of an indrawn breath. At other times it seemed to have gone on for centuries.

Ky said quietly, perhaps a little hesitantly, "I've had sex with other women before." He felt the curve of her smile in the dark with his fingertip, and a reciprocal smile crept into his voice. "That's the human in me, I guess. I didn't know..." and now his tone dropped a fraction, became infused with that same cautious disbelief they had shared together on more than one occasion that night. "About this. About the bond. I don't know why it was with you and no one else. But I'm glad it was."

Amy let her hand trail up the length of his arm, stroking and massaging. Touching him was all she wanted to do, forever. "Maybe I've got werewolf ancestors somewhere," she murmured.

"Maybe."

He did not sound so tense when she said the word now. She thought that tonight, in some odd way, had begun to show him more truths about his nature than all the rest of his life put together had done.

And then he added softly, "I know now why they mate for life."

She searched his eyes in the dark, though she really did not have to see him. She could feel what he felt now, almost without touching him.

"Does it feel like life to you, Ky?" she whispered.

"There is absolutely no possibility," he told her sincerely, "of it ever being anything else."

She smiled, tracing the shape of his nose with her fingertip. "Because I really do adore you, you know."

Ky kissed her fingertip. "You put parsley on my dog's plate," he said. "How could I not love you?"

And as she laughed softly, he grew serious again, bending to silence her with a gentle lingering kiss. "And I will love you, I want you to know," he told her quietly, "every single day that I live, for the rest of my life. Believe that."

She did.

In late morning they arose. Ky went across the street to attend to Voodoo, and Amy showered and made breakfast. They sat before the plant-filled window with the patio doors open so Voodoo could go in and out, and drank coffee and talked of little things, and basked in the surety of each other until the sun was high in the sky.

Amy asked, "Why do you think St. Clare chose you?"

By now they were too well tuned to each other's thoughts for the query to require preamble or explanation. Ky sipped his coffee. "I'm not sure. I'm a pretty good tracker, but I don't know if I'm any better than the rest of them. He kept saying I was the only one who could do it. Maybe it's because, well, sometimes people don't notice me. It's not that I become invisible, but there's something about me, my body chemistry, maybe, that makes me invisible to human tracking senses—you know, that sixth sense that lets you know when you're not alone or when someone is watching you. Maybe it works for werewolves, too."

He was silent for a moment, thinking it over. "He had my blood on his fingers," he said, looking at her. "He knows my scent. He should have found me by now. That's the only thing I can think of—that he can't. He tracked me to my apartment because the trail was fresh and it was close. Then he lost the trail and couldn't pick it up again and it must be frustrating the hell out of him."

Amy asked curiously, "Could you have tracked him across the city that many days later?"

Ky nodded. "If I'd had his blood, or something else that held his scent. As it was, I just had my memory, and it would take years to crisscross this city, looking for something to trigger that memory again. In fact, that's probably what he's been doing, trying to find me."

Amy said, holding his gaze, "What are we going to do?"

Ky dropped his eyes. He knew he couldn't lie to her, not directly. "I need some time to think about it."

"Will you call your friend Trey? He could at least—"

Ky shook his head sharply. "No. Promise me you won't do that. We can't have any humans out there, there's no telling what might happen tonight and we can't take any chances. I need your promise.''

Amy hesitated, then said, ''All right. I promise. But you know there's no way you can talk me into staying behind. Maybe he can't sense you, but he'll know immediately if I'm not there, and that's going to tip him off.''

Gazing into his coffee cup Ky said, ''Maybe neither one of us should go.''

Amy was silent, staring at him.

He looked up, his expression suddenly intent. ''I mean it, Amy. Why can't we just leave this place, just get out and go somewhere he can't track us? With the way your career is going now, you can name your own price at any station in the country, or maybe the network. I could live in New York,'' he decided with a nod. ''I could really get used to that.''

''Do you mean just run away?''

''Why not?'' he demanded. ''This isn't our fight. We didn't ask for this. We've both been used and manipulated but that doesn't mean we have to be stupid enough to go on with it.''

''But...'' Amy got up from the table and walked over to the door, looking out at the garden without really seeing it. ''What about St. Clare? What about your deal? What about finding your father?''

''I never wanted his money. What I spent he can deduct for expenses and have the rest of it back. As for the other...'' He shook his head. ''It's not important anymore. Especially not when weighed against you and the life we could have together.''

''But what about him? We're supposed to just let him go on killing?''

''St. Clare can find someone else to do his dirty work,'' Ky said. ''Someone who's willing to take the chance, someone who has nothing to lose—one of his own, for God's sake. I don't owe him anything, I don't owe any of them. Amy, don't you see? We just found each other. How can you ask me to give you up so soon?''

Amy whirled with her hand at her throat, her eyes bright with tears. ''Ask you?'' It was barely a breath. ''Oh, Ky, I was trying to find a way to ask you not to go!'' She flew into his arms, a fierce, hard embrace that tasted of desperation and relief, hope and despair. She pushed a little away and looked up at him. ''When?'' she asked.

''There's a flight to Atlanta at two-thirty,'' he said. ''From there we can connect to anywhere. I want you to be on that flight. I don't like to ship Voodoo so I'll drive. I can meet you there in the morning.''

But long before he had finished speaking, she was shaking her head. Her hands tightened on his arms. ''No,'' she said firmly. ''Either we go together—all three of us—or we don't go at all.''

A shadow passed over his eyes, and then, almost forcefully, he smiled, as though he had expected her reply. ''We've got time,'' he said. ''We'll be safe until nightfall. But for now...'' The smile grew more relaxed, almost genuine. ''I'm starving. Let's go sit in some sunny café and order something really spicy, and we can make our plans from there.''

They took Voodoo with them and spent the afternoon walking around the city, stopping where the notion struck them, holding hands and acting like lovers. Seeing the city she loved through the new and enhanced eyes of the man she loved was like seeing it for the first time, even though Amy knew they were saying goodbye to it.

They returned home around sunset. Amy dropped her keys on the table and looked around her house a little wistfully. ''I should pack some things,'' she said. ''I'll arrange for a moving company to do the rest when we settle...wherever.''

She turned to Ky and smiled. "I kind of like the sound of that. Adventurous.''

But Ky wasn't smiling. He reached into his back pocket and took out a folded airline ticket, which he handed to her. "You have forty-five minutes to make the evening's flight,'' he told her. "There's a cashier's check in there for the rest of St. Clare's money. When you get to Atlanta, put half of it in a bank and get the rest in small bills. You may have to move fast if...well, it might be a while before you can get to your own money. Check into the downtown Hilton under the name Amy Londen. I'll call you there as soon as... I'll call you. But if for some reason I can't, wait for me there until six o'clock tomorrow night, then leave. Don't check out, don't make any calls, just leave. And whatever you do, don't come back here. Not ever.''

Amy looked at the ticket. She looked at Ky. She said, quite distinctly, "Like hell.'' She dropped the envelope on the table beside her keys. "If you were expecting to shock me, you didn't. This is what you were planning all along, wasn't it?''

He didn't blink. "More or less.''

"Well, it's not going to work.'' She looked at him sadly. "I love you too much to let you do this, don't you understand that?''

"Yes,'' he said quietly, "I understand. Just like you have to understand why I can't let you stop me.''

With a gesture of helplessness and frustration, Amy half turned away. She had not even completed her breath before he seized her, pinning her arms behind her back and snapping cold metal circlets around them.

"I am so sorry," he said. And he swept her into his arms.

"Ky, are you insane? What are these, handcuffs? Put me down!"

He carried her into the bathroom and set her on the floor beside the sink. Before she could even struggle to her feet, he had linked another pair of cuffs through the first, securing the other end around the support pipe of the sink.

"If there were any other way," he told her, "you know I wouldn't do this."

It was only then, only when she looked into his sad, dark eyes, that she fully realized he was serious. This was not a joke. He was going to leave her here, chained to her own bathroom sink, while he went out and faced a killer for her sake.

"Ky, you can't do this! Please, don't do this alone! Let me come with you—or let's leave like you promised, please, Ky, we don't have to do this! You don't have to do this!"

He turned and left the room.

Hot tears scalded her cheeks and she didn't even try to stop them. "Ky! Ky, don't leave me!"

He returned in a moment with the cushions from the sofa, which he piled around her. "There's enough room for you to lie down if you want to," he told her. "I don't want you to be uncomfortable, but it can't be helped." He looked intently into her eyes. "I swear to God, Amy, if there were any other way to stop you from following me, I wouldn't do this, but you're the most reckless, stubborn woman I've ever known."

"I thought we were supposed to be a team!" she accused angrily, still crying. "How can you do this to me? How can you go out there and risk your life—"

"This one time," Ky said firmly, "there's nothing you can do to help me. It's me he wants, and I'm the only one who can stop him. You've done your part. Now let me do mine."

"But I can help!" she gasped, more than desperate now. "Ky, listen, I can be the decoy, I can—"

Ky shook his head and said, "I really don't want to do this, but I can't take the chance that your screaming might alarm a neighbor."

He took one of the linen finger towels that Amy's grandmother had given her for Christmas and, despite Amy's furious, indignant struggles, got it into her mouth like a gag and knotted it securely behind her head.

He wiped her face with a tissue, then held it against her nose. "Come on, blow," he commanded, his tone brisk now. "And don't start crying again. I'm not taking any chances on your not being able to breathe."

After another moment of glaring at him in hurt and anger, Amy did as she was told.

He discarded the tissue and knelt beside her. "I'm going to leave a message on Trey's machine at home. He gets off duty at ten and he always, always checks his messages. If he doesn't hear from me before then, his instructions are to come over here, okay? I know it's a long time and I know you're going to hate me for it, but I'd rather have you hate me than die."

Amy shook her head back and forth against the tile wall helplessly. What she wanted to say was that she didn't hate him, could never hate him, but of course she couldn't speak. She could only hope that he already knew.

And then it seemed that he did. He smiled tenderly, and leaned forward to kiss her hair. Then he cupped her face, very gently, in the fingers of one hand, and looked into her eyes. "Every day of my life," he told her softly, "for as long as I live."

He stood and left the room. Amy heard him say, "No, Voodoo, you stay here. Take care of Amy."

The dog made an unhappy sound, but in a moment came into the bathroom and flopped down on the tile beside her. Amy heard the front door close, and the lock turn.

She spent a long moment, squeezing closed her burning eyes, holding her breath, desperately struggling not to cry. And then at last she opened her eyes, gathered her strength and went to work on the pipe.

"Bloody hell," grumbled Noel, slamming the telephone down. "Either the man is as deaf as a toad or he's deliberately ignoring his telephone. I've been calling for three hours."

"Maybe he's not at home," suggested Victoria. "Shall we go over and wait?"

"Not without an introduction. Sebastian surprised him once, we're not likely to do so again. And may I remind you, we know nothing about this creature? He's as likely to turn on us as not."

Victoria shrugged gracefully and went to the window of their elegant suite at Le Meridian, gazing out over the busy lights of Canal Street. "This is incredible, isn't it? So French. And so warm. Do you think I'll have time to shop tomorrow?"

Noel smiled indulgently at her. Victoria had never traveled farther south than New York and everything was new to her. Rediscovering the world through her eyes still delighted him, and always would.

"We'll make time. Where shall we dine tonight?"

"Arnaud's?" she suggested.

He wrinkled his nose. "Rather common. Everyone goes there now. How about Brennan's?"

"I want a crème caramel for dessert."

"Broussard's, then. I'll call down. An hour?"

"Is there anything to snack on?"

"I believe you are taking that old saw about eating for two too seriously, my dear," he drawled. "You really are in danger of getting fat."

She made a face at him, then spied the fruit basket. "Ask the desk to send up ice cream," she said.

Noel was reaching for the phone when it rang. He snatched it up. "Noel Duprey."

"Noel, it's Aggie."

Her voice sounded breathless, and Victoria put down the mango she had been about to peel, turning toward the telephone.

"I just got this off the Internet. It's from her—Amy Fortenoy. Listen."

Victoria came over and sat on the arm of her husband's chair, listening.

"'Tell Sebastian St. Clare,'" Aggie read, "'that the confrontation he wanted is going to take place tonight at moonrise, in the St. Louis Cemetery Number One. If he wants it finished, he must send help. I don't think we can do this alone.'"

Victoria looked at Noel in alarm. Noel said, "Damn."

"The message was posted this morning, 10:41," Aggie went on urgently. "Moonrise there is at 8:14, I looked it up. Listen, Michael is on his way but—"

"No," Noel said sharply. "No, Michael is not to come here, do you understand? I need him there, if anything happens . . ." Victoria's hand closed around his arm and he broke off. "He couldn't get here in time, anyway," he finished. "It's after seven here. Listen to me, Aggie, do you think this woman is telling the truth? Because it could be a trap, Londen himself could have sent the message trying to lure us—''

"Are we going to go through that again?" Her voice was sharp, on the edge of a shriek, and Noel held the phone a little away from his ear, frowning. "She knows what he is, she knows the deal Sebastian made and she's trying to help the man she loves! What is so hard to believe about that? As for Ky, he's only doing what any werewolf of honor would do. He's keeping his bargain and protecting the pack!"

"He doesn't even know about the pack!"

"It doesn't matter! Didn't you tell me yourself his own character would tell how much of his heritage he'd retained? Well, what more could you ask? Damn it, why am I arguing with you? Let me talk to Victoria."

"No need, she's here." His voice was brusque, but his expression was thoughtful. He glanced at the clock. "I'll do this for you, Aggie. I'll go and see this woman, and determine for myself whether she's telling the truth."

"If she's telling the truth, there's no time for that. What are you *doing* in New Orleans, anyway? Did you come to help or to watch him die?"

"That will be enough, Aggie," he said sharply, and somewhat to his surprise, she was silent. In a moment, he went on, "Where does she live?"

Aggie mumbled something and came back to the phone in a moment with an address.

"All right," Noel said. "You're still in Alaska?"

"Yes."

"Stay there. If all is as it should be, by tomorrow I'll bring Londen back with me. I want an end to this business once and for all."

"Good," Aggie said. "I mean..." For a moment, he almost thought she might thank him, but she repeated instead, "Good."

Noel hesitated. "Perhaps," he said, making his voice deliberately casual, "if you don't hear from us by noon... you'd best send Michael down, after all."

A silence. Then Aggie's voice, brisk and competent, "I'll hear from you. You'll call the minute you meet with him. Victoria, do you hear that? Call."

Noel hung up the phone and turned to his bride, a rueful expression on his face. "Will we ever, do you think, get our honeymoon?"

She smiled. "Or even our dinner."

She sprang lightly to her feet and caught up the Burberry coat she had tossed on the bed less than an hour ago. "Come on, then," she said. "There isn't much time, and we still have to find this dreadful cemetery."

"First," Noel reminded her firmly, "we find the woman."

The cemeteries of New Orleans had a reputation for danger, and St. Louis Number One was the most dangerous of them all. Even in broad daylight, it was a haven for muggers, rapists and cutthroats; tourists were warned away in droves and even the bravest of natives did not stroll through the gates alone.

At night, the narrow paths were shrouded in shadow and moss-encrusted mausoleums stood out in stark relief; cherubs, angels and ghoulishly grinning gargoyles seemed preternaturally aware as they loomed overhead, gazing down upon the unwise visitor. Spanish moss, thin and wiry, dripped from the bony fingers of twisted oaks, and with every breeze there were whispering, crackling, dry-breath sounds.

St. Louis Cemetery Number One was the oldest above-ground cemetery in a city that thrived on death, and at night all the tormented souls of three centuries past seemed to moan and try to break free of their confines. Evil crept out of the ground like black swamp water, swarmed out of the sky like a fog, clung with a soul-choking stench to every branch and bench, to each chipped marble angel and spiked iron fence. Ky smelled it as he moved silently through the shadows, felt it like a cold dank breath on his hands and his face. Evil. That was why he was here.

He felt them there in the dark: the hungry, the hunted, the quarry and the prey. They searched the night with greedy darting eyes, but they did not see him. Ky walked among the living and the dead alike unnoticed, a shadow among shadows, knowing them but unknown to them. He was the predator now. It was a role that suited him well.

The time was seven-thirty. He had forty-five minutes before moonrise. He went up the steps of a Gothic-columned temple and settled down in the pool of black-ness provided by the portico, waiting with the dead for the arrival of the werewolf.

CHAPTER FIFTEEN

The ringing of the bell set off a cacophonous barking and growling from inside and Noel winced.

"Sebastian said Londen had a dog," Victoria said.

"A lot of people have dogs. I don't smell werewolf here, do you?"

"Well, no, but that's the point, isn't it? We don't know his scent."

"I suppose." He rang again, and the dog seemed to be launching itself toward hysteria.

"No one's here," Noel said, and turned to go down the steps.

"Wait." Victoria put her hand on his arm. "Do you hear that?"

"The dog? How could I not?"

"No—beyond that. It's muffled, weak."

She cocked her head, listening, and Noel waited. Victoria's ears had always been better than his.

"It's a woman," Victoria said urgently. "She's in trouble."

Noel did not waste time trying to pick the lock. He aimed his foot for the weakest point in the doorframe and kicked. The door popped open like a pressurized can.

The dog stood in the middle of the room, barking and shivering and lunging back and forth. Victoria paused to speak a few soothing words to the animal, and it responded, as all living things did to her charm. Noel moved

quickly toward the back of the house, following the
sounds of distress he could hear easily now.

"Good God," he exclaimed when he saw her.

He bent down and pried the gag from her mouth, de-
manding, "Are you Amy Fortenoy? Who did this to you?
Where's Londen?"

Her eyes were big and terrified and she looked as
though she did not know whether to answer him or kick
out at him. She might have done the latter had Victoria
not stepped in quickly.

"It's all right," she said. "Aggie St. Clare sent us. Do
you know who she is?"

Amy's head dropped back and she whispered in a dry
and raspy voice, "Oh, thank God." Then, hoarsely, "We
have to hurry. Ky is gone, he went without me, we have to
stop him. Please, get me out of these things."

She struggled against the metal handcuffs that held her
bound, a gesture of helplessness and frustration more
than anything.

Noel glanced around. "I don't suppose he left a key."

"No! Please, do something. You don't understand—"

"We understand," Victoria assured her.

Noel looked at Victoria. "Hairpin?"

"Don't be absurd. No one uses hairpins anymore."

"Then forget about me," Amy cried. "Just find Ky.
Stop him, don't let him go up against the monster alone!
Don't you see what he's doing? He thinks if he gives the
killer what he wants, if he offers himself as a sacrifice, I'll
be safe. But Ky can't fight this creature, he's only half
werewolf and he hasn't changed since he was a child—I
don't think he believes he can! He doesn't have a chance,
oh, please, you've got to stop him!"

Noel frowned a little. "He doesn't sound very bright,
then."

Amy sobbed and kicked the sink in frustration, and Victoria knelt beside her, patting her shoulder. "What about a straight pin?" she suggested. "A safety pin, or a turkey skewer?"

Amy stared at her for a moment, breathing hard, then she said, "In my desk. Top center drawer."

Victoria returned in a moment with a handful of straight pins, and thirty seconds after that, Noel had manipulated the tumblers on the locks and the handcuffs fell free.

Amy stood up, rubbing her wrists, and did not waste time thanking them. "Hurry," she said, rushing for the door. "Please."

Ky caught the scent on the evening breeze and his heart started to pound. Immediately and forcefully he calmed it. The other werewolf might not be able to smell him, but surely his ears were as good as any, and Ky did not want to give away his position until he could do so on his own terms. Still, there was a sick feeling in the pit of his stomach and cool prickles of perspiration broke out on his upper body. He thought about Amy, about the life of magic and discovery they might have lived together, and he wondered if every man thought about the woman he loved when he knew he was going to die.

He turned his head, following the scent as it moved east, away from him now. Good. The werewolf couldn't stalk him. The advantage still was Ky's.

He moved silently from his hiding place and slipped through the shadows like a specter himself, from monument to mausoleum to heavy-trunked tree. Moonrise was still fifteen minutes away, and the darkness was his friend.

For the first time in three years, there was a gun in his hand.

He kept hearing St. Clare say, *"Who else is there?"*

Then he saw him, crouched behind the base of a scarred and moss-covered angel, looking down the path. Ky had no doubt it was him. His scent was so strong, Ky had to breathe shallowly to avoid it. Ky could hear the werewolf's heartbeat, whose rhythm was slightly different from a human's. If he had been facing the other direction, his night vision would have easily picked up Ky, less than twenty yards away. But his back was to Ky, and for those few seconds, he was unaware he was being watched.

Ky lifted the gun. He had chambered a round before he entered the cemetery; now all he had to do was aim and fire. It was long range for a handgun, but Ky's marksmanship was flawless. In less than a second, it would be over, and Ky would be an assassin.

They never attack in human form. From out of nowhere, Aggie St. Clare's words came back to him. *They are forbidden by ethical and practical considerations to use weapons...* Was that why, in all his years on the force, Ky had never killed a human being, despite the many he'd encountered who needed killing, badly? Was that why, even now, the gun felt heavy and awkward in his hand and even though he knew, with his superior coordination and reflexes, he could not fail to hit any target at which he aimed? Was there something woven deep into his genetic code that reminded him of those things even when there was no logical reason he should know them, or care whether they were true at all?

No. That was crazy. The only thing that made him hesitate now was his natural and completely understandable reluctance to shoot a man in the back. *Turn around, you bastard,* he thought.

And then he did.

Less than two seconds passed while he turned and straightened, his quick sharp eyes seeking and finding Ky in the dark. But that was plenty of time to pull the trigger. Plenty of time.

Then he smiled, and it was too late.

"Hello, my son," he said gently.

"He hates you all," Amy said tightly, trying very hard to keep her voice from shaking as she mentally urged the car to go faster, faster. "He thinks you're all like his father, heartless and amoral. He thinks you turned his mother and him out into the world to die."

"His father was neither of those things," Noel said, "at least not as far as we know, and neither are we. What has happened here is a great tragedy, and hopefully, the only one of its kind. We would have prevented it if we could."

The two werewolves had a limousine with a uniformed driver. Amy sat in the back with them and watched the traffic creep by and she wanted to bang on the window to urge more speed, she wanted to get out and run. She struggled to keep her composure. They had asked her to tell them about Ky. She tried to focus on the task at hand.

"It was hard on him, growing up alone," she said, "the only one of his kind, with no one to tell him what to expect or explain the rules to him. I don't think you can imagine how hard."

In the darkness of the seat across from her, there was a small movement—Victoria slipping her hand into Noel's. It was a simple gesture, but it touched Amy enormously. And when Victoria said softly, "Yes, we can." Amy believed her.

Noel said carefully, "It's a wonder, under circumstances like that, that he survived to a normal adulthood at all. That he wasn't damaged, mentally or otherwise, in some important ways."

"Apparently his mother went to extraordinary lengths to make sure that didn't happen. And she did an outstanding job. Ky Londen is one of the most purely good men I've ever known."

In the passing headlights of another car, Amy saw Noel lift an eyebrow quizzically. "And you say this even after he left you chained to a bathroom sink with a towel in your mouth?"

Amy shook her head impatiently. "He was trying to protect me. He knew I'd follow him, and now I think he was also trying to give himself the best chance for survival. I didn't understand at first, but he knew he couldn't worry about me and do what he had to do. Does the driver know to turn at the next corner? It's not far."

"He knows," Victoria said. Then, gently, "You are mated to him, isn't that right?"

"Mated," Amy repeated softly. "What an interesting way to put it." Then, "Yes, I am."

A look passed between the two werewolves that Amy couldn't read. She leaned forward urgently. "You can stop him, can't you? I mean, there are two of you—"

"Four," corrected Victoria. "There are bodyguards in the car behind us. Five, if you count the driver."

"Werewolves?" Amy said hoarsely. There was a part of her that was surprised she could speak at all. "All of them—all of you werewolves?"

Victoria said, "Of course."

Amy sat back against the seat in a sudden wave of weakness. "It's all right, then," she whispered. "We can stop him."

"I think you misunderstand," said Noel from deep within the shadows. "We have no intention of stopping him."

His hair was jet black and tied back at the nape. Beneath a thick dark beard his features were sharp and his eyes ice blue. He wore jeans and a black T-shirt; he could have been any one of the dozens of predators that lurked in the shadows of this dark place, but he was the most dangerous predator of all. He was the Werewolf Killer.

He came down the path toward Ky easily, his hands thrust into his pockets, the smile still on his face. Ky kept the gun trained on him steadily, his finger on the trigger.

The werewolf said, "You came. I'm glad. It's long past time we talked."

Ky asked hoarsely, "What did you call me?"

He stopped a few yards in front of Ky, still smiling in that easy, confident way. "Don't tell me you're surprised. You must have known, or at least suspected, since the first time we met."

And the worst of it was that Ky had known. Yes, since that first moment, he had known...

Ky did not lower the gun. "If you think that's going to change my mind about killing you, you're very much mistaken."

He laughed softly. "I can understand how you might harbor a certain resentment toward me. I won't insult you with excuses and apologies—except to point out the obvious, which is, until a few days ago, I didn't know you existed. Now I want to make up for lost time."

"Don't come any closer," Ky said as the werewolf took another step toward him. But his heart was pounding like thunder and the command in his voice was less than convincing.

"As you wish." He stopped still, his tone unconcerned, his stance relaxed. "But you won't kill me. You've waited all your life for this moment, and if you kill me now, all those questions that have been burning a hole inside you, keeping you awake at night and torturing every waking hour will go forever unanswered. This is your chance, Ky. This is your chance to see from whence you came."

True, all true, a desperate voice inside Ky cried. A lifetime of searching and hoping, hating and waiting, only to discover a truth that he had always known deep inside— that his legacy was evil, his parentage was perverse and his basic nature, when all the so-called humanity was stripped away, was nothing more than that of this amoral killer. None of that surprised him. What did surprise him was how desperately he had wanted it to be different, how deeply he had needed to believe Aggie St. Clare and the fantasy world she spun. Now there was no hope for him.

Ky looked into the eyes of evil, and saw himself reflected there. "What do you want from me?"

"Just a chance," said the werewolf, "to get to know the son I never knew I had. I'm old, you must have guessed that by now, I can't live much longer. I've made mistakes, Ky, but none I regret more deeply than losing you. I want you to know me, maybe to understand me, and when you do, make your decision."

As he spoke, he walked toward Ky and Ky didn't try to stop him. There was no question of his pulling the trigger now. He did not even know why he still held the gun.

Sensing the same, the werewolf reached out and took the gun, tossing it casually aside. "We have no need for weapons, you and I," he said softly.

He lifted his arm as though to embrace Ky. That was when Ky looked into his eyes, really looked, and the spell which had held him enthralled suddenly shattered like glass. He stepped back, throwing up an arm to ward him off, but it was a moment too late. He heard the werewolf laugh, and felt the bite of claws on the back of his neck.

"What do you mean you won't stop him?" Amy cried. "Why did you come here—"

Through the intercom, the driver said, "Which gate, sir?"

Noel demanded of Amy, "Which gate?"

"I don't know!" Her voice was high with near hysteria. "Talk to me! What did you mean—"

Noel told the driver. "Nearest gate."

"Amy, listen, we only mean the best," Victoria said. "We'll help Ky if we can, we don't want anything to happen to him—"

"But we'll do him no favor by interfering in his fight," Noel added sharply as the car made a turn and slowed, "and we may even get him killed. That goes for you, too. If you can't stay still and stay quiet, I'll have you restrained, is that clear? I'll not have you putting all our lives at risk."

Amy stared at him, wide-eyed and numb. There was something compelling about this werewolf—about both of them, really—that made her inclined to obey his commands. She spoke with an effort, "You won't let anything happen to him."

The car stopped and Noel opened the door. "I can't promise that," he answered simply, and he got out.

The three of them stood in the shadow of the shrouded cemetery for a moment, Amy biting her lip with anxiety while the other two stood still, their heads cocked and their noses turned to the air. Then Noel murmured, "Have you got that?"

Victoria's voice sounded a little weak as she answered, "God, it's sickening."

Noel glanced over his shoulder to Amy. "This way," he said, moving forcefully ahead. "Stay behind us, and don't make a sound. The moon is just up. There's still a chance—"

But then a sound rent the night that tore through Amy's soul and seemed to shake the very foundations of the city of the dead. It was the fierce, furious, ear-shattering growl of an animal.

Amy began to run, not away from the sound but toward it.

Ky managed to tear away from the werewolf's grasp but only for a moment, then he was on him again. Again Ky struck out with all his superhuman force and again he spun away. His heart was roaring and heat was rising; adrenaline pumped acuity to his vision and length to his muscles and hunger to his soul, a sensation that was both shocking and familiar, welcome and dread. The other werewolf's scent was growing sharper, a strange sweet-sick, electric-sharp odor that was both nauseating and compelling, almost hypnotic. Ky stumbled backward, trying to clear his head of it, gasping for breath and struggling for control.

And then he heard the roar, a magnificent thing that thrilled him to his core and drew his gaze, helplessly and inexorably to the miracle that was exploding before his eyes. The miracle of the Change. Ah, yes, he knew it, the explosion of power, the rage of becoming, the raw thrill of instinct unleashed. And now as he watched, he felt the pull of it from deep within his belly and he fought it, with dry throat and cramping muscles he fought it . . .

The wolf launched itself at him with greedy eyes and bared teeth and Ky flung himself aside. Sharp teeth tore at his leg and he fell hard on the ground, kicking out to try to free himself while with his hands he swept the ground for the gun. *I am better than this,* a voice inside him screamed while pain seared his muscles and his vision strobed with effort and he couldn't find the gun. *I'm not like him, I'm not...*

He scrambled away a few feet, panting, and his hand struck the metal barrel of the gun. He had the gun in his hand, clumsily searching for the trigger as he turned in the grass to get his feet beneath him, when the wolf was upon him again. Sharp teeth sank into Ky's side, sending a paralyzing explosion of red-hot pain all the way up his spine where it exploded inside his head, blinding him. And then he couldn't fight it anymore, didn't want to fight it. The monster inside him broke free.

The gun slipped from a hand that was suddenly unable to hold it, and Ky turned on his assailant with a roar.

They arrived in time to see Ky, bleeding from wounds on his leg and flank, fling aside the wolf and stagger backward, his head thrown back and his throat emitting a heart-stopping, inhuman roar. They could see in the filtered moonlight that already his hands had begun to change, and the bones of his legs. He tore at his clothes, which came apart in ribbons. The sound that was torn from him was a scream of agony—or triumph.

The black wolf charged him from the shadows and Ky launched himself into the air to meet him. Amy sank to her knees, breath stopped, heart stopped, hands pressed to her mouth to capture a soundless cry, mesmerized by the spectacle and the wonder that was unfolding before her.

It was as though the air itself shattered, exploding into a cacophony of light and movement, of splendid human form and sleek dark animal power. *Magic* was too mild a word. *Miracle* too tame. It was majestic, it was magnificent, it was almost beyond the capability of the human mind to absorb.

Noel murmured, "My God. He is one of us, after all." And there was admiration and a little amazement in his voice.

Victoria knelt beside Amy, holding her shoulders. Amy could feel the other woman's muscles quivering with excitement, anxiety, or the mere wonder of the spectacle.

But it was beautiful for only a moment, for when the two dark animals met, it was in a clash of blood and thunder, of howls and tearing flesh. Amy's breath came back in a choked-off sob as Ky—was it Ky?—was thrown to the ground and the other wolf tore at his throat.

She screamed, "No!" and tried to throw off Victoria's restraining hands, struggling to her feet. "Ky!"

But now both wolves were on their feet, panting and salivating, growling and circling. Both were limping, both were bleeding. They were both jet black. They both had blue eyes.

And before Amy could draw another breath to scream, it was over. One of the wolves attacked. The other swiftly sidestepped, redoubled and caught his adversary by the throat. With a single snap of his head, he tossed the wolf to ground, where it lay dead.

It was only then that Amy realized that the broken, wheezing sounds that she heard were the sobs coming from her own throat. She whispered, "Ky, oh, God, Ky..." in a senseless, high-pitched monotone that bordered on hysteria. She stumbled forward toward the limp and bloodied corpse.

"No," Victoria said sharply, and she seized Amy's arm. "No, Ky is all right. It's the other one."

Amy looked in desperate hope from the wolf who still stood with head low and chest heaving, near the body of the other, to Victoria. Victoria answered her unspoken question simply. "The scent."

Amy clasped her hand to her throat, squeezing back tears of joy and relief. "Thank God," she whispered. "Oh, thank you . . ."

And once again she started to move forward. This time it was Noel who stretched out an arm, blocking her way. He was frowning. "He should have changed back by now," he said.

Amy saw the look that passed between Victoria and Noel, and it frightened her. Victoria said softly, "Maybe he can't."

A stab of fear went through Amy that was so cold, it seemed to freeze her blood. "No," she said.

Then Noel swore sharply. "He's noticed us," he said.

The wolf raised its head in their direction, baring its teeth, obviously exhausted but lowering into an attack crouch. The growl that came from its throat was low and deadly. Noel stepped in front of the two women, trying to shield them, but Amy pushed past him.

"Ky, no!" she cried.

Noel grabbed for her arm. "Don't be insane, woman! He won't know you!"

Amy twisted away from him, moving toward the wolf. She heard Victoria say, "They are mated. She has to try."

"He'll kill her! He'll kill us all if he gets a chance."

"No," Amy said without looking around. "He won't." Yet there was no assurance of that in the gaze of the wolf, which was narrow and wild and glittering with fire.

"Ky," she said softly, "they're werewolves, but they came to help you. They're like you, Ky, not like the other one. He's dead, it's over. You've got to come back to me now, Ky. Please."

The wolf flattened its ears and bared its teeth further. The growl held genuine menace now, and it frightened Amy into pausing, just a half step.

Noel said to Victoria, "Go back to the car and get help. There's still a chance we can take him alive."

"No," Victoria said. "If he attacks you, you'll need me here."

"He's not going to attack," Amy said quietly, and moved forward again. She was only a few steps from him now and she dropped to her knees, holding his gaze with tears burning her own eyes. "Ky," she whispered, "every day of your life, remember? You can't leave me now. Please, please don't leave me now."

The wolf launched itself at her, and Amy opened her arms to him, ready for whatever might happen. And what happened was that her arms closed around warm fur and a familiar scent as he pushed himself against her, the wolf body trembling with exhaustion and confusion, and then growing stronger as he inhaled her fragrance, tasted the salty tears that bathed her face. She could feel his muscles stiffen and his bones start to straighten, and then the fine electric quivers that overtook him; she could taste the hot strong chemistry in the air. Then it was Noel taking her shoulders, pulling her gently but quickly to her feet, saying, "Give him room, be calm, don't confuse him. Hold his eyes. It's all right, Ky Londen. You're welcome here."

And then Amy was privileged for the second time that night to witness the miracle, and this time it brought the man she loved back to her. Naked and bleeding, dazed and exhausted, he staggered as he looked from one face to the other, finally finding the one he sought.

The faint curve of a smile touched his white lips, and he said huskily, "For as long as I live."

Then he collapsed on the ground, unconscious.

CHAPTER SIXTEEN

Noel carried him out of the cemetery wrapped in Victoria's coat. He regained consciousness when they reached the car, but wasn't fully coherent until Noel made him drink some brandy from a small bottle that he got from the limo's bar. Though still in obvious pain and more than a little confused, Ky was alert, and cautious.

Amy used the car's first-aid kit to clean and bandage the wound on his leg while Noel and Victoria went to search the luggage in the bodyguard's car for clothes that might fit Ky. Ky sat with Victoria's coat draped over his lap, his skin prickling in the humid night air.

"They must be very rich," Amy said in a low and breathless tone of voice as she applied adhesive tape to the gauze pad on Ky's leg. She was talking just to be talking, just to communicate with him, to say the words and know he heard them, to have him near because that was one thing she would never take for granted again. "And important, too, to travel with bodyguards like that. But they came as soon as they got my message. I sent it to Aggie this morning, while you were asleep, asking for help. I knew you couldn't be talked out of this, I knew you'd try to get yourself killed..."

A single tear rolled down her cheek and she sniffed it away impatiently. Ky laid a gentle head atop her hair.

"Amy," he said quietly. "The monster I killed back there was my father. Those are the genes I carry in my blood, and this is the man you're in love with."

Amy raised her eyes to him slowly, and saw that the pain that haunted his was beyond the physical.

Then Noel's voice spoke behind them. "It wasn't your father, Londen. That's what we came to tell you. That creature killed your father, some thirty-odd years ago. Killed him, I would suspect, for the same reason he intended to kill you. Because he was another werewolf invading his territory." He thrust a folded pair of khaki pants and a stiffly starched white shirt at Ky. "Here, try these."

Ky stared at him. "Who the hell are you people?"

Noel's lips twisted dryly. "It's a rather long story, I'm afraid. But your young lady is right—we're important. At least as important to you, I hope, as you are to us. Well done, by the way," he said with a change of inflection so subtle it was almost unnoticeable.

He held Ky's gaze for a moment, and something passed between the two men that was completely unreadable to Amy. Then Ky accepted the clothes Noel offered, leaning heavily on Amy to get to his feet.

Amy gasped as the coat fell away and she got her first good look at the ugly bite mark on his side. "Oh, Ky, please let us take you to the hospital. You need stitches and antibiotics..."

"Not necessary," said Noel, giving a perfunctory glance at the wounds. "He'll heal straight away."

Amy glared at Noel and Noel ignored her, offering Ky his arm to steady against as he pulled on the pants.

"Tell me," Ky said, his voice tight with pain as he fastened the waistband near the gash on his side, "about my father."

Amy said, "Sit down first. Let me bandage that before you bleed all over someone else's clothes."

Noel said soberly, "He was a distant relation to our ruling family, the St. Clares. My wife, also, is from that branch of the family. We thought—well, not I, of course, as I hadn't even been born at the time—that he was lost in a train crash here in the States all those years ago. He was an architectural engineer, perhaps you know that, and brilliant even among his own kind. How he came to meet and love your mother we of course can't say, unless she told you, but this much is certain—he never knew there was a child. To even imagine such a thing would have been beyond his capability because, you see, as far as we can determine, you are the first."

Both Amy and Ky stared at him, and he explained, "Until now, we did not believe it was possible for a human and a werewolf to produce offspring. Until recently, in fact," he added with a dry undercurrent neither one of them quite understood, "we believed the actual mating of a human and a werewolf to be aberrant, if not impossible."

Victoria appeared from the darkness and slipped her arm through her husband's. "Of course," she said, "we are learning new things every day."

She looked at Ky, "What my beloved is trying to tell you, and probably not doing very well, is that if ever you had any doubts about the character of your father, please put them aside. He came from our strongest and most noble line. He was among the finest werewolves that have ever lived. As you no doubt know, now being mated yourself..." She smiled, but her smile was for her husband, not for Ky. "It would have been literally impossible for your father to have betrayed your mother, having once mated with her. There was none of the deviancy in your line that spawned the creature we just buried."

"If there were," Noel said matter-of-factly, "you would not be sitting here now. I'm afraid I would have had to make sure of that."

"I'm not sure that was necessary to say," Victoria told him tartly.

"He's one of us," Noel responded. "He understands."

"One of you," Ky repeated softly.

Amy lay her cheek against his, knowing exactly and without a doubt what he was feeling. To be alone for all of your life and to suddenly be a part of something, to know where you belonged for the first time in your life... it was overwhelming.

Ky slipped his arm around her, and they simply held each other in silent communion for a long time.

"We were going to dine at Broussard's," Victoria said when they were in the car again. "Will you join us?"

Neither Amy nor Ky was able to respond to that, so Noel supplied, "I'm certain they're too tired, my dear."

Then he said, "Of course, there is a great deal more we should talk about. I'm sure you have a thousand questions." And then he hesitated, seeming for the first time almost uncomfortable. "As a matter of fact, there is something in particular. I hesitate to bring it up in your present condition, knowing you need time to adjust to everything that's happened but, well, the fact is, I made a rather rash promise, and it's one I hope you'll help me keep. True, the promise was only to a human..."

"Honestly, Noel," interrupted Victoria impatiently, "I fail to see how you can hold on to those foolish prejudices when you're constantly meeting nothing but humans of the very highest caliber. Look at Amy. She's strong, honest, loyal, and for all she's seen this night, has she even once collapsed into human hysteria? Do you know what courage it took for her to even send for us? She's the perfect mate for Ky! And Aggie—''

"Aggie St. Clare is a human?" gasped Amy.

"Actually," said Noel a little stiffly, "she is the person this is all about in a way. She married my cousin, Michael St. Clare, who is—was—a powerful werewolf in our pack."

Amy squeezed Ky's arm, sharing a moment of silent exaltation in the fact that she had been right to trust Aggie, that, in fact, she and Aggie had a great deal in common. Ky covered her hand with his and smiled down at her.

"She believes—it's foolish, of course, but she believes that you—that something about your genetic structure might provide a clue as to the manner in which humans and werewolves might produce a single offspring. She wants children of her own," he said simply, and, reaching for his wife's hand, added, "I can't say I blame her for that."

Victoria said, "We'd like you to come back to Alaska with us, Ky. Whether or not you agree to the genetic testing Aggie wants—and we certainly have no intention of coercing you into that!—we want you to meet your family, learn about your heritage. I think you'll be pleasantly surprised."

Amy said softly, "Alaska." Then, completely at a loss for anything else to say, "Wow."

Ky tightened his fingers around hers, understanding. He said, "It's been a lot, for one night. I have to think about it."

Noel nodded, appearing relieved. "Of course."

The miles passed. Headlights flashed. St. Louis Cemetery seemed very far away—and as close as their next breath. Ky shifted his weight, drawing Amy into the circle of his arms. "I almost didn't make it back," he said softly into her hair. He knew the other two werewolves could hear him, but he didn't care. "After what I'd done, what I'd become, and believing that the monster was my father—I thought you would be repulsed, that you'd hate me. Even if you didn't, I couldn't bear to inflict myself on you."

"Don't ever say that," Amy said fiercely. "Don't even think it."

"It was . . . strange," he said, still very quietly, almost to himself. "Until tonight, that part of me had always seemed abhorrent, evil. I never wanted to change again. But when I knew you would be left behind if I lost the fight—when I sensed you there in the cemetery, and the other werewolves . . . I can't really explain it, but it was as though *not* changing would have been the aberrant thing, the evil thing. I never even imagined feeling that way before." His voice was gentled with wonder.

Amy pressed her face gently against his sleeve. "It was beautiful, the Change."

"Yes," he said slowly, as though still not quite comprehending it all himself. He reached up a hand and stroked her hair lovingly. "First you gave me a reason to live," he said, "then you saved my life. I don't want anything else but to spend the rest of it with you, Amy. Wherever and however you choose."

Amy tilted her head to look up at him, smiling. "Then I guess I have to choose what's best for you. For us. I want you to go to Alaska, Ky," she told him. "I want you to find your family."

She could tell by the way his muscles relaxed that this was what he wanted, too. "Not unless you come with me."

"Wherever you go," Amy replied, and settled against him contentedly. "Every day of my life."

Ky bent to kiss her hair. "For as long as I live."

They turned their faces toward the window as the limousine sped home.

* * * * *

SILHOUETTE Shadows

Welcome To The Dark Side Of Love...

COMING NEXT MONTH

#60 'TIL WE MEET AGAIN—Kimberly Raye

Mishella Kirkland had the healing touch, and she desperately
sought to harness its power to save her sister. Yet stranger
Raphael Dalton knew the truth behind her gift—particularly the
evil source bent on reclaiming its power. To save her, Dalton
assigned himself to act as Mishella's protector—and lover—
only to discover that he was her greatest threat.

COMING IN TWO MONTHS

#61 MYSTERY CHILD—Carla Cassidy

Night after night, Forest Kingsdon heard the haunting cries of a
child—and he remembered.... Then Julie Kingsdon, the seductive
widow of his late brother, arrived with her little boy to claim their
legacy and build a home. Yet Forest knew mother and child would
never know peace. For sweet Julie and her angelic son had just put
their faith—and love—in the wrong man....